Isle of Dogs, Part 1

Isle of Dogs

Jon Frankel

ω
Whisk(e)y Tit
VT & NYC

This is a work of fiction. Names, characters, places, and incidents are the product of the author's imagination, and should not be confused with your idea of reality. Resemblance to actual persons, living or dead, events, or locales is entirely coincidental.

Published in the United States by Whisk(e)y Tit: www.whiskeytit.com. If you wish to use or reproduce all or part of this book for any means, please let the author and publisher know. You're pretty much required to, legally.

ISBN 978-1-952600-01-2

Library of Congress Control Number: 2020941447

Copyright ©2020, the author. All rights reserved.

Cover design by Richard Buchanan.

First Whisk(e)y Tit paperback edition.

For my mother, Marjorie Eustis Frankel, and my father, Raymond Frankel, without whom....

*I have seen such beautiful things in the world which, apart
from desire, I should never have seen. I bless desire,
the fault of its satisfaction: the fault of the world.
I bless that fault: that, in its offering
denying us all, denies us nothing,
offers the world to us, not to have.*

William Bronk, "Unsatisfied Desire"

A Note to the Reader

Isle of Dogs is Volume Two of *Drift*, a multivolume saga set in a world that was first described in the novel *The Man Who Can't Die* (Whiskey Tit, 2016). It is the immediate prequel to the first volume in the series, *GAHA: Babes of the Abyss* (Whiskey Tit, 2014). *GAHA* takes place in Los Angeles, in the years 2540-2543. *Isle of Dogs* takes place mostly in New York and surrounding areas and begins in the year 2500 with the birth of Sargon 4, a character introduced in *GAHA*. Note that the publication order is not the order in which the books should be read. *Isle of Dogs* is divided into four parts of approximately equal length.

While in most respects *Isle of Dogs* is a stand-alone novel, it is assumed by the author that the reader will have read *GAHA* first. *The Man Who Can't Die*, set in 2180, has many more details about the world from which *Drift* arises, a world devastated by climate change and the political, social, and individual responses to that disaster. But it is not necessary to read that book to understand the action of *GAHA* and *Isle of Dogs*. Future volumes will complete the story of *DRIFT*.

Acknowledgments

Many thanks go to the following people for their insights, useful criticisms, encouragement, friendship, love, support, intellect, company, disagreement, understanding, indulgence:

Maja Anderson, Oskar Eustis, Michael Salwen, Philip Shelley, John Fousek, Eric Maroney, Miette, Nancy Moss, John Newman, Cara Hoffman, Svetlana Lavochkina, Steven Adkins, Judy Swan, Bob and Sandra Stratton, Julie Copenhagen, Billy Cote, Ubaldo Valli, Bridget Meeds, Roman Tsivkin, Teresa Hartmann.

Introduction

Readers familiar with my speculative fiction may be surprised that I have turned from the future to the past with *Isle of Dogs*, and, moreover, that I would write a work of historical fiction. I actually set out to write a conventional history, based on papers left by my grandparents, Robin Micawber and Tiriel Harvale, in the archives of Georgetown University. The story that unfolds in those papers seemed to me of real importance and, now that we are able to write more openly about the period, I felt, and my editor agreed, that there is a vital public interest and need to know the actual events of a century ago.

I am an old woman now, and, while I could read through the archive, I found my ability to construct an actual scholarly history of events in New York City in the early twenty-sixth century was limited both by training and advanced years. A work of historical fiction, with all of its liberties, however, seemed within reach. Once I made this decision, work proceeded rapidly.

I have decided to make the archive available to professional historians and journalists in the hopes that they will be able to take advantage of the plethora of materials available. Harvale was a reporter for the *New York Times*, as well as Press Secretary to Vice President Sargon, and her notes and research, unpublished in her lifetime, paint a Boschian picture of life on the Isle of Dogs, as Sargon 3 affectionately and scornfully called Manhattan.

Micawber's writing is more scholarly and thorough, taking the deep perspective of the historian. It is my hope that his work will be edited and published. Much of it was composed for the education of Sargon 4, the subject of this book, and is unusually frank for a Ruler narrative. Many Rulers commissioned such works, but few allowed the secret history to be recorded. Whether truer versions of events were communicated orally or not is not clear. Certainly diaries and written communications that have been preserved suggest that, but the decisions and behavior of Rulers in the late period indicate that they did not learn the lessons of history, and were doomed to repeat it.

Isle of Dogs, Part 1

My object has been to recreate in as much detail as possible the insular world of the Rulers, their intense and constant competition and conflict, and also show their human side, which has been lost in the rapid reversal of fortune that was their fate. Should I have the longevity suite of my grandmother (I have never been tested and never will be), I will finish the story in subsequent volumes, but given the realities of time, and of publishing (seven centuries separate us from the triple-decker tomes of the nineteenth century), I am publishing this novel as it stands, unfinished, in four separate parts. I wish to express my deep gratitude to the librarians and staff at Georgetown, as well as my agent, Andrew Springbok, and editor, Babylon Sippar, for their devotion and confidence, and my husband, Brandy de L'amour, for reading multiple drafts. All mistakes, however, are my own.

— Eleanor Harvale Micawber

1

The Birth of Sargon 4

COLD SPRING, NEW YORK, AD 2500

On the day of his clone's birth, Sargon 3 was out riding and didn't reach home until after the cord had been tied and cut and the placenta expelled. He rode Herculaya, a black Arabian stallion with white feet, to a halt and dismounted, boots crunching into red gravel.

"Wait here, my friend," he said gently, stroking the horse's neck, and hurried towards a service entrance to the Winter Palace.

At the door, he turned back to look over his land. It was late fall and the maple leaves were glowing as they broke free of the branches and fell. The sky blackened the cold water of the pond, which lay below a grassy hill and a split-rail fence. At the top of the hill, across from a gravel path, was a leafless orchard of dwarf trees. A few apples and a butter-yellow quince brightened in the low sun against the slate-colored cloud overhead.

A giant, brindled American bulldog ran up to him. Sargon squatted down to scratch behind his ears. The dog licked his face and Sargon smiled, wiping the saliva off with the back of his hand.

"I love you too, Balfour. Come."

Balfour followed him beneath a high stone corbel through the servants' door, trotting behind him as he strode down the back hall, between the billiards room and the pantry. The Palace was bustling with cooks, maids, and footmen preparing for the Birth Night feast. He passed the liquor closet and the lift down to the wine cellar and took the backstairs to the birthing quarters in the North Tower, his shoulders squeezed in by the walls. In his war days he wouldn't have fit, but forty years of politics had left him thin and weak.

The fifth-floor landing led to the family apartments. The narrow halls were hung with paintings he and his Sires had done, portraits of people, dogs, horses, and sailboats. He had added three: a juvenile work of a young Balfour, four clones back, painted in oils in the manner of Vermeer; a picture of his yacht, the *Rosamund Fair*, sails trimmed, in the style of the Hyperrealists; and one he had done a few decades ago, at Hommocks Cottage on Long Island Sound, of Uncle Osiris holding a forty-pound striped bass in both arms. Rulers didn't trust photographs, but they loved to paint.

Sargon heard laughter and voices coming from the birthing room. He paused outside the open doorway and observed shadows of legs crossing a trapezoid of light. An obscure, cold feeling of fear stirred up from his gut and froze him in place. Even sixty years later it still came upon him all at once, without warning, followed by the sickening smell of acid and burning flesh.

It was his first battle. He was twenty-two. He saw himself riding a carnivorous horse out of the Santa Monica Mountains with his childhood friends, Bard and Otis. Heat rippled the horizon. Sun blazed across desolate land charred black by fire, still smouldering, poisoning the air.

They rode into combat behind their Commander, Everest of Texas, thirty-eight, eagle-nosed, tall in the saddle, his glowing indigo beard forked with coral fire, spangled uniform sparkling. A Birth Law fanatic and sadist, Everest had come to take LA back from Mexico, under orders from the new President, to reunify the nation. Everest didn't find a Mexican province but an independent city-state, a wealthy, decadent and depraved outpost that specialized in blasphemous entertainment, real estate, and rocket ships. From Santa Barbara to San Diego, from the coast inland to the Mojave, it was Ruled by *Deadbeats*, illegal bastards with bootleg DNA. Differences between human and Ruler were lax. Intermarriage and natural breeding were common. Everest set about eliminating both.

Sargon's job was to *break and scan*, an operation he had been trained in since childhood, which required, among other things, a load of indignation and hatred. He felt with bland lucidity the pain in his bones, training as a child on horse and baton, in all weathers. The forced marches. The jousting and sparring and ice cold swims. Like the nonconsensual sodomy, it was meant to build character, and turn children into killers.

They followed a road pounded to rubble by artillery and descended at a gallop from the Hollywood Hills into town. Smoke, dust, and dirt broke against his visor, the beast beneath him surging forward. He rode as he had been taught, and dropped a grenade down the intake tube of the first adobe dome he came to. Flames shot out the vent and smoke puffed from cracks in the dome. He wheeled around, tossed two more grenades, and rode into the spewing smoke and fire to strike down anyone who fled with his baton. He could feel the heat warp his visor. Two people charged out, frantically slapping at the flames immolating their heads. Dizzy, choking down the rising vomit, he watched them die before riding on to the next dome.

The city was broken. Water mains gushed like severed arteries and wildfires poured down the canyons like magma. He went door to door, searching for Deadbeats. Off patrol, he coughed up a slurry of dust and soot and washed it down with shitty beer and tequila, in bars full of gringo rough trade.

Neighbor informed on neighbor, friend betrayed friend, families turned each other in—a web that spread through the city block by block, home by home. Everest compiled lists and sent them out with transport trucks, to arrest the accused. Sargon pushed them into the containers, half-dressed, ill, stupefied by relentless fear, hunger, and violence, their bony arms small in his mailed grip.

Everest's troops registered 3,000 people with legitimate genetic modifications and 30,000 bastards, mutants and hybrids with no legal claim to their genome. They discovered synthetics no one had seen before. Many simply lacked registration papers for obscure mutations they had inherited from generations back, but that didn't matter, there were no appeals. Soon the jails of LA were packed with actors, agents, singers, athletes, musicians, politicians, accountants, brokers, lawyers, doctors, financiers, real estate moguls and independent barons, and lots and lots of nobodies. Everest ordered that they execute the Deadbeats in acid.

It was late October. The air was incendiary. Armored vehicles rolled up and down the palm-lined streets of Hollywood and Beverly Hills like armadillos. Dark-green tankers, their paint scarred and dirty, tires balding, ACID written across their sides, stood by greasy black dissolution tanks. Wisps of vapor wafted off their surfaces in the morning. Sargon, Bard, and Otis were assigned to the Beverly Hills Jail, where 1,000 bastards were housed in cells sufficient for ninety-three.

Sargon's job was to enter the jail and bring three Deadbeats out at a time. They were packed against the bars, half dead, rotting in their own shit and piss. He gagged on the reek. Outside, Bard and Otis, in rubber suits, seized and hooded the trembling, weeping prisoners, who began to shriek as soon as they smelled the acid, spreading panic through the cells.

The acid melted their writhing bodies into a sludge that was pumped into the waiting filtration truck. Normally they would kill them first, but Everest insisted that the pain would purge and cleanse the Republic of sin. Anyone showing mercy was to be burnt alive. Even so, after the first few dissolutions Sargon wondered what the fuck he was doing there.

"Sorry Balfour, stay."

Sargon took a breath, and went in to greet his replacement. Balfour remained seated, his nub of a tail vibrating back and forth, the light glinting off of his worried eyes. It was sinful how much he loved that dog.

The air was cold but the smell was warm, of sweat and afterbirth in a crowded room. Standing next to the bed on the left was his Consort, the Ruler Renee, her face pale, draped in loose wraps of black silk. In her arms was Phaedra, the Surrogate Ruth's one-year-old natural child. On the other side of the bed stood Doc Hughes, the family Geneticist. He had white hair, a bushy white mustache, white bristling eyebrows, and sideburns like ski slopes. Next to him were the midwife and the nurse, in platinumweave scrubs, webmasks, and hoods.

The Surrogate Ruth lay on the bed holding the Baby Sargon to her bare abdomen and chest. Yellow hair, tangled and dark with sweat, fell against the pillow. Capillaries burst by labor speckled her chest, cheeks and forehead. She let down and brushed a pendulous nipple across the Baby Sargon's lips. His tiny delicate mouth swelled and sucked the air, but he didn't latch on. Exhausted, she laid her head back on the pillow, gazed down at the baby, and smiled. The midwife sat next to her and said, "I thought we wouldn't make it in time."

Doc Hughes made two fists, shook them, and said to Sargon, "Congratulations, son." He winked at his own joke. Sargon was eighty-six, but there was speculation Doc Hughes might be over 350 years old; no one knew exactly. If it was true, that would put him well past Dr. Vesuvius, who was known to have cloned 250 years before. Doc Hughes had been old for all of Sargon's life, anyway, and his Sire once confided that he had been old *his* whole life too. Doc Hughes beamed, proud of his work. "He checks out. One hundred percent HomoZygotic. You even have the same eccentric swerve in your iridophore. I'll just leave you to log these tissue samples, if you'll excuse me, Sire?" He wiggled forward on his aged cage and held aloft a glass bag of sparking, clicking sample logs. "Congratulations again, my Sire."

Ruth got up on one elbow and looked around the room like a stray cat. "Where is Phaedra?" she asked. In a certain mood Ruth had a striking face. In another mood it was hardly visible. She came and went like a ghost in the house, sometimes a shadow, sometimes luminous. Ruth had learned quickly the art of disguise. She came from Transylvania as a young girl and was raised to bear Sargon's and Renee's clones. Surrogates lived as family members, and retired, if at all, when the Scions were grown. Many continued to live with their families, as nannies, aunts, or cousins, into extreme old age.

The Ruler Renee clung awkwardly to Phaedra, as if she were afraid she would escape. Phaedra watched Ruth and the Baby Sargon on the bed. She reached out her hand and opened and closed her fingers. "Momma baby," she said to Sargon.

He exclaimed, "Imagine, my munchkin, you have a friend now, almost like a brother." Not almost, he thought. The day she was born was the happiest of his life. He trembled when he first held her, the unfamiliar heat pulsing in his hands. That was followed by an incredible calm, a calm he hadn't known existed. When he was with Ruth and Phaedra, they were enclosed in their own peaceful bourn. Every night, after Ruth fell asleep, he would come to their rooms to sit in a chair, the dark dimly and warmly illumined by the ambient night light, cradling Phaedra's tiny sleeping body in his hand, her face framed by a triangle of blanket.

As he rocked in the chair his mind would eddy into fugues of lying in bed with Ruth. He came to her for sex but found her sleep deprived, focused entirely on the child. He had gone from being a god to practically nonexistent, except in the strictly formal observance of protocol. It was wounding in the moment but he could not look at her without feeling her exhaustion.

Would he do the same for his Scion? He had no answer. But somehow it was all different, a natural child and a clone. He was still stunned that they had been able to conceive at all. Rulers were usually sterile.

It was different. Phaedra was conceived in love, his Scion in a medium. It was him, budding off. He felt diminished by it, like he was being robbed of his future. His younger self would mature and he would die. It did not feel like a continuance at all. Just an end.

Phaedra was an *abomination* that could cost them

all their lives and bring down his line. Yet he felt only joy and a present happiness, without worry of the future or of consequences, when he was with her. *He felt safe.* Why? Another thing he couldn't explain. He was known for his ability to explain anything. He thought he knew it all. For so long it was a matter of making the correct moves, which was hardly any work at all. After war, life is boring, he thought. All the excitement happens in your head.

Sargon held out his hands and Renee, managing somehow to look both irritated and relieved, abruptly handed Phaedra over. He parked her on his ribs and gazed at her with his leonine eyes. She pulled his glasses down his nose. He pushed them up. She paused, looked at the glasses, looked at him, then looked away. Sargon turned his head and as he did so she yanked the glasses down again and giggled. He pushed them up and giggled back at her.

Sargon overcame his reluctance and decided to get a closer look at his future self. Ruth lifted the Baby Sargon and as she did so Phaedra reached out and hugged his head like a monkey. The Baby Sargon smiled blindly and all the old faces in the room smiled back. Then he opened his arms and seemed to hug her back and they laughed out loud. Tears welled in Phaedra's eyes and she cried, "Mommy! Nurse," twisting around in Sargon's arms like a snake.

Sargon laughed gently. "OK, back to Mama," he said, putting her down beside Ruth. Sargon ran his fingers through his hair. It felt like a shoe brush. It was time to hold his Scion. "OK. I'm ready now," he said.

Ruth looked at her lap. "Forgive me, Sire, I did not offer first."

He hated that she had to show deference. "No apologies," he said, whispering *Mausi*, "except for mine."

He took the Baby Sargon up in his large thick hands and held him against his heart, resting his cheek on his head, inhaling the sweet animal scent, damp and warm from the womb. *My son*, he thought. *You are the fourth generation of our father, Mr. President, Sire.* He saw them riding the inaugural carriage down Pennsylvania Avenue, the wild empty streets choked with trees, the winter leaves swirling by in a hot wind. The boy as a man riding the same carriage, the gleaming white uniforms and gold braid of the marching bands, the red, white and blue bunting disguising the burnt hulk of the Capitol as the wraith-like Chief Justice of the Supreme Court administered the Oath of Office. He imagined the boy's first words, then long discussions on horseback, teaching him how to hunt with a crossbow, and how to Rule, beginning with Manhattan. It crushed him how many hopes he had. He tried to chain them up but they would not stand down, except when his doubts were aroused, and they chased one another, doubts and hopes, like dogs in a yard.

Phaedra curled up and suckled at Ruth's breast. The nurse left quietly. The midwife got up and dictated data for the birth certificate. Sargon held the baby while the midwife scanned his hands, eyes and feet. When he started to squirm and cry Ruth said to Phaedra, "OK, enough now. Baby Sargon wishes to nurse. Remember what we promised." Phaedra let go and fell back on the pillows, half asleep, milk pooling on her lip. Ruth sat up and said, "He'll nurse now." She cradled him against her bare belly and chest. As he cried, he reached out towards her with his hands and lips. She lowered her breast over him and let him find her nipple. Sargon watched him latch on and suck, lips buried in the bumps of the areola.

"Well done!" cried Sargon, then to Renee, "We should let them rest."

"Yes. Good afternoon, Ruth. We'll see you at the party."

"Yes, My Lady."

Sargon kissed Ruth's cheek and took her hands into his, where they disappeared. How odd, he thought, how love works. He saw in her blue eyes his own Surrogate's eyes. Anna. One of his earliest memories was of awaking from a nightmare, alone in his room. He ran to the door and peered down the long dark hall to Anna's room, the light flickering under her door. Shaking with fear, he groped his way to her room as if it lay at the end of a black tunnel. He pushed the door open and peered in. Anna was in her nightcap, propped up on pillows watching TV, her eyes half-shut, a glass of red wine in her hand. Without turning from the TV she said, in her soft Austrian English, "Come in, *Bärchen.*" Little Bear. He ran to her bed and got under the covers, head sinking in the pillow. There was a girl with golden pigtails in a swamp full of Swamp Creatures. Anna took a gulp of wine and said, "It's called *Heidi in Swampland.*" They watched the swamp-creature Heidi's pigtails become like the golden fan of a lizard.

Sargon held Ruth's hands a second longer than was necessary, breathing in the fragrance of her body, savoring it on his tongue, letting it permeate his mind. He sighed. Always the forbidden. He felt a tingle in his nerves. He had never been so stricken with love, not for any man, woman, or horse. He looked at Phaedra and then at the baby. Phaedra would never know he was her father. No one would. He would become President and protect her from Everest and his acid tanks.

✶

Sargon paused in the hall by a stone casement, disturbed and distracted, and stared at the unsettled hills of November, tawny, warped by the lead-paned windows. The brown banks and bluffs of the river below were eroded by cold, featureless matter. He could feel time wearing him down. Yet this was a day most joyful. Self-birth. Continuance. The family capital preserved for another turn of the wheel. There was no reason for his feeling of loss.

The walls were covered with portraits of the Sargon and Renee branch of the family, going back to the Oil Age, a lineage his Grand Sire, Sargon 1, researched obsessively in old age. He would sit with Yni, his gruff, powdered and gowned Librarian, a Ruler without portfolio, at a mahogany desk under Edison lights, poring over genealogies kept in enormous hand-bound folios that still crammed the shelves of the Winter Palace Library.

As a child, he wandered the narrow catwalks with low iron rails that circled the stacks, climbing the ladders and stairs between tiers. The tower seemed a steeple, with a vanishing point deep in space. Lost birds swooped through the giant, mote-filled tunnels of light, banging the stone walls in panic.

By then, the post of Librarian had gone to a classicist from Budapest who specialized in maps and hated children. When she died he didn't bother with a replacement, but now that he had two children to educate he would have to change that. As soon as Robin Micawber, his counselor, friend, and closest confidant, returned to work he would tell him to hire a Librarian. Robin would know what was necessary. He had grown up with the collection and was a historian and a bibliophile. Robin had come to the house when he was ten or so, while Sargon was in LA, the child of poor foragers working the river and woods. Every Ruler needed humans, with short lives and only their wits to sell, to look out for them. That was one of the few things the Old President taught him that was of any use.

He would tell Robin to hire someone who was not just knowledgeable and dignified, a role model, but also willing to indulge a child's imagination. In addition, it should be someone who could be a research assistant for the family history Robin was writing, a project he would have no time for once

Sargon became President. It was hard enough as it was, with Robin sitting as his proxy in City Council sessions and maintaining all of the accounts. But one thing he was certain of: even as President he would not send his Scion to boarding school. He would keep him close, and safe.

The oldest pictures were of natural humans with strong family resemblances—Renee's stark white skin and black hair, his lion face. He came to Sargon 1's portrait, painted in his very early twenties, dressed in a platinum spacesuit, helmet tucked under his arm. As a child, he took it for granted that he too would wear a spacesuit and fight the Martian Rulers, who had become legendary, almost mythical figures, a part of his childhood play. When he was older, he learned about them as actual Rulers. He studied the space battles at West Point. The battles between Iocle and Ocba were a touchstone of every Ruler childhood and some of the idiots never let go. The only analogue was chivalry, which made him laugh out loud.

At twenty, Sargon bore no resemblance to the Ruler in the spacesuit at all. He wasn't in space, he was in the desert eating bugs, or in the city kicking down doors. His life was a pile of greasy ashes smoking in the street, not heroic battles. He was hollowed out. He lurched from task to task for decades, a dissociated husk. No kind of Ruler at all. Twenty years of California. Earthquakes, mud, fire, dust. He did not want to think of it again, but he knew he must. Robin was reaching a point in his research where oral history would take over from documents. It was the most vital part of the project, but one he dreaded. None of his Sires had left more than skeletal memoirs, a few diaries and appointment books from which to reconstruct a world. They never told him honestly what it was like to be a young Ruler in combat. It was all ho ho and patriotic songs, drinking and young men. Resentments and betrayals, yes. Those, the Old President rehearsed at dinner with relish, as if he could taste every rotten thing ever done to him.

Staring at the image of himself as a young man, who was not himself, he wondered, what were his Grand Sire's twenty years in space really like? It was brutal now, and even more so then. Prison labor rebellions. Jovian gas ships exploding. Space salvage and recovery missions. Mars defiled in every way imaginable, inhabited by transgenic mutants. Space was America's last fuckup.

His only memory of the actual Sargon 1 was of a shriveled sack with a raspy voice, buried in bedclothes, glasses the size of saucers balanced on his nose. He was 162 years old and hadn't said a coherent thing in years. He could play cards and was sensible, if terse, in American Sign Language, which Rulers of his generation learned for space war. That was when the 400 fought as one, at the head of the 20,000. Rulers were the Guardians of the Earth. The old-school phrases came back to him with a clanging clarity. What bullshit! But, he reminded himself, the world is as stupid now as it was then.

In Sargon 2's generation, they corrected the mutation. Now, the cognitive senses degenerated all at once, resulting in a catastrophic breakdown of consciousness. The world disaggregated into granular static, followed by blackout and death. Bloop.

Sargon 2, the Old President, was in his nineties and vigorous when Sargon was a child, before he was sent off to Phillips Exeter Academy at age six. The old man was so distorted by age he never saw his own nose, eyes, or mouth in him, which was by design. What clone would want to grow up in the shadow of himself? But the shadow was always there, the echo of the Sire saying *you are me* and *you are mine*. He was a moon until his Sire died. Only then did he become a star. Senator from New York, and President, *if* things broke his way on the Executive Committee, a big *if* churning away in his gut.

Now he did see his Sire in the mirror, and himself in the full-length portrait of Sargon 2 and his beloved horse MacDuff. The Old President who bent over him as a babe in the crib and taught him to ride when he was four. The man had lived on MacDuff. He supervised his feeding, grooming, and training. Spent hours in the stables. He kept a herd of carnivorous battle horses, but stabled them miles away. Even in war, the old man despised them. It was said that Sargon 1 had gnawed his way through the enemy in the Battle of Lower Manhattan. Sargon himself only rode them on parade. Like his Sire, he couldn't stand to watch them eat and despoil corpses. The Lord Otis relished the sight. His horse would browse in the rubble of a defeated town, licking guts off of construction blocks.

✯

He felt Renee watching him from the doorway to their living quarters. "Drink?" she asked.

He nodded. He could use one before greeting all those people. They walked towards the main stair, their heads high and eyes forward, in a deliberate, military gait. Sargon said, "The replacement has arrived."

Her face was a cold sheet of daisy-white, indigo eyes fixed beneath the high forehead. "Yours has."

Her voice was edged with angry humor. He wondered why. After all, it was his most joyous day. He asked, "Is something wrong?" knowing it would incite her. But his voice was lost in the expanse of the atrium. Fifty feet below lay the black-and-white marble floor. He stared down at it. The statues circling the galleries were reflected in the marble and seemed to turn around the axis formed by his eyes and the intersection of two black and two white tiles.

"The way you dote on them, honestly."

"Phaedra's a beautiful baby! Surely you don't begrudge me that?"

"You should not be concerned about me, but other people."

"Oh, what will the neighbors think? Are we living on *Peyton Place?*"

"Hgh!" she imploded, and yet the guttural emerged—"You behave as if this were all a joke, with your silly erudition. I have no idea whom your Peyton is, but I do know we are not invulnerable. We have not got a fortress around us, just perilous alliances with scoundrels and dependents. Within our own city, behind the walls of Manhattan, we are at risk. Federal troops patrol our streets when Congress is in session. How hard would it be to turn that into an occupation? Even within the nanodome, we have staff. If Phaedra's genome got into the hands of our enemies, what then? They would kill both of them, mother and child, and we'd be attainted."

"We took Ruth from her home, her people, to bear our whelps. The least we can do is protect her."

"You've taken more than that," she said, with dry precision. A lawyer by training, her fearless, Jesuitical, literal skepticism ballasted his tendency towards romantic excess. They were siblings, Consorts, originally cloned from a single Egg, designed to be two vessels of a single family genome, which had been accumulated over generations, and paid for many times over in blood and diamonds. The Consorts were to function as One, to act as each other's second, complement, breeding partner (in the old days), and closest ally, to preserve the family line. Well, there was the line, and then the tangle of the world it was designed to thread, he thought, both perhaps undying, though it never felt that way. The only undying things he could think of were pain and separation.

★

They descended the great stair, spiraling a chandelier of cascading water and light, and turned down a crimson-carpeted hall with black walls and gold trim to the second-floor TV room, which enfolded them in its quiet pocket. It was a place they came to to talk and relax, away from retainers and family. One grey wall was a TV. Opposite was the carved cherrywood bar, ivied columns framing a Martian mirror, and glass shelves of bottles. He looked at her in the mirror. Her hair had turned as white as her skin and grew straight to the shoulders, with a bang across her forehead. "Do you want gin and tonic?" she asked.

"No. Bloody Mary. With egg in it."

Renee clapped her hands and Albion, the butler, entered from a door at the other end of the bar, dressed in a black linen tunic and pants, the restrained uniform of the house. It was said you could judge a house by the feet of its servants. Albion's were clean and high arched, his toenails painted carmine. There were four bar chairs with black leather seats trimmed with gold tacks. Albion flipped two coasters down and said, "My Lady."

Renee said, "Bloody Mary with a raw egg."

"Quail or chicken?"

Sargon said, "Three quail."

"And for me a gin and tonic with lime and lots of ice. Make it a double in a tall glass and garnish it with mint."

"Very well, My Lady." He fell to making the drinks.

Renee turned on the TV. The wall lit up with pictures. Albion put the drinks before them and sat still at the end of the bar, glazed in silence and the color radiating off the wall screen. Renee and Sargon sat down and turned around to watch, elbows on the bar, toes propped up on gold footrests. Gangsters fired machine guns at each other and drove fast cars. She changed the channel. Brigands in medieval armor contended bloodily with swords and pikes, on a ridge of red rocks and blue sky.

"The thing is, I have no feeling for children or babies," Renee said. "None whatsoever. I fear I'm devoid of those instincts. Children are beasts, running about, shouting, smearing food all over the walls and furniture, and later, with the foul odor of hormonal sweat, rutting. There are days when the Palace feels like it's infested with swarms of young fornicating Rulers. It's ghastly. I think of copulating bugs when I should be feeling a gush of warmth and grace."

"That *is* a ghastly, paranoid view of things."

Isle of Dogs, Part 1

She considered him with unblinking severity. "And I wonder, was this love of children bred out of me, and on purpose? It's something no one speaks about. I try to remember if My Lady was cold."

"I don't remember her being a cuddly bundle of joy. And I don't see what purpose it serves, if it's by design. Life without love is nothing at all."

She nodded slowly, licked her lips and said, "My Lady *was* funny."

"In a cruel sort of way. Once, when I came in from a ride, she looked at me critically, sort of the way you are now, and said, 'It's a shame you'll never be any better than your Sire.'" He stared at the TV while he spoke, although his attention was on Renee. The images flashed by in a wheel of carriage spokes, dust, and gunfire so hot it warmed his face. "That might be the only thing I've ever wanted, to be better than my Sire. Certainly as President," he practically spat, "but also in the raising of children."

Renee said to his profile, "Scions, please. And you're not getting off to much of a start. You were out riding during the birth."

He studied her eyes. They were still and quiet, brightening to cobalt, set in ceramic. "Oh, I see, you mean like the Old President, I prefer riding to the birth of my Scion. Sorry, but it's stress. This whole business with Iocle and Everest is giving me ulcers. My heart races, I'm faint-headed, short of breath, can't remember my own name it seems. Riding calms the acid reflux, incipient asthma, abstract ideations, spells of annoyance and fretfulness."

"Why are you drinking a Bloody Mary, then?"

"I like the way it tastes, and the egg coats my stomach."

"You've got it all figured out." Her face relaxed as it did when she took off her clothes for bed. She cleared her throat. "I am not looking forward to entertaining half the Senate, the Admiralty and—"

"—*all* of New York."

"And California! I'm stunned Bard and Otis are coming East."

"I know. It's not like we went to LA for the Baby Bard's Birth Night."

"He must have some other business here."

"I hardly think so, with Slim and Orchidia to take care of things. He doesn't like to get his hands all grubby with business."

"You sound like a scold now. It's not becoming of a future President. Did you have a chance to speak to Bard in private?"

He had. They'd spoken for the first time in many years. They had last done so over a glass of rare apple eau de vie from the Bánffy estate, where they unfolded, slowly, over the course of the night, their mutual horror of events in California, and swore they would never let another purge happen, even if it meant seizing power. In this, silence was their most powerful weapon. Now the thing they feared most was a possibility, as Everest had maneuvered his way into President Iocle's inner circle.

Genetically, Bard was his and Renee's uncle. The family alliance dated back generations. For centuries, the Bards and Sargons Ruled New York together, and served as President and Vice President of the country, contending with the other Rulers: the Iocles, the Imogens, the Ocktomanns, and names now lost to time and history, dissolved in acid or burned in battle, extirpated from official records and memory.

It was this alliance President Iocle sought to break when he first came to power, and he used California to do it. It was all clear to Sargon now, almost clockwork, but at the time none of them knew what he was doing. Everest was the first move. His Sire was powerful, but a regional Ruler content to terrorize the frontiers with Mexico and root out Texan Deadbeats. But Iocle needed his support, so he gave the California command to his Scion. Iocle must have known the Younger Everest would overreach and fail. He also knew that his own troops would detest him. In the end, they overthrew him, and he barely escaped with his life.

Bard, a popular and talented General, with Otis and Sargon as his Lieutenants, won back what Everest had lost and restored California, and the rest of Aztlán, to the American Ruler fold. They were heroes.

After years of desultory fighting, at age forty Sargon did something Iocle didn't expect, but that fit his plans exactly: he retired abruptly back East, to Rule New York and enter the Senate, a move moreover that both mystified and pissed off Bard. Bard and Sargon were now, both emotionally and spatially, estranged. It was perfect. Iocle elevated Bard to Ruler of California, a position he would never abandon, for in New York the best he could hope for was Co-Ruler. And Iocle pursued a quiet vendetta against Sargon, fueled by transgenerational disdain.

Sixty years later, President Iocle was a mad old man kept alive by machines and potions concocted by Dr. Nerval, his Geneticist. And the equally mad Everest, for many decades Senator from Texas, and Ruler of the South, had come to dominate President Iocle's inner circle in DC. If Sargon wanted to be President, and stop Everest, he had to make his move, but he lacked the votes on the Executive Committee, primarily because the Senior Senator from California, the Ruler Adelaide of Sacramento, was willfully mercurial. He needed Bard to make her knuckle under, form an alliance, and support him for President.

Sargon said, "Yes, we spoke, but he was his usual enigmatic self. It was like nothing had changed since the goddamn forties. I took him to Lucretia's. Private room, foie gras, caviar, Dom Pérignon. They flew the Dover sole in that morning. We drank delicious wine; he joked about Slim and Orchidia not being there. And I have no idea what he's going to do. I don't know if he knows. He's certainly worried, more alarmed than we are, even, because we've adapted to the madness. The worst thing so far is giving Ocktomann the Martian Portfolio. You can thank Adelaide for that. She cosponsored the bill appointing him, with Imogen. Iocle must have been in suborbital consciousness when he signed it. If Everest has his way, he'll break the Quarantine."

"Did you tell Bard that?"

"Nope. Not in so many words. I need California. Insulting his Senator won't get me there. Massaging Bard's balls will." He growled beneath his breath.

"Bard's brilliant, honest, and he has self-control," she observed, pushing her empty glass across the bar.

"He'll come around. Where else can he go? You are old allies."

"Don't get me wrong. He is a man of honor. But Bard doesn't need anything, except to be admired. And California does a lot of trade with Mars. Half the rockets launch from there."

Renee sat thinking. "President Iocle didn't want to see Tobor Ocktomann running the Mars portfolio. He's angling for something else. It must be Imogen's price for supporting the Younger Iocle. Iocle really wants *him* to be President, not Everest."

"Would we be having this conversation if it mattered anymore what President Iocle wants? Holed up in the White House like that, with long fingernails," he said, grinning like a skull, clawing the air with a hiss.

"Is he really that far gone?" Renee's voice rose an octave, as if to laugh.

The black door opened a crack and Balfour thrust his head in, looking sideways at Sargon. Without turning around he said, cheerfully, "Come, Balfour, have a treat. Albion, a biscuit for Balfour?"

"Sire." Albion drifted behind the bar and got out a jar of dog treats, which he arranged in a circle on a Martian porcelain plate and placed on the bar.

Sargon tossed Balfour a biscuit, which he caught in midair.

The only thing he knew with certainty was President Iocle's undisguised hatred of him. There was rumor, and then his own observations on the very rare occasions he went to DC.

"The old man is no longer in control. Everyone says he's bonkers. Repeating himself. Calling people by the wrong name. He's confined to that wheelchair, a barbaric, Oil Age contraption. Nothing a normal person would use. So now Everest makes his move. He's been waiting for decades, ever since slinking home from California. We should have killed him when we had a chance, but Bard wouldn't do it, said there was no honor in it. Now Everest's little pricks Rule the President. Utkasting," he sneered, "Utburd, and Aeppar. Political nihilists. They care for nothing. Religion makes them evil. That Census Bill of theirs keeps spinning its wheels in the Council; using Birth Laws to pick up Deadbeats and send them out to space, to work on gas ships and mines, is evil. There is no other word for it. I hear this crazy shit in the Senate all day long now. It's a tide of stupidity that overwhelms anyone who is sane and intelligent. It is astonishing even by common accepted standards.

And those three fanatics are that psychopath's mainline into Iocle's brain."

Sargon inhaled and continued:

"That son of a bitch in the White House doesn't care what Everest does, so long as I never become President. He rambles on about injuries committed by Sargon 1 against Iocle 2! The stuff of fairy tales and children's cartoons can exercise him to the point that those great hanging globs of flesh on his face actually twitch. It's as if the rage were animating the dead slough he lugs about."

"But Bard does share our thoughts about Iocle?" Renee asked, ballasting.

"Well, we'll have an idea of how it stands tonight, I hope. They'll all be here, even Imogen."

"We can convene in the Parlor during cocktails. It will look perfectly normal to an outside observer, just old friends celebrating the birth of a Scion."

"I'll have Albion summon each of them after the meet and greet."

"This is coming together better than I had hoped," Renee laughed aridly through a wisp of a red smile so slight it didn't dent her cheeks.

Sargon drained his Bloody Mary, bit the lemon wedge and patted his lips with a napkin, "Lemons have burned the Teflon off my teeth."

Isle of Dogs, Part 1

★

In a White House bunker, two levels below the West Wing, sat Utkasting, Utburd, and Aeppar, advisors to President Iocle, formerly of Senator Everest's staff. With them was the Ruler Pike, Senior Senator from Oklahoma and Everest's enforcer, a leather-faced man, dour and practical.

The bunker was designed to feel like a typical corner executive office, with *Freshett* sighing and *Ambi* whispering from the contracting ostia of the living walls, but instead of the usual sylvan prospect, the windows looked out on dioramas of the Holy Land, which resembled Texas, in both the lunar landscape and the bright primary colors that robed their Saints. For the Texas Christians had adopted the iconography of Mexican folk religion. This they shared with their neighbor to the east, New Orleans.

Aeppar sat at the head of the table sipping a glass of bourbon, her back to a view of Calvary: a cobbled road leading up a blasted hill of bleached rocks and dirt. At the top, three shadowed crosses stood out, black against a rising sun. She was staring out the window at a vision of the Virgin of Guadalupe, dressed in folds of red fabric, clasped hands pointing to her lips, and haloed head to foot with golden needles, round face beaming above the parted robes. As she stared at the radiant Saint, it came to her quite suddenly that the halo was in the shape of a vulva, that the robes were like labia, that her hands came to a V in prayer, and that her face seemed to swell up above it like a clitoris. She had gazed reverently on Our Lady's image her entire life and never noticed it before. She shook her head and looked down the table at Utburd.

Utburd could not stop looking at the Road to Calvary. Whenever it detected an eye, a little claymation Jesus would carry the cross up the cobbled road, to the top of the hill, where two black, silhouetted figures hammered nails into his hands and feet. When he needed to think, Utburd liked to watch the crucifixion over and over again. And, if there was a meeting in progress, it served to remind him that Our Lord God and Savior had suffered too. Utburd reached for his bourbon, swirled it, and sipped.

Between Aeppar and Utburd, across from Pike, sat Utkasting, leaning back in his chair, holding the bourbon out. "Which one will he be tonight?" he asked.

"Shut up," Pike said, pointing at the device on the table. "You don't know whether that thing is alive or not."

A moist, spongiform cube eructed an image of President Iocle, a screen just big enough to contain the baroque topography of his face, which floated drunkenly before them. His synthetic voice was pinched, and delivered sarcasm in a nasal, rising voice:

"Now that his Scion is born, Sargon's strategy will change. He means to put you Texas fanatics down. Don't think I'd bloody weep! The only thing I'll miss in death is seeing Everest run out of the Senate and boiled in acid. Only one dog gets the meat. If Everest wants that Census Bill to pass, I won't stop it. But he'll have his old friend Sargon to contend with. They go way back, all the way to California. I can't wait to see the catfight that erupts between those two, a man who believes everything and a man who wouldn't know a conviction if it bit his dick off. When Sargon makes his move, you'd best be ready for it. He'll have Bard with him. They're meeting as we speak. I know what they want and I know their hearts; I know what they think before they do. Look for a bastard. Turn one against the other. That is my—Sara? Sara—I must be off, Sara's here."

The four looked at the table. Pike said, "Sara's gone, Mr. President, Sire. For almost a hundred and forty years, Mr. President, Sire."

"Bard is at the Birth Night party," Utkasting said.

Utburd said, "That hardly establishes the existence of a conspiracy. Everyone is attending, with the sole exception of those who live in toxic pestilential quagmires infested with mosquitos. One can hardly sleep for the volume of nocturnal stridulations. Yellow Fever is reported in town."

Pike said, "So what? Your air is screened."

"I'm especially eager to know what transpires at that party," Aeppar said. "Bard's not the only one who'll be there. Otis will be there too. What are they up to, then? It's been a long time since the three of them got together to take down the Senator. And I can tell you he doesn't forget, nor will his Scion and his Scion's Scion."

"I know what lurks in them. We are destined to see young slithering vipers turn into serpents. Arrest them all!" bellowed President Iocle, shaking the cube and wobbling in the air.

"Mr. President, Sire, that lies beyond our current interest and ability," Utburd said. "As to your point, Aeppar, I have been speaking to Imogen, in the hopes that she would bare her soul to me." He pointed to his chest with his thumb and Aeppar had to remind herself that he wasn't joking. "She did, and, in her serpentine way, assured me we still have her vote when we need it."

"Well done," said Pike. "But we'll see when we get to the vote where she really stands. Did she name her price? Did you get what you were after when you gave Ocktomann the Martian Portfolio?"

The cube bulged as Iocle's artificial voice exploded within its confines. Fluid was beading up in the surface pits. "Idiot! I fell for that, and I'm not such a fool as to fall for it again. The vanity and stupidity of old men is limited by what they can remember of their own goddamn experience! If that piece of shit Ocktomann lets one molecule of Ocba's hoard of outlaw DNA out of the dusky asshole of Mars' lowest surface depression I will nuke the goddamn planet. I will nuke California, I will nuke New York, I will nuke Chicago, Detroit, and Dallas, I'll nuke Everest's goddamn Alamo just to make him feel bad."

Utburd looked at the window and watched Jesus drag the cross up the hill. He was increasingly unable to digest the heavy dose of madness he was forced to ingest each day, all in the promise of a pure future. He said to Pike, "What she desires most is a transport station in the East. He'll never agree to that."

Pike said, "I agree. We need to pry a Ruler loose in the Northeast who will allow Kuiper Belt to build a transport station. And if we want to find a bastard, we need a spy inside. Let's make it an operation, devote resources as needed, off budget, and run it out of this basement." He paused, sipped his bourbon, glanced up at Our Lady, was momentarily confused, then looked away rapidly and continued, "The Old President was rumored to have fathered several, but it wasn't proved. I've searched the archives in Georgetown; never found a thing. It's a shame. We might have burned the whole line and not be dealing with this today."

Utkasting said, "Alive, in acid I hope. Why not someone from the navy, on Renee's staff?"

"Aeppar," Utburd asked, tearing himself away from the crucifixion, "Naval Intelligence?"

"Every time I look into space, my heart breaks!" the President screamed. "Sara!" Two distorted hands pushed an oxygen tube into his nostrils and the cube fizzled out, leaving a small mucilaginous puddle on the table. Aeppar snapped her fingers and a Scythian Guard in gold armor took a clean handkerchief from his pocket and wiped up the fluid, carrying it out on a tray for incineration.

"I know someone reliable, a Ruler named Euclid," Aeppar said, sadly. "We came up together in the

SEALs. He's on Renee's New York staff. Maybe he's available."

Pike said, "If Sargon does have a bastard, that would serve us well, from blackmail to arrest and dissolution. Rid ourselves of the lot of them."

Utburd said, "It's time to brief the Senator. He'll want to know."

2

His Birth Night Party

His Sire's ambivalence notwithstanding, the Baby Sargon's birth was a joyous occasion, a public event to be celebrated that night in the Great Hall of the Winter Palace. Extended family, friends, and colleagues were attending the Birth Night celebration. The Baby Sargon would meet the faces of his world, where finance, war, and politics crossed with art and commerce.

The outpouring of emotion was genuine. Rulers only cloned once, and they worshipped their Scions, though they were never meant to express that. What they could do is throw lavish parties on the Birth Night and they did. The balls and parties would continue unabated through the New Year.

Isle of Dogs, Part 1

It was time for Sargon and Renee to stop bickering and descend the grand staircase, in full platinum dress, their heads draped in diamond nets. The cascading light of the chandelier sparked off of their jewels, medals, ribbons, and gem-encrusted kill stars. They held hands and circled into the awaiting guests below.

Faces, rounded by the light, crowded the length of the hall, lit by candles in asteroidal iridium chandeliers and sconces. Beeswax melted on the air. Shadows moved in the vaulted ceiling sections, in the stone archways, and across the busts of warriors, monarchs, and the prophets of peace, set in arched niches along the wall. There was a relief of the Emperor Asoka and a floor tile mosaic of Alexander the Great. At the very end of the hall, a dark, undecorated Christmas tree towered over the entrance to the Fire Chapel.

Sargon looked out, smiled, and felt Renee's fingers dig into his palm as he dove into the midst of the crowd, like a dog chasing after a stick. He loved nothing more. They greeted the guests, waving their hands above their heads while everyone clapped and cheered. Then they turned to the dignitaries who had gathered at the foot of the stairs.

Closest, naturally, was the Ruler Maximilian of the Bronx, the other Senator from New York, a Ruler able to elbow his way to the front of any line. He was dressed in battle armor that had never seen a day of war, blue-green and shiny, like a frog. His scarlet hair barely covered his head, the long wiry strands glowing bright against his mottled pate. His face, sitting in the armor like a head in a jar, was perpetually worried, and his eyes ran, sensitive to odor.

Just as he could muscle his way forward, he could fall back and escape a room without a peep, as if he'd never even been there. But the most notable thing about Maximilian was his extreme punctuality. He was known by all as the most clocklike of Senators, with unbreakable habits, maintained by him to uphold traditions that didn't exist. Maximilian was a Ruler who found his love in the Chamber, at a young age, and never did anything else again. He sat at his desk, desiccating into his boots. "Max!" Sargon cried with delight.

"Sire, congratulations." They shook hands and Sargon slapped his back. When Maximilian recovered his breath he said, "I am most honored to attend this great occasion. Blessings on you, my friend."

Sargon smiled and turned his back on him to greet Bard, his Consort Orchidia, and brother Slim. At ninety Bard was still striking, with a nutmeg complexion, deep-set blue eyes, and a stoic mouth that exploded easily into an exuberant smile, infectious to all around him. Orchidia and Slim were nearly identical to him, differing only in hair color and complexion, Slim a shade darker and Orchidia with a rare, orange tint, and olive-green hair that was braided and wound on her head like a paper wasp's nest. They wore black dress armor of obsidianweave, Bard's black opal epaulets studded with six gold stars. Sargon shook hands with Slim and Orchidia and embraced Bard, muttering under his breath, "We'll meet in the Parlor. Albion will call you in." Bard blinked.

They had been talking to Tobor Ocktomann of Michigan, a tower of sophomoric flesh, his face a block craning downward, in a uniform of white gold, with Family Orders in precious metals and jewels stitched across his chest. Even his battle awards for valor and Purple Heart were done in gemstones and gold.

Sargon contemplated Ocktomann with loathing. There were boobs who made pleasant dinner companions. Senators you could drink and ogle boys with. Ocktomann was not one of them. Part of his dreary personality was a total lack of reflection. He had no idea who despised him and who did not. He was at home in any company. He was one of those

Rulers who think a friendship in boarding school is a lifelong commitment. Thus, despite Sargon's own evident lack of interest in anything resembling a conversation, Ocktomann would probably bug him later to go play a game of billiards, drink brandy, and reminisce about the old days. That was not going to happen. Yet he had to remain civil. He did not give a damn what Ocktomann thought or even what deal he and Imogen had cut with Iocle for her vote on Council. But he did need to care about that. He did need to play the long game now.

At Ocktomann's side was the Ruler Imogen of Illinois, his Consort and polar opposite. She was Senator from Illinois and Ruler of the Great Lakes States. Between them, they controlled the world's largest reserve of fresh water, in addition to a big piece of terrestrial US industrial production, and a controlling interest in US space operations, transport, production, and logistics, from the Moon to the Oort Cloud. Her Great Lakes Fleet was essential to any alliance.

They were a mother-son pair that decided to clone at the same age and grow up together in perpetuity. They produced, in the old days, a covey of inbred pinheads, before losing interest in sexual relations in the second generation. Imogen was two and a half feet shorter than Ocktomann, with hair like flames, starting to crinkle and yellow at the ends, and eyes like periwinkle glass. Sargon felt a lump in his gut as he inclined his head to them. Was she looking at him? Imogen tried to communicate with looks. He could not figure out what most of them meant, even after decades together in the Senate. He bowed his head to Ocktomann and tried, but failed, to fathom what Imogen intended by her bulging eyes and flared nostrils.

They waded deeper into the crowd, shaking hands, kissing cheeks. Commander Roosevelt, head of the City Police and the Black Guard, stood stroking his considerable mustache, listening with his usual menacing focus of attention to the Lord Otis, who stood like a horse, golden hair loose against his shoulders, relating a tale of urban warfare in illustration of a point about the unavoidable evil done by good people in a wicked world.

Sargon waited for Roosevelt's smile, a broad flashing of teeth so wide it squeezed his eyeballs shut, to subside before interjecting, "Pardon my intrusion, but when I see two of my favorite people in the world laughing together, I can't resist. My friends, welcome." He took Roosevelt's hand between his hands and gently shook. "It's good to see you out of the office. And Otis! Otis. It's been a decade, I think."

"At least." The Lord Otis of San Diego kissed Sargon on both cheeks and slapped his back. Sargon looked into his old pal's scarred and weathered face and saw Bard's Hammer, as he was known. Bard's legendary ninety-day drive, reuniting the old state of California, would not have happened without Otis's intense and relentless offense. Otis drove down the Valley, attacking from the mountain passes in the east, while the navy shelled the coast from the west. Otis battled heat, starvation, and thirst. At every siege, his army rode in, cutting down all who stood in the way.

Otis put the most vicious horse to shame for anger and hunger in battle. He had a sweet, copper face, cupped in a wave of yellow hair with a slight, innocent smile, even with a bloody machete in his hands. His line had chosen well. They weren't peacocks, they were wolverines with long lives, cunning minds, and sweet smiles. Otis had no Consort. They were self-fertilizing hermaphrodites, descended from the San Diego branch of the old California Outlaws, and were legalized as Lords centuries ago. Otis put his arm on Sargon's shoulder and said, "Congratulations, my old friend. I hope I know your happiness soon."

"I pray that you do. And that he will be born in California and Rule in San Diego. I hope we will have time to catch up later?" His voice dropped to a whisper. "Albion will call you into the Parlor." Otis nodded and Sargon moved on to shake hands with the next ten heavily decorated Senators, men and women in their nineties and hundreds, their shriveled lips stretched over sharp Teflon teeth.

Sargon greeted knots of cousins and aunts and uncles, the natural children of the family, and their large families. He handed each a black pearl and took their hands in his and kissed them each on the cheek. He put his hand on the shoulder of anyone he knew well, and hugged old friends and cronies until the greetings became remote and generic. Servants in red-and-gold livery passed trays of smoked fish, aged cheeses, sliced venison, and bread. They poured the best cider, beer, and wine. The room grew loud with laughter and conversation. Renee pulled him along, and he missed Robin. It irked him that his unease all day might simply have been Robin's absence.

Finally they entered the tall doors into the Parlor, and closed off the crowd behind them. This is it, he thought. It was hard not to feel in his gut that he had it in hand, but he had been in the game long enough to know he had to be ready to give something to get Imogen on board. He hoped that she would reveal what she was after, so he could at least make a counteroffer.

It was a magnificent room, built to awe. It had a star-shaped vaulted ceiling encrusted with spacemetals, semi-precious stones, glass, and enamel work from every rock in the solar system. It was furnished comfortably with dark leather sofas and chairs, tall palms, ferns, and Bacchic statues. Paintings of Arcadian scenes hung on the walls between drapes with silver sashes. He stared up at the ceiling, created to look like a Martian ice cave, facets frozen into sharp angles and mirrored clefts.

As a child, he approached the room as he did all rooms, shivering and tongue tied, as if it were a crypt. He toddled about in the marmoreal shade of his Sire's monumental leg, where there was no warmth, only the command to be silent and listen to him rehearse generations of ancestral grievances, betrayals and desertions. Sargon 2 had annotated every one of them and the appended commentary could go on for hours. It was intended to be his inheritance. Now he was seated in the same chair, casting the same triangular shadow across the floor.

Isle of Dogs, Part 1

Even as an adult, his helmet bloody and burnt and many horses lost, he licked his lips with trepidation going into the Parlor to kiss his Sire's ring. The old Ruler's body was bound to the chair. The curvature of his spine was so severe he had shrunk down to six feet. He scowled in discomfort, moving only his jaw. Sargon would look up at the sparkling pins of light in the ceiling and realize it was going to be his one day. He would be the Ruler Sargon and then President. The Old President would be gone. And won't his boy want to kick him off the throne too?

✶

One by one, Albion escorted Bard, Orchidia, Slim, Ocktomann, Imogen, and Otis to their seats in the Parlor. The party murmured on beyond the doors, and strains of waltzes and marches came and went in waves. Balfour lay stretched out at Sargon's feet. A Siamese cat walked across the back of the yellow sofa, pillows embroidered with peacocks, upon which Ocktomann and Imogen were seated like a St. Bernard and a poodle. A fire burned in the hearth. There was a bottle of iced vodka on the table and six vodka glasses.

Bard poured himself a shot and asked, with a stricken face, "Have you heard about the fire?" The others stopped chatting and looked at him. "No? It's all over the news. There was a fire in DC." They were staring at him now. "In the Presidential quarters of the White House. Totally burnt up." He paused and let a mischievous smile steal across his face. "But don't worry, Iocle's just as dead as he was before."

"Ha, Ha!" chortled Ocktomann. "You really had me going there."

Laughing, Imogen said, "Did you know that JFK would have lost the Presidency but for the dead of Cook County? In Chicago, in the old days, the dead voted."

Bard said, "Not much has changed."

"Indeed. But we've outdone our ancestors. For many years now, we have had a dead Mayor. The people keep reelecting a guy named Richard F. Daley, a hanged thief, because they believe he is a clone of the original Mayor, Richard J. Daley."

"Maybe he's not actually dead, maybe he just doesn't want to step down with a noose around his neck," Sargon said.

"Or he'd rather hang than spend more time with his family," said Bard. He poured vodka into each glass and handed them out. "A toast." They raised their glasses. "To my oldest and dearest friend,

Sargon. May you know the happiness of love I have known these four years with my boy. Prost!"

"Prost!"

Sargon said, "Thank you Bard. Thank you for traveling all this way to share our joy, and allowing us the company of your great General, Otis. Surely this is a sign if ever we needed one that California is a secure and peaceful state of the Union. I wish I could say the same for the rest of the country. My friends, I fear for our nation, as I'm sure each of you do. I think it is time we do something about it." Sargon felt a crump in his head. "Ocktomann, can you tell us a little about your position on Mars? I have heard Everest wants to violate the Quarantine."

Ocktomann said, "Everest?" He was surprised. "No one escapes the Quarantine. I'm convinced of that."

Sargon said, "Except for the Martian Princess." They chuckled.

"It isn't a joke," Bard said.

"That wasn't a joke," Sargon said.

The Martian Quarantine had been established two hundred years earlier to prevent Rulers with Martian genes from spreading alien DNA on Earth. They were afraid to unleash all the bizarre synthetics created on Mars in the colonial days when labs engaged in forbidden R&D, led first by Monozone

Inc. and other biotech giants, and later by Dr. Vesuvius, under Ocba's Rule. Conditions on Mars triggered mutations, and synthetic DNA was already mutation-prone. No one knew for sure what they had cooked up in the ice mines because no one had returned, except for the urban legend of the Martian Princess, Iocles 2's Consort, Sara Istar, who disappeared behind the Quarantine in 2360 and whom many believed returned to Earth as a poltergeist on a slave ship called the *Saint Dominick*.

The long-standing policy came under criticism rarely, but Everest and his allies saw its violation as serving several purposes. Primarily it was a way to differentiate Rulers definitively from humans. Martian DNA had unique markers and the hybrid products intercepted in the past were dominant, not recessive. Importation of quarantined genetics would be a badly needed infusion of novel genes into the market. Everyone would *have to have it*. DNA hunters had spread over the world to strip natural human mutants, or Uniques, of their genome to supply that demand, but the returns were diminishing. There were fortunes to be made getting Earth patents for Martian genetics.

Ocktomann scoffed. "Really, would it be the end

of the world if Martian DNA were for sale on Earth? We overreact, I believe."

Sargon said, "You can't possibly question the need to maintain the Quarantine."

Imogen, looking at Ocktomann as if he pained her, stepped in to explain, "What he means is, we have sufficient safeguards here on Earth to prevent the introduction of alien DNA into the genome. But I believe we do have an interest in increased trade. If I could transport more Deadbeats to work the gas ships, mining operations, and surface factories, we could regain a position of global dominance. China's got the Moon, Europe and Africa dominate Mars, but we have the quarantined mines and caverns, the factory ships and space stations. We have the infrastructure. We don't need to kill the Deadbeats we arrest, we need to put them to work, so we can grow. Otherwise, we won't survive."

Bard's face froze and he asked, in a cold contemptuous voice, "Why kill them all when you can work them to death?"

Ocktomann waved his hand and honked, "There I go with my foot in my mouth again, I'm like a cattle disease tonight. Everest is right. We can't afford to let our stuff out there. It erodes our wealth. Felons yes, Deadbeats no. Kill 'em all. Consolidate, consolidate, wherever you can. I like it when Everest says, 'Labor doesn't redeem, fire does.' If you said things like that, Sargon, you'd be more popular."

"And less powerful," said Renee.

Otis said, "We're virtually infertile, and homosexual by culture and inclination. But we must stay pure. Otherwise fertile humans will overwhelm us. Billions would have our genes, but we would disappear into the mass, showing up here and there as glowing hair, or albinism. Martian DNA could preserve us. Our speciation would be complete. We'd be like angels, every Ruler a unique species."

Ocktomann whooped. "I've never thought of you as so poetic."

Otis said, "I was aping *you*. I believe in mutts. It keeps the line healthy. That's what we San Diegans are all about. Muttitude, dude."

Sargon said, "We have to face facts. Sterile Speciation will mean our extinction. Cloning can't be the sole means of reproduction for us. This is about Drift, Ocktomann. Drift. Genetic purity is madness. That is what Everest is after, and his Census Bill is the means. I need all of you to support me. I'm going to defeat that bill." He paused and thought, *now I've done it*. "You haven't seen a purge. Otis and Bard and I have. Is that what you want in Michigan and

Illinois? He has President Iocle's ear and we do not." He looked to Orchidia and Slim. "Tell me Bard, can I count on Adelaide to vote with me? What does she need?"

Orchidia and Slim stirred slightly. Bard was alert but mute. Slim spoke up, his voice quiet, incisive. "She doesn't need a thing."

Sargon said, "I'm sorry, but she often votes with my friend Imogen." He let that hang in the air.

"There are deals," Orchidia said. "Adelaide has acquired a controlling interest in the SoCal Aerospace Corp., which subs for Kuiper Belt and Oort. And we have state concerns."

Imogen said, "To answer your question directly, Sargon, Adelaide supports me, and the census, because California needs my water. What do I need? That Census Bill, and more transport stations. If you want my vote, you can always allow us to build a transport station in New York or New England. It would save us transport costs and let's face it, the East is full of Deadbeats."

Blood rushed into Sargon's face and he blurted out, "That will never happen. Build it in Cleveland! Bard, certainly you can make Adelaide—"

"Allow me to interrupt," said Bard. "There isn't time for this. From my discussions with each of you this week, it is clear that I should come East as Senator from California. My goal is to make a strong stand against Iocle in Council, and prevent Everest from taking over, which I agree, Sargon, would be a disaster for this country. So, Ocktomann, allow me the chance to offer you the appointment of Ruler of Southern California. Senator Adelaide will retire and Rule the North from her Tower in Sacramento, and I will take her Senate seat. Does that earn your support, Imogen?"

Sargon felt his stomach buck violently. The thoughts drained out of his head into his chest, replaced by a scream. He looked at Renee. She showed no reaction, but her jaw was tight enough to crack a molar.

Ocktomann said nothing, an idiotic smile dusting his doughy face, a sign of Drift, Sargon thought, the slow drift into inanity, the entropy of empires. Cruel when young, strong, and stupid; cruel when old, feeble, and perverse. Ruler of Southern California. Ally. Tobor Ocktomann barked like a seal. "Isn't that something? California! I never expected such a plum. The jewels fall into your lap there, like ripe fruit."

Stunned, Imogen said, "You see how much he appreciates it."

Bard leaned forward. "Yes, he's quite

demonstrative. But I want to know, how much do *you* appreciate it?"

Ocktomann said, "I'll be in California." He was at peace with his own imbecility, so he didn't attempt to hide it from others. He said, "I think out West I can finally stretch the wings a bit."

"You need your head about you in California," Bard said. "Or those wings will be pulled off for sport. You will have a guard at all times."

"Oh, I intend to ride in formation down Hollywood Boulevard." He suppressed a laugh, a boyish smile on his eighty-eight-year-old face. "I'll design a new uniform for my guard. And I'm looking forward to getting down to Mexico. The *young goat* they say is excellent." A silent laugh disturbed the room.

Otis said, "Yes, there's plenty of young *cabrones* for your delectation."

"That's what I heard. Also nicely grilled over mesquite wood with lemon." Otis smiled and winked at Sargon, but Sargon didn't smile, it was all he could do not to let the screaming in his head loose on the room. He was hoping for it to cool to invective.

Ocktomann chuckled, "Now you're acting like Exeter Middle 3 boys. These two at school, we all thought they were going to scandalize the Ruler world by eloping in Budapest."

Renee clapped her hands and said, "Another elaborate thought, I'm so proud of you."

Albion entered from a discreet door in the back and approached Sargon from behind. Balfour opened his eyes and wrinkled his brow. Sargon smiled as if at Renee's insult and rocked back slightly, allowing Albion to lean down and whisper in his ear, "Sire. Senator Maximilian wishes to have a moment in the hall."

Just what he needed. It was Maximilian's way of getting asked to join the party. That blabbermouth, he thought. He whispered back to Albion, "Tell him I'll be out shortly and to wait by the stairs. I'll see him going up. Remind me when I get there." He really needed Robin to talk him down, his heart was racing and irregular. A bad time for a fib. Sargon said, looking distantly, "In LA you're always thinking, What if there's a bomb, how do I get out of here? Remember that?"

Bard shook his head and said, "I've had enough war and killing. It's time for a President to work for peace."

There was a commotion by the stairs. Albion returned to say the time had arrived. All stood and proceeded out the French doors into the Great Hall. The guests parted for the Rulers as they made their way to the grand stair, and Ruth, aided by the midwife, descended with the Baby Sargon in her arms, drenched in dazzles of light shed by the chandelier. Sargon and Renee took their places in front and Maximilian stood just below them. All began to clap and cheer until an ovation thundered through the room.

Ruth stood before Sargon and Renee. He fought back tears looking at her, so beautiful and vulnerable. He wanted to lie in her arms and forget the pain drilling into his forehead. Renee kissed her and kissed the baby and then Ruth gave the baby to Sargon, who kissed them both and held him up for all to see. The Baby Sargon's face was squished shut, but as the crowd cheered it opened briefly, and he peered out at the room with dark eyes. The swirls of hair on his head lit up neon green. Swallowing his rage, Sargon cradled him. The crowd stomped its feet and sang "Happy Birthday" as Ruth, with the midwife's help, walked back up to her private rooms.

✶

Ruth sat down on the bed, sore and exhausted. All she wanted was to close her eyes and sleep dreamlessly for one hour. When she laid the Baby Sargon down in the cradle by her bed, he opened his arms as if parting a curtain and she held her breath, resisting the urge to touch him, and the urge to fly away. As his arms slowly lowered to his side, she squeezed her eyes shut, seeking dark and peace.

But that was not to be. She couldn't shake the agitation of appearing before a crowd. The singing, the clapping, the smiling continued as if she were still there, trying not to tremble as everyone looked at her. She was worried her uterus was going to flop out as she walked down the grand stair. In such crowds big chairs and arrases were her friends, but she was exposed now, like a feather hanging in the empty sky. In her mind, she projected herself out of her body and out of the hall. The shadows fled from her face like bats racing up the stone walls. She smiled. She waved. Her eyes snapped open.

Ruth stared at the ceiling for a while and then sat up in bed and turned her eyes towards the hands folded on her lap, wondering whose they were. On the front of her cotton gown was a small red dot. She watched it spread slowly through the fabric and darken until a puddle covered her lap. She yanked her shirt up. The pad was saturated with blood. She shrieked, "Ew! Duck, help! I'm bleeding to death!"

Frau Duckworth hurried in from the hall in time to see the midwife take the pad, hold it up to the light, and say, "No. You are not dying. You lost some blood on the stairs, that is all. Lie down. I'll get you juice and water." She tossed a clean nightshirt and a bundle of fresh linens on the bed. "Rest. Change it whenever you have to, and put the old one in that garbage—" she pointed to a can by the bed with a glass-bag liner and lid.

From the doorway Frau Duckworth said to the midwife, "I'll see to her now. You can go." Ruth relaxed a little when Duck touched her with her small familiar hands. Duck bathed her as she used to do when Ruth was a child. Frau Duckworth's stern, disapproving mouth was clamped shut, encircled by faint wrinkles and edged, along the top, with an old woman's mustache. But Ruth paid her mouth no mind. She looked into her grey-blue eyes and saw gentle, loving Duck. As long as Frau Duck was there she would be OK.

Duck was the only mother she had. Her real mother had visited once, and she thought about her from time to time, but that was more like a dream. And, ever since Phaedra's birth, she had come to judge her mother harshly for sending her away. What mother gives up her child? She would never let

Phaedra go. What else did she have? She had outgrown the clothes she had arrived with in less than a year. Even her bones and flesh were made within these walls, not those of Castelul Bánffy, where she was born. What she had come with was long subducted. Everything disappeared with time, but Phaedra would not.

Unless she was forced to give Phaedra up. The fear never left her that armored guards would seize them on the street and test her. She would murder Phaedra and kill herself first. Ruth told Sargon that, the night she was born. Her voice was so certain, so calm, it was like another person speaking through her. He looked at her strangely and smiled, as he did when she was a child and amused him, or when they were being playful in bed. She would not give him the smile he sought but made him swear on his life he would help them escape to Montreal and make their way back to Hungary if there was trouble. He took her hands and swore on his life he would do so and she rewarded him with a slow kiss.

Two servants came in bearing towels and a basin of hot water. A third moved the crib.

Frau Duckworth said, in lilting Austrian German, "Take off the shirt and lie on your side, dear." Ruth did as she was told. Then she rolled onto her back and sank into a warm fragrant towel, drifting into a trance. Frau Duckworth bathed Ruth with a rough orange sponge, turning her from side to side like a baby. When she was covered in creamy soap, Frau Duckworth dipped a washcloth in the basin and slowly wrung it out, steam rising between her strong red fingers, and wiped away the lather. Ruth's skin tingled. Frau Duckworth rubbed her with geranium-scented oil from neck to foot and she slept.

An hour later she awoke, stretched out her arms, and put on the fresh shirt. She lay back on the pillows and kissed Phaedra's small warm head. They wheeled the cradle back in and left her in the silence. She had wanted it so desperately, no sound and nothing to look at. But now that it was here, she felt a wave of panic. All day, people, talk, faces. Before that, a heavy blur of agony and isolation. Long waves of pain. Relentless, stabbing spasms that never ended. And then the breaking open.

The Baby Sargon stirred and cried. The cry was quiet and a little crooked. He hadn't gotten his lungs yet. Ruth got up on one elbow and gazed at the baby. She loved him, but he was not hers and she knew it. She was just the hired vessel. Sometimes she felt like she was one of their collections, a collection of one. At least the other collections had their own rooms, like the miniature instruments, or the dwarf zoo. She'd lost hers, in the East Tower, on the second floor, overlooking a courtyard with fig trees, abstract sculptures, sand and stones. They could make a miniature version of her and put her in there if they wanted to. As long as she had something to do. Little books to read and portfolios for drawings. A guitar. Maybe leather to make shoes.

She lifted him from the cradle and laid him alongside her. He had his Sire's face. His sister's face. While he nursed, they dozed off for two hours. When he awoke to nurse again, the Ruler Sargon was seated in the corner with Balfour, watching them with dark, unhappy eyes. She was too tired to acknowledge his presence. She pulled up her shirt, gave her nipple to the baby, and shut her eyes.

The next night, after dinner, Sargon came and sat with Ruth and Frau Duckworth. "Do you mind if I sit on the bed?" he asked. Ruth was too tired and lost to smile. A hurricane of sadness was approaching, she could feel it. With Phaedra she'd been free, but now she looked at the walls when she was awake and felt like she would scream.

As he sat, the bed sank down low. He took her hand. It was the smile that made her feel safe, the one she grew up with. He didn't look at other people the way he looked at her. In her few, isolated years she knew one thing well and that was her Sire. And he knew her, as no one else did. When the color in his eyes spun around, it was hard to look away. It felt like he was probing her. Doing to her mind what Doc Hughes did to her body to prepare her for the births. And other times, like now, he had the still, kind eyes of deep-blue water. And yet, she trusted him, even though she knew she should not do so.

"How are you feeling?" he asked.

"How would you feel if you'd pushed a watermelon out of your ass?" He laughed. "I am feeling OK, very tired. He weighed ten pounds! I think he's twelve now." She laughed. "He is beautiful, look at him. A little you."

They had marked Phaedra's birth with fraught meetings, secret medical procedures, and fear like permafrost. The Baby Sargon's birth would be celebrated with six weeks of balls and banquets. Sargon leaned his big face in and moved his crinkled eyes over the Baby Sargon, and the Baby Sargon kicked his legs and grimaced for Papa. When his hair lit up, Papa Sargon clapped his hands and beamed. He stroked Ruth's forehead, kissed her on the cheek and said, "I love you, *Mausi*. And our Baby Mausi too. We are a family, never forget that. I love you more than life itself." But there was something in his voice, a quaver of loss, that both saddened and alarmed her.

✶

The Baby Sargon's celebrations ended after the New Year, on Altar Day, when they reconsecrated their Fire Altars. January was unusually cold and dark, with several wet snow storms and a genuine nor'easter, the likes of which the city hadn't seen in centuries. Four feet of snow fell on New York City in thirty-six hours. The Ruler Sargon, shrouded in black wool, drove a team of blindered percherons down Fifth Avenue behind a snowplow. He stayed out on the street all night, checking in with road crews, handing out bonuses, and pouring coffee in emergency shelters set up for first responders. It was his job. He was still Ruler of the city. His lungs burst with energy as he drove the team of horses, great clouds of vapor obscuring his face, serene banks of snow sparkling in the lamplight.

The crisis passed and he returned to the Winter Palace. Each morning, he rode over miles of trails through the deep forest that lay to the north and east, breaking through the morning ice. He rode his thoughts out, through woods he had explored as a child with Bard, Slim, and Orchidia. They'd each had a pony with silver bells on the saddles. It was where he learned to hunt with his Sire, who liked to go out on a cold Sunday morning, alone. And these were the woods he would take his Scion into with his first crossbow.

There was much to think about. Bard's decision to come to the Senate upended all of his plans. Without Robin or Renee, he had to explore it himself, working through details he was too depressed to care about. He worried about preparing his boy for office. He wondered how he would protect Phaedra. He swore he saw a strand of her hair light up when she was laughing. And then there was Ruth. He wanted to marry her and live like an ordinary human couple, something he knew nothing about. It was really a mad fantasy. But all of his fantasies—including the Presidency—seemed mad to him. In the morning, he awoke with a spike-like desire to fuck her, vivid ideations and fantasies of her body, her breath on his neck, his cock in her mouth, her thighs against his cheeks. It was an obsession. Sometimes he was frightened it wouldn't last; others feared they would pay the price of his old man's folly, as Renee never ceased to remind him. She thought he should send Ruth and Phaedra back to Europe and let Duck raise their Scions until they were ready for school. He wouldn't hear of it.

He would return, bathe, dine, and head up to the South Tower with Balfour to watch movies with Duck and Ruth. They sat in a dark room, he on the floor against cushions, his legs stretched out like fallen trees, the back of his head resting between her legs. He lost track of the days until the end of the recess approached and he found himself drinking late into the night alone in his room with the television grinding through dramedies and detective stories, his hopes destroyed with nothing yet to replace them but self-recrimination. Because he should have seen it coming. That was the truth. He spent all of his time dreaming of a crazy married life with a woman sixty-five years younger than he was and not of the political crisis that was all too real, a mad and dying President.

3

The UN

On March 3, 2501, the 356th Session of the United States Congress convened in New York. In Cold Spring, at 6:00 a.m., Robin Micawber and Sargon left for Manhattan aboard his private train. Sargon's car was paneled in mahogany, with fused asteroidal, regolithic fixtures, and Persian carpets on the floor. There were two desks inlaid with extinct woods, ivory, and spacemetals, and seats of crimson velvet for four. Sun fluttered in and out of the curtained windows.

That day's Senate business was the election of members to the Executive Council, a body of twenty Senators. There were fifteen open seats and five permanent members of the Executive Council: New

York, California, Texas, Illinois, Virginia. They formed the Executive Committee. Because there were two Senators from each of forty states, each of the five permanent seats had two potential candidates. Theoretically Bard could be opposed by the other Senator from California, Philomel, but that would never happen in the Senate, where celebrity and power were rewarded directly and Senators were loath to alter tradition.

Sargon conceded the necessity of a nomination process that was unrelieved drudgery, blindly obedient Senate Ceremonial at its worst. But he did not have to be there for the whole numbing process. He planned to meet Renee for lunch, followed by a game of bridge at the Waldorf with his kitchen cabinet: Lugalbanda Uruk, President of the City Council, Monozone CEO Arthur Bell, and the Ruler Darius of New Haven, Senator Titania's Consort.

Robin brought documents, and coffee in a thermos, which he poured when the train pulled out. He was small by Sargon's side, but he wasn't particularly short for a human, just over five-eight. He had thick brown eyebrows with grey threads, and stout limbs. His eyes were pale blue, set in a face of seasoned oak. He was dressed in an olive-green corduroy vest and crimson button-down shirt tucked

Isle of Dogs, Part 1

into green wool trousers. He sat at his desk sorting through the documents.

"Sire," Robin began.

"Thank God you're back!" Sargon said, surprised by the vehemence of his outburst. "All hell has broken loose. But first, how is your father?"

"I thank you for asking, Sire." He bowed his head slightly and continued. "At eighty-six, not much on his feet. They don't last long after that."

"Not if they're lucky." Sargon shook his head. *He* was eighty-six. "Eighty-six. A long life for a man." He looked away.

"The old horse won't leave it to luck. He has a vial of poison he carries around."

"Hardcore." Sargon glanced around the room and loosened his neck. He said, "I don't suppose you've heard the news?"

"I'm afraid not Sire, unless you refer to the birth of your Scion."

Tears of shame strained Sargon's eyes. "Bard is coming East to take the California Senate seat."

Robin Micawber rarely expressed surprise, but he couldn't veil his consternation at the news. Sargon probed him silently and waited for him to speak. Robin looked out the window and back at his Sire, his face grave. "Sire, I don't understand. Surely he was here for the Birth Night celebration? Did he ask or announce the decision?"

"Announced. In front of everyone! And it gets worse. He is making Ocktomann Ruler of Southern California, to get Imogen's vote against Everest. And he gave no warning whatsoever, even though we met privately in the city the night he arrived. I took him to Lucretia's! We had a private room, foie gras, caviar, Dom Pérignon. They flew the Dover sole in that fucking morning! But does he ask me if I mind him destroying my dreams and plans and putting LA in the hands of an idiot?" He wrung his hands as fury overtook sadness. "I can kiss the Presidency goodbye."

Robin Micawber nodded with understanding and then, in a gentle consoling voice, said, "Sire, you have my deepest sympathies. But you mustn't lose hope for the Presidency. You still have the Senate, where your power is unquestioned, and your position on Council and the Committee is strengthened by this. Surely Bard will be a more reliable ally than Adelaide?"

Sargon laughed bitterly. "Sure he will be, but not for my bid for the Presidency. That vote goes to him, the war hero, the Ruler of unimpeachable honor who, moreover, is a lot of fun. He'll seduce those hapless idiots. I can herd them, I can whip them, I can squeeze a vote out of a recalcitrant backbencher with a dam or a highway bill, but I can't charm their asses into tits."

"It remains to be seen, Sire." He took a small volume from his pocket, thumbed the pages and came to a heavily underlined passage, which he quoted, in Greek and then in English: "'Ο μὲν φιλόδοξος ἀλλοτρίαν ἐνέργειαν ἴδιον ἀγαθὸν ὑπολαμβάνει, ὁ δὲ φιλήδονος ἰδίαν πεῖσιν, ὁ δὲ νοῦν ἔχων ἰδίαν πρᾶξιν. Ambition means tying your well-being to what other people say or do. Self-indulgence means tying it to the things that happen to you. Sanity means tying it to your own actions." Robin held up a sheaf of papers. "Shall we go through these now?"

"Yes, of course." He settled into the desk, took up a pen, and focused on Robin, who had put on his reading glasses. "What are we going to do?"

He handed him several packets with yellow tabs. "You need to sign these."

Sargon glanced through the pages, but could not concentrate on the mathematical notation and molecular blueprints. "Why bother? I don't know what the fuck I'm doing anymore. Why am I even here? The shame alone, of going before that chamber full of cattle, knowing what they think in the back of their tick-sized brains, swelling with my blood."

Robin plowed ahead: "Fiberoptic hair, heritable, one license; single generation, seventy-two licenses; and finally this one authorizes payment of the annual management fee for city properties."

"Fee!" he pronounced with loud guttural scorn. "Everyone kicks up. Gangsters I could arrest and execute pay me to leave them alone. We kiss each other's asses. It's a fucking isle of dogs." He cleared his throat. "All I wanted was four months off. But you weren't there; Renee moved into the city on the first of the year to screw that waitress of hers. Couldn't get out fast enough. And I don't blame her. You weren't there."

"So you have mentioned, Sire."

"We had what, two months of entertainment at the Palace? Making merry when you feel like sticking your head in the oven. For Renee, entertainment is like a disease she barely survived. Without anyone to organize my life, I couldn't order my thoughts. It takes two to strategize."

"Strategy *is* a process of dialectical reasoning. The papers?" He pointed with a pen in the direction of the packet.

Sargon turned to the page and confirmed the date and commenced to sign. "Next," Sargon said, dispatching the business quickly.

Robin reclined slightly, facing him. "When the session has been called, the first order of business will be nominations to the Executive Council. Have you decided who will nominate Bard?"

"Well, it won't be me. I feel like killing him."

"Have you spoken since?"

"I couldn't. He has been courting me like a teenage boy, sending over bottles of wine, a brace of geese, Hawaiian flowers grown by his cousin. I taste bile thinking about it."

"Sire, please don't take this amiss, but you do yourself an injustice with self-pity. Master your feelings. Treat him as he should be treated, an old friend and an important ally. Not since your California days have you had such need of him. And the stakes are very high. Consider what would happen if Iocle dies. That must be your focus, not your own ambition to be President." When Sargon didn't reply, but instead stared off into space, Robin said, "Someone must nominate him."

"I don't see what difference it makes."

"Might I suggest Senator Imogen?"

"Imogen can't. It will tip our hand and Everest will make a counteroffer, which she's likely to take."

"Vizier Holland will do it."

"Why would Holland split with Everest to do that?"

"Spite. They fell for the same boy last year in St. Moritz and Everest won."

"Is that all there is to it? Why would he turn for that? There must have been a woman involved. Go find out if that's it."

"We need his vote now."

"Then we'll have to promise him something. What do they need in Georgia, besides brains?"

"He wants to rebuild the Blue Ridge Dam. There's a bill you could move through the Executive Council to the Senate."

"Isn't that Appropriations?"

"Sire, it's Water."

Sargon sighed. Imogen was the Chair of the Water Committee, since she controlled nearly all of it. And the little she didn't, she battled over constantly with the Canadians, ten different Indian nations, and Pennsylvania. He would not escape her now, it seemed.

"Sire, why the sigh? She's our ace in the hole. Kuiper Belt Earth will get the construction contract. It's perfect."

Sargon shrugged and said, "It's, it's the way she looks at me, like she's trying to get information, and getting it. She thinks I'm telling her things with my looks, and I'm not. Sometimes, most times, I'm not saying anything at all but what I'm saying, do you understand?" he paused, his face incredulous. "Renee says I have to look her in the eye!"

"Sire, I have had this experience myself. It's just the way she looks at one."

"I was hoping we could do this without her involvement. You touch her, I don't want to."

"I have always had cordial conversations with My Lady Imogen."

"And I'll talk to Vizier Holland. Now, while we're on depressing business, is the rest of that Mars?"

Robin Micawber rubbed his large, bloodshot eyes and looked at Sargon, blinking. "Word is Everest has Iocle's support for the Census Bill now. I've read it. It authorizes and funds random scanning on the street to create a genomic registry for every municipality in the country. Red Suits would conduct the survey with local police. It was obviously penned by Utburd. It has his flair for absurd circumlocutions and loquacious embellishments of simple phrases.

"Then there's Imogen's Convict Labor Bill. It authorizes the secret transfer of healthy illegals to labor on Mars, gas ships, and asteroid mines. The scariest part is an obscure footnote that would identify pregnant women and small children for deep-space mining. Those are one way, multi-generational voyages to the Oort Cloud. With Ocktomann in charge of Mars, and now, apparently, Southern California, they have everything they need, and even with Bard's and your opposition, assuming of course he makes it to the Executive Council, these bills could pass. It will spread panic when they became generally known. Civil unrest will likely follow, which will justify the use of Federal troops. More Red Suits means more scanning, more convicts, more space traffic."

"That's Imogen's plan exactly! Bard is a fool. He doesn't understand how this works. He's used to marching around on a horse issuing orders, General Bard to the rescue. How the fuck will we keep her vote? A dam in Georgia is chicken feed."

"Let's hope that Southern California is a big enough plum."

"Ha. That's just how Ocktomann described it."

Robin said, "He should not have made the appointment before the vote." Sargon grunted. "The remainder seem like routine executive appointments but they are in fact all traceable back to Everest, operating through the President's office. We will need to stop them somehow, which will take votes on the Council and probably in the Executive Committee sessions. That's all the President pays attention to. That's where you can block him."

"With Bard and Imogen, we win," Sargon said.

"Getting and keeping her vote is key. It's not like we're going to bump off Everest."

Sargon smiled. "Like the old days." The train rocked along the Hudson levees. Thick stands of bamboo shivered and swayed against the cobalt sky, scattered with pink petals of cloud. Sargon, feeling more confident as he considered the dynamics of the Senate, said, "Stick by her side. She won't be lugging her manchild about, so you won't have to watch him too. Don't let her talk alone to anyone until the vote. And keep your eyes on Pike. He will try to make the deal.

"Everyone will assume Bard has come back East to challenge Iocle for the Presidency. Part of the Senate will fall under the spell of his face, and another faction will dismiss him as a vainglorious playboy without guts or conviction, a man who likes a grand parade and a boy in the bed but doesn't know how to cut a deal, doesn't have the discipline for the actual work of governance. Everyone knows without Otis, Bard wouldn't have taken, never mind held, all that land in California. He needed a hammer to do what he could not do. Otis was cruel and terrifying. I still shake in elevators thinking about it. The sound of horses clopping over cobblestone freezes me in the saddle, and I have vivid waking dreams of driving a hammer truck through a crowd, followed by horses and dogs. I can hear the femurs, ribs, and skulls cracking beneath the syncopated mallets. What was left of the living begged to be shot."

Robin quietly hit the record button and looked out the window at the trees in new leaf, hazed with green and yellow, red budded, as Sargon spoke. When he was done, and he felt it was safe, he said, "Bard could be a great leader with the right guidance. But he doesn't need a hammer now, he needs a key. You are the key to New York and New York is the key to Bard's future, and he knows it. He cannot make it without you. And that makes your price very high."

Sargon rubbed his hands together and thought about being President. Unlike his Sire, he would know what to do with the job. He wouldn't waste time on juvenile revenge fantasies and the venting of resentments. His cool self-assessment said yes, he would be a better President than anyone then alive. But he was realistic. His control of the Senate had made him as many enemies as friends and he was seen as a conniving insider, a corrupt baron from a corrupt city. And if, in the Senate, he had merely made political foes, in President Iocle he had an implacable and irrational antagonist whose loathing of the Sargon line was universally known.

Sargon mused in a chilly, objective voice, "I am disappointed. But my power in the Senate is undiminished. There is much that I can do on the Executive Council that Bard and Imogen can't. And I do realize that the only way to stop Everest from becoming President is to sacrifice my own ambitions. Everest's plan is clear. He is going to come after us. That must be prevented no matter what. I must protect my children, and my city, my people." It was beginning to sound like a mantra to him.

They rode on in silence until Robin, sensing his Sire's mood lighten, said, "Sire, I know you prefer to avoid discussing your early days in California. Perhaps we could go over your earliest memories?"

Sargon nodded grimly. "At least I still have early memories! Recent ones aren't worth shit."

"Sire." He recorded Sargon's restless, somewhat disordered recollections of his Sire and Grand Sire.

★

They crossed into Manhattan and rode through dense woods. At 61st Street, the earth swallowed the train, and it proceeded by dry track into Grand Central. He and Robin got out and climbed the incline from the Lower Level, into the high marbled expanse of the station. They went out the Vanderbilt Avenue doors and he inhaled the air. It smelled sweet to him, as it always did, even on a summer's day when the gutter and sidewalk were ripe with stagnant puddles and urine. Under the portico, they paused.

"I'll get your car, Sire." Robin said.

"You take it," he said, smiling at rushing pedestrians and the concrete laddered with light and shadow. Cars chugged by. A man was grilling satay on the sidewalk on a small iron grill, which he fed with chunks of burning charcoal. "I'm going to walk."

"Under normal circumstances, Sire, I wouldn't say anything, but surely you intend to wait for the Red Guard? It is by Presidential order."

"Goddamn the Red Suits. Goddamn Iocle. It's my city. I should be able to have my own guard, or not, if I want. That's how it's always been. I'll be fine. They don't gun Senators down on my streets." He escaped on Vanderbilt to 42nd Street and headed east.

It always made him feel more alive, walking beneath walls of old glass, and the almost total lack of deference shown by the city's citizens. Yet he was their Ruler, their life and death. He could order what he pleased. All restraint was that of will, not prior constraint of law or custom. There was no constitution in force that would prevent him from torturing his enemies and murdering his opponents. But that absolute power was elusive and distasteful. There is no killing without consequence. Disappearances, executions, torture, Rule by fear, were stupid. His power was great because it was restrained. And he bribed his citizens with pleasure. There was nothing that could not be had in Manhattan. They were free to buy and sell, to make art, music and theater, play sports. There was an active press and he even allowed forbidden political organizations to operate quietly, so long as they never made a move against him. Vice was tightly controlled and taxed circulating gems, gold, and silver up from the street to the city coffers.

Absolute power had always been in some measure rhetorical. Especially here, in the city. Like LA it was a city-state, under its own control, by means of compromises, allegiances, and sworn limits. The city posed the threat of perpetual war, should every faction take up arms and fight it out on the street. Stalemate was the only possible outcome that worked for everyone. Yet nothing stayed the same. Conflict came. Drift was not a distraction to be explained away. There was a force at work that he could feel, not a platitude of conversation. A force that didn't want them to lock it down. The wind that blows through things. Most people he knew had no sense of the tenuous web that held it all together. He was a student of Drift. He tried to see its action in the world. He had learned to smell its plume. To feel the heat of Drift, to taste it in the air.

Like all Rulers his being was torn between the two laws, the determined and the random, genetic Drift and metaphysical Drift. The tendency to go awry was essential in preventing genetic Drift, while cloning, the exact replication of an individual, prevented random mutation from determining fate. That was why the Geneticists were the Druids of their age. What they did in weaving together chance variation and precise duplication was an art upon which the entire civilization stood. They were the weavers of the Ruler cloth. But where would Rulers be otherwise? Where the nursery rhyme verses say: *On skating rinks and variety shows, tying professional wrestling bows*? Who needed Ocktomann? He had four feet too many on him for his own good. And with all that height you'd think they would have remembered a neck and a brain. The Ocktomann line had one heroic moment in the Great Rebellion and then for 300 years, nothing. And Sargon always wondered, who marries their mother? But wasn't that what all Rulers did?

What irked him most was that Ocktomann was only manageable when close at hand. On his own, he'd be exposed at the first sign of trouble as a Moron and a coward. Their plans, his plans, rested on an idiot's broad but useless shoulders. They still had Otis. There was no one more loyal than Otis.

Sargon crossed Second Avenue, passing blocks of brick apartment buildings, his stomach starting to knot and grind, anticipating his first encounter with Bard. He would have to keep his trap shut. The streets were quiet and tidy and there was little traffic. A full bus drove by but did not stop. As he approached First Avenue, sensor fences became apparent, and all entrances were under guard. The Red Suits were on every corner. It stuck in his throat. He wanted to spit. Iocle!

The House and Senate were housed at the UN Headquarters, the House sitting in the General Assembly, and the Senate in the Security Council chamber in the Conference Building, which formed part of the Turtle Bay Wall, the East-Midtown section of the Levee Works. The Plaza was thick with cars and teams of Red Guards. Their suits and black visors stood out in the muted glare of morning sun. He took a breezeway from the Plaza to the Conference Building, passed through a gaggle of guards at the door, and took the elevator to the Senate Chambers.

Senators milled about in semi-dress uniform. No chest spangles and brush epaulets. He scanned the room and found Bard seated at his desk, reading a sheet of platinum electraweave. He swallowed his anger and disgust and reminded himself of all he had just discussed with Robin. *Treat him as he deserves to be treated, like an ally and a friend.* He deserved whipping. "What's it say?" Sargon asked.

Bard looked at the electraweave sheet for a moment longer, shook his head and said, "Sargon! How did you find the wine, cheese and Christmas flowers? Those poinsettias are grown on volcanic soil. I'm just now reading about the harvest. Apples are down 40 percent in the Northeast this year. The cider makers got most of them."

Sargon sighed. "Our rural districts somewhat depend on apples, but cider is a lucrative export."

Bard said, "Yes. Here and in California, where scientists said you couldn't grow apples. So I reopened the universities. And in fifteen years we had apples again, and stone fruit. We made it happen in the hills. It was old fashioned plant breeding. None of the hocus-pocus. Now people want apples at Christmas. If they get oranges, and not apples, they complain. I say give the people what they want."

"Mine complain too. Because if they don't get apples, they don't get much of anything at all."

"You would complain too, if you couldn't eat fruit each day."

"Certainly," Sargon said. "In any event, shit happens."

"Not without fruit it doesn't. We spend more money breeding people than plants."

"When you breed better people you breed better plants."

Bard looked at Sargon severely and said, "The idea that breeding better people breeds better plants is the problem I came East to address. For sixty years, I sat out there looking at the world through the wrong end of a telescope. I thought California was where the power was. Slowly, I came to realize I was being kept there because Iocle fears me."

Sargon looked around. No one was nearby. "Be careful what you say in the Chamber. Never assume we are alone here."

"After today, Iocle will assume I am here to unseat

him. Everest will be plotting a countermove." Bard looked about and continued, "I'm going to work on agricultural reform. Even Utburd and Aeppar and Utkasting can support that." He smiled. "For too long, this Chamber has been content to sit on its ass and let the President Rule from DC. He keeps us fighting each other, fighting with other nations on Earth, and in space, something our Sires—"

"Grand Sires!" Sargon managed to insert, glaring out the corners of predatory eyes at the room, a land he knew as well as any he hunted.

"—prevented. I am the only Ruler of territory in this country who is at peace with all of its neighbors—indigenous, Anglo, and Mexican."

"I'm at peace with my neighbors. Look, there are things you can't hope to change. We go to war. That's what Rulers do!"

"We need a nation that isn't run like a racket."

Sargon swallowed a burst of laughter and said, louder than he intended, so that the seven-foot red-headed Senator from Kansas, the Ruler Amuna looked up and smiled at him, "We've been a racket since 1492."

Bard stared at Sargon, who could not stand to be stared at. "We can give up wars with each other, with Mexico and Canada, and the Indian nations, stop

Isle of Dogs, Part 1

fighting on the Great Lakes, in the Northwest, and in the Rockies. We can stop fighting on Mars, disarm trade in space, go back to automation and robotics, and end this barbaric practice of convict labor. But what difference would that make if we can't reform the Blood Laws? Who would we be then? Because the primal sin, the basic flaw in our Rule is—"

Sargon put up his hand and hissed, "Shshsh! This is not a fucking dorm room, it's the Senate. Spies are everywhere. And that's not all." Sargon reared back and looked around for some sign that the calling to order would end this conversation. "Let me show you something. You need to learn this. We're going to look over the room. You see those Senators up there? Look at their faces and tell me if you can see their lips moving."

Bard looked at the upper seats and squinted. "Yes," he said.

"Then they can read yours. Read the room the way you'd read the desert. If you see someone sitting alone, watch them and see if they don't start signing out of nowhere. That's how we communicate here. If someone reads your lips and starts to sign it to others, a coalition can form quickly, like a tornado." Sargon paused. "I've got to find Holland. He's going to nominate you."

"Holland? Why Holland? He's as Red as it gets."

"He wants to fuck Everest, over a boy. Purely personal. He knows the nomination will piss off Everest and Iocle, and he gets a dam for it, which Imogen's Kuiper Belt Earth will build. Everyone wins."

"That's why I was hoping you would nominate me. I have to uphold the standards I set for others, don't I?"

"It doesn't work that way around here. You've got it exactly backwards. If I nominate you, I'm just doing a favor for a friend. But if Holland nominates you, it shows you have trust across the aisle. You're asking to be a permanent member of the Ruling Executive Committee. All the factions on the floor will have instructions. Some are waiting to see who comes out for you. See? It's politics. This way, the old shit gets something he cares about, and you get his vote. I've got to go now."

✶

Sargon found Robin standing in the Cloak Room with Maximilian, Imogen, Vizier Holland, and Philomel, the other Senator from California. Robin said, "Here comes Sargon."

"Wonderful news about our friend," said Vizier

Holland. Filaments of his hair incandesced and floated off his head. "It would be an honor to nominate him."

Imogen engaged Sargon's eye and he attempted not to notice, but after some moments of doing so she seemed to draw him to her against his will. His neck was aching with the effort not to look at her. Renee said to engage. Still, he resisted. Finally he turned his head. Her eyes were fixed on his, dilating. Compulsively, she ran her tongue across her teeth, bulging out her upper lip. She said, "We are discussing a dam project."

Vizier Holland replied, animatedly, to the point of expostulation, "Many former Peach State dam sites could be restored. But," he rapped the palm of his hand with a roll of imaginary plans, "I have actual *blueprints* prepared to restore the Blue Ridge Dam. It's a shovel-ready project, only in need of a little spacemetal. And a suitable contractor." Holland's eyes were glowing the color of his hair, but their attention was directed entirely within now. His voice was possessed by an energy he used to reserve for meting out justice after battle with his machete. His beard remained stiff and dark, as dark as blond gets when it's caked with blood. Sargon noted a slight tremble in his hand, the ragged edge of his words.

Robin said, "Souvanouphong is about to call the session to order, Sire."

Maximilian seized Sargon by the elbows, the apparent glee in his eye undermined by dark fidgeting. Like most fools, he was transparent. "Sargon!" Maximilian boomed, smiling broadly.

"Hello Max. How goes it, my friend?" He took Maximilian's hand in his. It was damp, cold and small-boned, like a toad. When he disengaged, he wiped his hands on Maximilian's jacket and together they walked into the Senate Chamber. There they parted, Maximilian for row five, and Sargon for the front.

Sargon flipped through pages of a document without reading, ignoring the other members of the Executive Council as they took their seats in the front and did the same. He had been sitting in the Chamber for so long it felt like an extension of his body. The desk was both his office and his token of authority. He moved between its spaces like a traveling actor going from stage to stage playing whatever part he had to, to get it done. There were only a handful of things people wanted—power, gold, sex, and drugs—so those were the currency of obligation, favors, punishments. Whatever is given can be withheld. It takes more than gems to put a skyscraper up. The room filled in behind him with mostly seven-foot-tall men and women, striking beauties eroded by age, going through files and whispering to aides. The gavel struck, calling them to order.

The President of the Senate, Vice President Souvanouphong, stood at the podium dressed in a cinder tunic over a yellow shirt. A horseshoe of twenty empty desks curved out into the dark behind him. That was where the Executive Council met. He cleared his throat and brought the Senate to order with another crack of the gavel.

"Nominations for the Executive Council of the 356th Congress are now open," Souvanouphong announced. "We'll allow one hour of debate for each nominee, to be followed by a voice vote." Elsinore, the ancient Senior Senator from Louisiana, rose up on shins like stilts, with arms like the legs of a bird and clawed hands. Her face, which only showed age by its severity, was frigid and calm. She said, "Mr. President, I place in nomination my esteemed colleague from Louisiana, the Ruler Long."

Mighty Jove Himself, the Senator from Arkansas, stood.

"The Chair recognizes the Esteemed Senator from Arkansas."

Mighty Jove Himself said, "Mr. President, I move

to suspend debate on this nominee and proceed with the vote."

"All who agree with Senator Mighty Jove Himself's motion to suspend debate on this nominee and proceed to vote, say *Aye*."

A broad, mumbling, shrug of an *Aye* issued from the red side of the aisle followed by restless noise.

"All who say *Nay*?"

"*Nay*," thundered a smaller portion of the green faction on the floor.

"The *Ayes* have it. We will move to a vote. All in favor of Senator Long vote *Aye*."

Again the slow eruption of a murmured *Aye*.

"Those opposed to the nomination of Senator Long to the Executive Council say *Nay*."

Again there was the enthusiastic, drumming *Nay* of a smaller number. The *Ayes* carried it.

And so on.

Sargon waited for Maximilian to make his exit, as he did each day at 1:22. He would not be seen leaving before him, nor be on a set schedule. He knew he was being watched. There were offices committed to modeling his behavior. People he couldn't remember by name spent hours discussing what he would do next, dissecting his moves. He had the nanodomes at home to protect him, but here on the floor he constructed his own dome, his own disguise, out of words and deals. Maximilian trundled out the third floor exit.

A half hour later, after the Chamber had thinned and the offices emptied out for lunch, Sargon packed his papers and left to meet Renee at Napkin, a French restaurant on East 63rd Street. As soon as he exited the floor, a team of Red Guards took up posts around him and followed him downstairs. They were silent, especially in the noise of the city, but on an elevator their respirators wheezed and gurgled and gave off the smell of the poisonous resin of smoke, acid, and disaggregated bodies that filmed the suits.

Robin chased after him through the breezeway to the Plaza, cheeks flushed, clutching his briefcase to his chest. "Stop," he panted, people in the breezeway pausing to stare. Those who didn't recognize him sniffed the air; those who did chuckled quietly and turned back to their own business. Even those who despised Sargon respected Robin for what he was, Sargon's man.

Sargon smiled at him as if he were a daft uncle and said, "I thought we talked about this? I'm going to lunch with Renee. Call if the vote is close; I can come back. But I don't see a problem. I count Bard winning by a comfortable margin. Only a few nuts from the South will vote against him."

"Yes, Sire."

"After lunch, I'm going to the Waldorf to review the City Council bills. Darius, Lug, and Arthur are coming by for a game of bridge and cocktails at five."

"I'll arrange for food and a bar. Will you have Albion?"

"You needn't bother. We can eat whatever is lying about and we know where the bar and glasses are."

"The delegates from the Haudenosaunee are in town. They want to meet in your Senate office."

"Why? I could meet them in the Waldorf easily."

"Sire, they will only speak to you officially as a Federal representative. As Ruler of New York, you have no treaty relations with them."

Sargon sagged. "Today? Well, if it must be. But ask them if they'd like to have cocktails with the CEO of Monozone Inc. and President of the City Council. We might conduct some business. Then I'll meet them tomorrow at the UN. Comp their whole trip. Put them up at The Sherry-Netherland. Advance them a hundred in gold at Margery Milk. Whatever else you think of." He narrowed his eyes and looked at the guards. He felt hunted. He blurted out, "Why are these Red dirtbags following me around? If I can't walk here, what kind of a Ruler am I? What kind of a *New Yorker* am I?" A black sedan with windows of negative space drove up and the guards escorted him to the backseat, one getting in on either side. He sank into the dark leather upholstery and watched the small oval picture floating two feet from his eyes. A reporter from the *New York Times* was discussing him. He *was* the news.

✱

At Napkin, seated on an inner wall, with a mirror view of Manhattan building tops and sky, Sargon and Renee drank blood orange juice out of Jovian-cut crystal tumblers and awaited their meal. "Bard has a lot to learn about the Senate," Sargon mused, his voice growing thin with strain.

"What happened?"

"We were on the floor, standing at our desks as you do, talking. It's the Opening Session. Everyone is there. And he's talking about ending corruption, ending war, and abolishing the Blood Laws. It's madness. If the wrong person overheard that, it would be all the Senate debated for six months, whether to expel or censure the Junior Senator from California. For what? In the end, it comes to nothing and you wasted all that time."

"I wouldn't abandon your ambitions to be President." she said, lifting the glass to red lips.

"Bard actually believes that he can restore the nation." He looked into her eyes a long time before saying, "Bard's a war hero. I'm a Senator. Maybe Vice President?"

The waiter brought bread in a basket woven from local rushes and a fava bean puree. Sargon aggressively applied the puree to the bread and loaded his mouth with the entire piece, chomping it like a horse.

Renee held hers aloft, turned it, and sniffed the surface. "Hm. Vice President. Not worth a bucket of warm piss." She wiped a thin layer of the puree across it and pushed it whole into her mouth, chewing as Sargon did, with equine avidity. When she had chewed sufficiently to swallow she said, "But it is a stepping stone. Was he confiding in you, or is that his public position? There is a constituency for those views. You yourself have advocated them."

Women in lab coats filled their goblets with young white wine. Sargon rinsed his mouth and took a good strong sip. "Excuse me, in private. I have never stuck my neck out in the Senate. I think he's reckless, probably bored, overestimates his own popularity. He's always been like that, since Exeter. But it is especially tasteless for a very powerful Ruler in his nineties."

Renee's expression didn't change but she nodded her head. "That's one side of his personality, certainly, but he is also capable of self-control, of waiting to see where others land before taking a position. I think he wants to win."

The waiter brought a plate of frogs legs browned in sunflower oil with garlic and Delaware lemon. A citrus fume of parsley and garlic bloomed over the table. They each took a few pieces and ate slower and smaller. The woman in the lab coat replaced their goblets and poured a white Burgundy.

Sargon, his eye stricken by the removal of the glass, embraced the new one and drank deeply. "Who doesn't want to win? We just don't all believe we deserve to win. But his war record will get him a lot of votes. And he's right, the country is ready for a message of peace. It's kind of brilliant in a way. He's a good gambler, a good bluffer. He's got the greatest poker face I've ever seen. But that's not enough in the Senate. He needs me there to make it."

The plates were replaced with clean china by brief hands and the waiter returned with a Salade Niçoise. He deposited little heaps of salad on each plate and left the bowl on a side table draped with a red cloth.

The woman in the lab coat poured a Gewürztraminer from Ontario.

Sargon continued, "I'm worried. Robin says that scanning bill of Everest's could pass, now that it has Iocle's support. It's not hard to scare a bunch of Rulers into voting for a purge. Bard has to stay focused on what we can get and what we *have* to get. All the power is with Iocle, ultimately, except for the budget. That is our only check on him."

"And states' rights. He has to stay in his yard."

"Tell that to Everest. Scanning would begin right away if the bill passes. What do you want to bet that Everest does his beta test in LA? He's never forgotten what we did to him. And then? Then there's pushback. If Ocktomann thinks he's going to carry out scanning in Otis's territory of Bard's state he better think again."

They each picked at their tablespoon of salad, unrolling it to see what it was. Renee gazed stonily into the bowl and then, with slow, stiff, deliberate movements conveyed more of the salad to each of their plates. Sargon ate the little chunks of charred tuna first, then the seaweeds, then the quail-egg-and-scallion slice, which he mashed into the filet bean and cube of potato.

"You have to consider that Pike will see an angle that we don't notice," she said.

"What does that spy of yours Euclid say? The man is like a mist."

"Extremely dextrous and useful. He's the mental equivalent of a fifth articulate limb. He said she met with Pike last month in Virginia. When you talked to Imogen in the Cloak Room this morning, did you look her in the eye?"

"I did, although I tried not to. It's like when your coat sleeve catches on a nail. Robin's tailing her. She can't do business without us. All her financing comes from New York. No one goes to the Bank of Tejas. Plus we've got her boy under our thumb in California. Bard can take back what he gives. Ocktomann doesn't go anywhere we don't put him."

"I'd put him in the ground," Renee said, popping an olive draped with an emerald artery of seaweed in her mouth.

"It's too soon for that. I must not be seen…"

"Your hand wouldn't be in it."

"It already is." They ate silently for a while. When they were done, at the same time, they leaned back in their chairs and relaxed, as if the race were now over. He asked, "Are you in tonight?"

"Yes, I'll be at 1220 Fifth. The magnolias are in bloom around the Conservatory."

"What a lovely picture. We should go for a ride in the park. Shall we plan on dinner then?" he asked. "I'm done playing cards at eight." Inspired by lunch, he was starting to put together a menu for that evening. He would have Robin call the chef and fly in Maine sea urchin, clams, and lobster; maybe oysters and monkfish; Gulf of Maine shrimp. He would also send to Scotland for some grouse. His cousin will have shot a brace. It could be there by drone in less than six hours. And there was also the button buck from Transylvania, hanging in the kitchen yard, next to a young doe he had killed by bow. A clean shot through the lungs. A carpaccio of Catskill and Carpathian venison.

Their places were cleared and brushed. They wiped their hands and faces with hot towels. Coffee, chocolate torte, and two bottles of brandy, with cigars, appeared on the table. Renee stirred sugar into the demitasse. As he examined the dates on the brandy labels, she said, "There's a benefit at The Public tomorrow night. I would like to go. Titania, Darius, and Lug will be there… Arthur Bell. Who else?"

Sargon turned away from the bottles and looked

at her. "Yes, Robin briefed me on our week on the train in." He smiled and returned his attention to the bottles. "That artist you like is having a show." One was an apple brandy, aged twenty-five years, from the Hudson Valley. The other a grape brandy aged fifty years, from Michigan, Ocktomann's home state. He selected the apple spirit and poured out two snifters.

"Was it a painter?" she asked, lighting a cigar.

He didn't really like cigars, but he smoked them. He deemed it necessary to pick one up off the tray and light it. When it was well lit and settled in his cheek, he puffed, removed the cigar, and said, as the smoke rose between them, "I believe so. A primitive abstract painter from Outer Tennessee."

"There are *so* many, let me see…" She tapped her head. A smile creased her face. "Lawrence Booth, from Kentucky. Paints with his fingers. Shall we have him to dinner?"

Before he could respond, Robin entered the dining room, trailed by a waiter. He bustled up to the table, his face pale and drawn, and said, "Sire, the vote is not going well."

"What do you mean? He had the votes. It was a done deal."

"Sire, Bard has been easily elected. But Pike

nominated Maximilian, Imogen seconded the nomination, and now it is under debate. It looks like the vote might go against you. Maximilian will hold New York's seat on the next Council."

"Maximilian!" He glared at Renee. "I've got to get to the floor, right away." Six Red Guards escorted him to the waiting car.

★

The pinnacle of the Chrysler Building was shrouded in a dirty haze. Robin was taking a seat behind Sargon, whose back was to the windows, facing Darius, his bridge partner. Darius was a robust blond with black skin and a hooked nose, his eyes like sapphires set in coal. He was absorbed by a bad hand of low cards and no obvious trump. To his right was Lug, a middle-aged Ruler with rumpled features, a bulbous nose and strong chin, walnut complexion and cool, pale-blue eyes focused on a perfect fan of cards. He was dressed in a black wool banker's suit with a white shirt, strawberry cravat, and matching handkerchief folded in a chevron peaking above the breast pocket. His partner, Arthur Bell, was seemingly human, slight of stature, with a ruddy, closely shaved face, small nose, and piercing brown eyes under heavy brows. Dressed casually, in a sweatshirt and stretch pants, he held his cards with manicured hands, rings on all of the fingers, the nails buffed and polished. Sargon put his hand down and sipped his Manhattan, eating the rapiered cherry with the slight wince sweets always induced. He said, "Robin, pull closer and join the conversation. Lug has an interesting point."

"Sire," Robin said. "It is an interesting suggestion, but radical."

Lug burst out, "Radical is yanking your Ruler's seat out from under him!"

Darius tossed his hand down with disgust and Arthur laughed gleefully. "Guess we know what you have!"

Darius said, "It wasn't the cards I was thinking of. Don't you think they'll be expecting this?"

"No way," Lug said. "He will not expect Sargon to do that."

"Because," Robin said, "it is dangerous and unprecedented, and that is not my Sire's way."

Darius drank down half his Manhattan, ate the cherry and said, "Pass the nuts. Killing a Senator is crazy. You will take the blame for it, no matter what. If he dies of a heart attack, if he gets hit by a truck, they'll see your hand in it. You'll be an outlaw." Sargon pushed the bowl towards him and raised his eyebrows. "I'm with Robin. Bumping him off would fuck up everything we've worked for. The Progressives in Congress would flee to Iocle's side. We sit on a knife's edge as it is."

"Unprecedented?" Arthur asked. "Maybe we haven't read the same histories. It isn't unprecedented, but it is unexpected. That's different. I've made a fortune doing unexpected things."

Sargon nodded and picked up his cards. If Darius had nothing, what could he do? Pass. He had a lot of hearts, nothing higher than a ten. Lug was impulsive in cards and politics. He would reveal himself. "I don't know," Sargon said. "I'm mad enough to kill him, but not crazy enough. Max is an asshole who will piss off the wrong guy. Let's let him suck his own dick for a while before he bites it off."

Arthur said to Sargon, "Your bid."

"I pass."

4

Hung Up on a Dream

Two young women and one young man sat around a brass bucket of cold muddy water, washing and sorting a basket of potatoes. Ruth didn't really belong in the prep kitchen anymore, but old habits and friendships lingered on. She came to catch up on household gossip and escape the nursery rooms that became hers with the birth of the Baby Sargon.

Ruth was the only mother the Baby Sargon would ever have. He grew in her lap; he was made of her milk. But in the first months after he was born Duck spent hours pacing their three rooms while he cried and she rode waves of postnatal depression and despair—a black, engulfing abyss throbbing with malevolent energy. Cloned babies were born with immature digestive systems and often suffered from bouts of extreme colic and acid reflux. They screamed with pain, their bellies hard and tight. Perpetual motion and nursing were the only palliatives. As he screamed so did she, silently in her head, at the walls of her hot, cheerful prison.

Since implantation with the clone, her world had contracted, first to the Winter Palace and its grounds, and now, the nursery. Sometimes she felt like beating her fists against the bars, but she never raised her hands to do so. It was an empty impulse. So she carried on. Wherever she went in her kingdom of three rooms, she felt walled off. Even the air pressed up against her face like a mask.

The nursery was three long, steep flights up, in the South Tower. Morning sun poured in the windows, when there was any. She had spacious rooms adjoining the nursery, where both babies were supposed to sleep, in cribs, and where they were to spend their days in stimulating activity with her, monitored hourly at first by an army of nurses who did not change diapers or wipe ass. That was something she did more times a day than she could count. The cuffs of her shirtsleeves were shit-stained. Shit permeated the stone, plaster, and wood. Shit pulsed in the air. The smell tainted the nursery, despite FantiSeptic scrubdowns.

Ruth was too exhausted by insomnia to bathe. Most nights they all stayed in her bed so she could nurse them, or, increasingly, him, and maybe catch a few minutes rest. There were weeks where Phaedra's night terrors exploded in the midst of a 3:00 a.m. diaper disaster. She would wail as the Baby Sargon writhed inconsolably beneath one hand, Ruth attempting to extract a warm, damp cloth from the dispenser with the other.

They were relentless, remorseless, implacable. At 5:00 a.m., the Baby Sargon was up for the day, followed shortly by Phaedra. "Mommy, I want to walk." They had the three rooms, the hall and the stairs. More like the plank on a pirate ship.

"We'll go to the stairs later."

"No, Mommy!"

Ruth fed them her body. She sang, read, and bathed them. Their environment was tightly controlled. She must wear certain clothes, nurse in certain postures. She was not permitted to leave. They didn't want her picking up microbes and bringing them back. But they did want *her* microbes, her biota, to colonize the clone.

As the Baby Sargon's colic subsided, his Sire, who

came each night with Balfour to take a walking and rocking shift, stayed to watch gangster movies. But that ended when the new session began.

The crisis changed everything. His mood, ugly when Bard made his announcement, collapsed into apathy, relieved by bouts of sudden rage or baroque strategy sessions. He spent most of his time at 1220 Fifth. Ruth had no company, no adult conversation other than Frau Duck, whom she adored unreservedly, but who was not enough.

Ruth tried to read from the Palace library but couldn't concentrate. If she could have gone herself, she might have found something she could read. But all she could think of were the classics she had not read. She requested *Moby Dick* and *The Brothers Karamazov* and *Middlemarch*. She found herself reading the same pages over and over. Finally, she gave up trying to read books like these and thought to order different ones. But her mind went blank as to what she might be able to read. All that came to mind were those books and other books like them. Rabelais. Swift. Montaigne. Schnitzler, Roth, Musil, Broch.

Ruth was not cheered by the cheery yellow walls and pink and blue furniture. Sunny days were bad, but worse were days when the bright winter sun flared briefly on the windows before dying under a cloud. She sensed when her mood was about to spiral, but could do nothing to stop it. As the bright days lengthened, she wanted only to close the shades and hide.

That Sargon could fall from power had never occurred to her. And she began to wonder what would happen if he couldn't protect Phaedra. What would she do? She didn't know anything about the world. She had traveled most of her life in the Sargon and Renee entourage! She had never cooked a meal. She had never booked a train and really had no money at all. The account into which her wages were deposited was established, when she was a minor, in her mother's name, and *she* collected all the earnings. This was explained to her when she was seven. But she hadn't understood what it meant. Growing up, she had everything. What more did she need? But she was not a minor now, and the world had just darkened. She had to have control of that account.

When the Baby Sargon was almost six months old, she'd had it. At that age, Phaedra had been out riding. She asked to see Doc Hughes. He was in his offices in the basement, at the end of a shiny steel tube, encased by glass. She sat on the glass bench and stared at his receptionist, Bronze, a small man with a goatee and sideburns shaped like scimitars. She wondered what he was like. Did he like to do things. She tried to think of the things she liked to do.

Doc Hughes opened the glass door. It was thick and tinted a faint blue, like a block of ice. They talked about her health and he swabbed her cheek and scanned her with the hand wand. She prepared to get into the stirrups but he said, "That won't be necessary." He was silent for a long time, his hair of the purest white light. "How are you feeling, dear? I sense you're not well. You wouldn't be the first to go nuts up there."

Ruth stared at his eyes, like turbulent tropical water, and wondered what he thought. She did not think she was going nuts. She thought she was being *driven* nuts by isolation and boredom. "Do I seem like I am going nuts?" she asked.

"What would you like, what would help?"

Tears stood in her eyes. She must not let them roll. She held her breath and braced herself, as if someone were going to hit her. "I must go for a walk in the Palace and visit friends, with the babies."

"A splendid idea!" Ruth never forgot that, the way he said the word *splendid*. He thought it a splendid idea. It was one of those words people used hundreds of years ago. He had always been gentle and kind to her, like a father, albeit one who examined her genitals. "But you will follow simple rules? The Baby Sargon mustn't be placed on or near the floor, nor can anyone hold him. They can look at him, but not too close. And no one with a cold, or rheumy eyes, yellow skin, open lesions… swellings, dirty or cracked fingernails, spittle on the lips, that kind of thing, may share a room."

※

Ruth stood in the doorway between the back hall and the prep area of the kitchen, hesitating to interrupt her friends, Nathalie and Griselde, women in their late twenties, and Clare, a man a little older. Clare had been born in the Winter Palace. His mother was a maid, long gone. His father was a chauffeur, a retired navy chaplain and recovering alcoholic, whom Renee had took pity on when she found him sleeping by a dumpster. Nathalie was from New Zealand, where she had been in service in a Ruler household. Griselde was a dancer from Budapest.

The prep area was an ill-lit, infernal region at the far end of the kitchen, heated by a leaky wood stove that kept a kettle of water boiling throughout the day for the strongly brewed English tea, served with lots of cream and sugar, that prep cooks and dishwashers preferred. This was where they washed the produce, gutted and scaled the fish, butchered the game. Wooden crates packed with carrots, turnips, potatoes, radishes, and bursting with kales, mustards, lettuces, and spinach from the gardens stood stacked against the stone wall. There were deep soapstone sinks and counters on the opposite wall, and a spinner for drying greens on the floor. The meat and dairy were prepped in a separate area, along the back wall, closest to the walk-ins and stairs to the cellar.

The three sat around the bucket, behind the butcher's block, on wooden stools. They were laughing hard, shaped by shadow and the varnished light of oil lamps on the walls and hanging from chains in the ceiling. Clare, scrubbing a gigantic russet potato, said, "This water will settle clear, too, if you give it time."

Ruth loved the warm kitchen smell. It reminded her of home. Even the grandest Transylvanian palace had a warm corner by the wood stove in the kitchen. Her mother had not wanted her hanging out with the prep cooks, but she liked to wash potatoes and listen to them talk. After a while, they'd forget she was there and she learned a few things she was too young to know, and what they thought about working for her mother and the butler Naomi, as cruel a bitch as has ever run a great house.

When she was seven, the Ruler Sargon came and asked her mother and the Ruler Bánffy if she could go with him to his home to live and one day become a Surrogate. This American family had been coming to Hungary for many generations. Ruth's great-grandmother Anna was the Surrogate who bore Sargon and Renee. Long before that, the Hungarian Rulers were close allies of the Sargons and Renees, and they exchanged Surrogates. And before that, during the Great Rebellion, the Sargons lived in Budapest and the Renees in Vienna. They had bred with Transylvanian Lords and Muscovite Rulers. Some lines vanished in the Carpathians, interlaced with Turks, Magyars, and Persians.

One day, her mother took her into the cool part of the pantry, where root vegetables and jars of pickles were stored. The room smelled of gourds and roots, of the earthen floor and fermenting garlic and dill. There were baskets packed with straw and apples, quinces and pears, and rough-hewn shelves filled with butternut squash, painted turbans, and cheese pumpkins. There were tall brown crocks of pickles and sauerkraut. Her mother never took her into such places. She preferred their rooms, smelling of potpourri, with the glass tabletops and lace, canopied beds, and curtains drawn across the small windows that fit into high towers. Light that slanted in, in rays that scissored about the room.

Her mother stood bent at the waist, eyes intense, the short hard curls of her blond hair hanging in her face. She took Ruth's hand and said, "You must remember what I say now. You will be going away soon. They will take you to America, to be in a great Rulers' house, the house of Sargon and Renee. And when you grow up, you will be the family's Surrogate, and bear their Scions. You must understand that this is a great honor for you, and for our family. Everything we have, all the lands in Transylvania, and Father's job managing the forests, come from your Great Grandmother, who bore Sargon and Renee seventy-five years ago. We would not be in a great house if it were not for her. We would still be eating shit for nothing in the stupid village.

"I'm sorry if you are afraid. Know that I love you. More than anything, my Little Bear... but it must be. We will see one another again. I made them promise me that. But for now, you must go with them, *Liebchen*." She pulled Ruth towards her, and gripped her to her starched-cotton chest. Ruth tried to understand. She knew she must remember, so she was repeating the words over, as she had learned in school. And even though she had said them many times, she still did not understand what the words really meant. So she pretended she knew.

"But first," her mother said, her hand gripping the back of Ruth's head. It was a harsh, angry hug, but she could feel that the anger wasn't directed at her. She knew that. Then her mother held onto the sides of Ruth's arms and smiled. "But first they will examine you, to make sure you're healthy. They aren't going to hurt you, but they will measure your hips, and shine a light in your vagina. This time it's OK to let the man touch you between your legs." Ruth swallowed. What did it cost her, she wondered, to say that? "You will write to me or call if anyone else does that? You understand? They are not to touch you. Only the doctor. You are free, not a concubine. You are a Surrogate. They will implant a baby in you with a special instrument, a teeny tiny baby you can't even see, with a needle that doesn't hurt. And you will give birth to heroes, a king and queen who will Rule the great City of New York and one day, all of America. Never forget that."

Her mother stood up and winced, her knees bad from a life of cleaning. "Now munchkin, listen. You do as they say, as here. You must obey the Rulers. But you must not trust them. *He* will be your friend. *She* will fall in love with you. They will treat you as one of them, one of the family, but you are not. You must never forget that. Not if you want to live. Remember. Only bear the clones. Never—" her voice dropped and she was silent.

She looked like she was going to cry. Ruth had never seen her mother cry, or show much of any feeling at all. She worked. She told people what to do. Ruth felt like an inconvenience, that she was on her own in the house from the time of her birth. "I don't know how to tell you. I don't know the words. Sweet Little Bear, *Bärchen*, never bear a Ruler's child. Never fuck a Ruler. Don't ask me what that means. One day soon, you will know. It is death for both of you. But there is a difference. The Ruler can be cloned. You can't. All you have is your body and your brains. Learn to use them well."

Her mother swallowed again and took her hand. As they turned to leave the room Ruth choked and screamed, "Mama! I don't want to go," and broke to the floor sobbing in the cold packed dirt. She could still taste that dirt.

★

Isle of Dogs, Part 1

So, at the age of seven Ruth departed with Frau Duckworth and Sargon for New York. They rode a dusty black barouche to the local train station and boarded a private carriage. It was her duty to remain silent and do what she was told. She was brought up to behave. When the narrow-gauge train hissed to a halt in the Budapest-Nyugati pályaudvar, and she saw the thousands of busy people in suits and dresses, the women in high heels and the men in narrow-toed boots, she moved closer to the old woman from America with the German prune face and smiled.

Frau Duckworth took her hand firmly, stood and said, in Austrian German, the tongue of her mother's bedtime stories, "You are with the Ruler Sargon now. You have nothing to be afraid of. Hold my hand, dear. We'll be in our carriage soon." The smile evaporated and they stood. She gazed at the red pillows, gold piping, and tassels on the seats and gagged, afraid she was going to throw up on them.

People rushed by the windows like starlings. Sargon was stooped against the ceiling of the train carriage. The doors slid open and a man in uniform escorted them out. Sargon walked quickly, the crowd separating around him. Duck (this is what she decided to call her) hurried them forward in his wake. Behind them came porters with trunks and railway agents in uniforms, chasing after the nursemaid, the girl and the Ruler.

The Ruler Sargon walked like a man who expected crowds to part for him. He was invincible, like the King in the fairy tales her mother told. But he didn't act the king with her. He was gregarious and gentle. He always squatted down to talk to her. She felt like he knew her, not like a piece of dust. She was a child then, she reminded herself, and now she was a mother and he was her lover. There was no time between. No time to get wise, and no time to get free.

In America, she attended the village school. There she learned to speak, read, and write English half the day. The rest of the day, at Sargon's insistence, she was tutored at home in literature, history, math, science, and music, plus rigorous exercise. He said, "You must learn so you can teach our children." Her tutors, Jacques (who insisted she pronounce his name Jay-kwees) and James went to work on her unruly mind and manners. Ruler history was their great obsession, but she was encouraged to use the library freely. She read novels, plays, and poetry in German and English. She learned well. She began to forget home. The wound of separation became a scar that ached and then faded.

Ruth had the run of the house, and was familiar

with both the Rulers and the servants. Ruler and human children played freely together. There were many people in the family entourage, cousins, cronies and neighbors, judges, lawyers, and business people, who filled the table each night. Dinners were long and elaborate. There were balls and hunting parties, brunches and sailing trips on Long Island Sound and up and down the Hudson. But Ruler children went to boarding school at age six. Except for holidays, when they all came home and she roamed with the pack, she was alone, a child in a world of adults. All the servants spoiled her.

Ruth moved with the family, from Hommocks Cottage to the Winter Palace, and from the Winter Palace to 1220 Fifth. Wherever they went, Paris, London, Saigon, Jerusalem, it was the same: she lived in the wing with the tutors, and shared rooms with Duck.

Ruth rode with Sargon, Renee, and Robin in all of the parades in the city, and attended ribbon cuttings, banquets, and openings. At home she sat to Sargon's left, across from Robin, while at the opposite end Renee held down whatever pair of mastodons she had been assigned, retired generals and admirals blustering over mashed potatoes with truffles.

Ruth loved Ruler boys. Their arrogance amused

her. And they were beautiful. The first boy she fell in love with was the Young Long of Louisiana, who came to live with Sargon and Renee every summer, to make connections on Wall Street before becoming Ruler of Louisiana. Because he had never seen snow, he stayed with them one Christmas at the Winter Palace. It was a cold year. There was actually a dusting of snow on the ground. The trails were good for riding. They rode themselves breathless. She wanted him. She thought, Mama said never fuck a Ruler. But that leaves everything else.

Their friendship had been forged in extremity. They became flirtatiously competitive and raced on horseback, or sailed across the Sound in rough weather. When she went overboard, she could swim, or stay afloat for hours. She didn't hold back. She couldn't stop thinking about it. He had to feel the same way, she was certain of it. It was in his eyes, in the way he lingered if they accidentally touched.

That Christmas, they were hiking by a stream slowing into ice. She took his hand and he reared back. His eyes dropped into ultraviolet. She saw the size of his face for the first time. And in that instant his look was empty. She was no one to him. She had made the whole thing up.

✷

Griselde had a pink face, crinkled black hair and teeth like shovels. When she smiled, it was like the first sun in the morning. She dropped a potato from her raw, veined hands and as it plunked into the brass bucket said, "Will you look at that!" Everyone looked up from their work and stopped joking.

Nathalie hooted, "Hello, Phaedra! Ruthie, you brought the babies." Phaedra hid behind Ruth's back, the hem of the dress rustling against red toenails. She held her breath, until she couldn't repress it anymore, and burst out giggling. The three chased Phaedra around Ruth until Clare gasped, "Can we see the baby?"

The Baby Sargon was asleep in the sling. Ruth looked down at his round face, peaceful in repose, yes, and not one you wanted to awaken. When, how, or if he slept was entirely up to him. Her rhythms and Phaedra's rhythms were his rhythms. They awoke when he awoke and slept, or tried to sleep, when he slept.

Ruth sensed from the start that the Rulers had an animal interest in her. If she was to be the vessel of themselves, then she must have the most perfect, robust human body, one worthy of bearing a Ruler. But one also able to nurture and protect the clone. It was a graft of an engineered human onto the stock of a natural one. For the clones, strong as they were at maturity, were endangered from the moment of creation, weak until years after birth, prey to unpredictable Drift and error caused by too many isonymic generations. Babies were born dead or monstrous, with gills instead of lungs or phosphorescent skin that poisoned them in utero. There were congenital defects and conditions, like asthma and diabetes, deformed hearts, failing livers, that plagued the clones. They could have eyes that didn't focus perfectly, or ears that lost depth perception. Other defects were mundane, like baldness, myopia, or collagen failing to regenerate. The Rulers came to worship the natural vigor of humans even as they despised them as inferior. Humans were the wild population from which they bred themselves, and the one they used to renew the lines. Rulers could not free themselves of humans.

Her part was epigenetic, epiphenomenal, even epiphanic, in the cast of Drift. The Scion took vigor from the stock, but also (it was thought) a wiggle, a virtually incorporeal influence, a wind to counter the tendency of mutation and error to compound and concentrate. And so the endless embarrassing samples, probes, scans, and tests. Scraping the uterus and swabbing the nose, throat, and rectum. The stirrups felt as natural as those of a horse.

Ruth said, "Of course you can see the baby, that's why we came to visit!" She played the part of ebullience without reserve or irony.

As they drew closer to her, she remembered Doc Hughes' words. She looked at each of them for evidence of his list of ills but found none. Still, her eyes said, don't come too close. This was how you communicated in a Ruler's house, with looks, nods, and lips. In a huddle, they peered into the sling at the baby's fat happy face and sleeping eyes, balled fists. "Oh, will you look at the Baby Sargon," they whispered.

"How was the birth?" Nathalie asked.

"How long?" asked Griselde, gazing down at the pronounced bump in her own belly.

Ruth said, "Phaedra was easy by comparison. I was not prepared. The labor was short but it was agonizing. Like shitting out a duffel bag! He weighed ten pounds."

"Ow," said Clare.

From the kitchen proper, a long, ambiently lit hall of stainless steel counters, ranges, and pot racks, came a cry of recognition as the chef, Mrs. Tucker, a tall woman with a chef's hat rising off her head, black eared and pink faced, came running into the prep area. "Next time you come to the kitchen first!" she shouted, pulling off the toque, revealing a tower of blond curls. They all laughed. "Let me see my little girl. Hello, Phaed. How's life been beating you?" She winked. "What's that hiding behind your ear?"

Phaedra showed off her four teeth and touched her ear. "Nothing."

"Oh, I think you're hiding something." Mrs. Tucker squatted down and reached behind Phaedra's ear, and with a flip of her scarred hand, pulled out a cookie. "Will you look at that!" She stood. "How's mom?"

Ruth touched the Baby Sargon. He was quiet. She knew better than to think the peace would last, was even hoping he'd wake up soon so she'd have an excuse to get away. She felt strange. It wasn't a new feeling, but it wasn't one she had been aware of among her friends before. What she had come for wasn't there.

"Damn," Mrs. Tucker said, gazing between the folds of the cloth carrier, at his face like a mummified dwarf. "Damn if he doesn't look a little like you!" Laughing at her own joke, as she always did, she looked at Phaedra and studied her face a moment. She froze. Standing abruptly, she asked Ruth, "Can you drink coffee? I was going to make espresso."

Ruth did not change her expression but her gut was empty and cold. She wanted to pull Phaedra to her but did not. They needed to get out right away, but she didn't want to arouse Mrs. Tucker's suspicions even more. She said, "Maybe a demitasse. I am permitted two cups a day. No more, no less." She faked a smile. "I did have two already this morning. But a demitasse hardly counts."

Mrs. Tucker asked, "And your favorite? Pogácsa?"

Ruth blushed to the back of her head. "Yes, please. It is permitted." She searched the exits. She could turn around and walk out. There was no one to block her way, and yet she remained.

They sat around the prep table and drank espresso and ate buttery pogácsa, a Hungarian scone Mrs. Tucker had made for her since the night she arrived, clinging to Duck's skirts. Her friends told stories and she pretended to laugh, not hearing a word but listening instead to the buzz in her head and chest. As soon as they were done, cups stacked and crumbs swept off the table, she escaped.

✭

In the back hall, she let out her breath and headed

for the stairs. Ruth was used to doing what she pleased. Even her pregnancy didn't alarm her at first. Rulers were particularly fascinated by Romantic love and children born of couples in its throes. Getting pregnant before bearing a Ruler clone was even encouraged. They liked to break a Surrogate in with a trial baby. After the age of fifteen pregnancy was celebrated and the child would be reared in the house with the Surrogate's freedom and status. As long as no one knew who the father was, she would be fine, or so she had hoped. Now someone else did know. And she had no idea of what to do.

She had been lying to her only friends. They had shared the details of their lives with her, treated her as one of them, and she repaid that friendship with secrecy. Clare taught her to ride a bicycle. Griselde showed her how to kiss the way grown-ups did, with an open mouth, and later she and Nathalie demonstrated how to give head with a banana. They made her feel safe, like family. But she had a secret that could not be shared. It was not her home. They were not her friends.

Ruth realized that she was never actually one of them. The aura of the Rulers had always embowered her, like the nanodome that secured their homes. Her life was not like the life of a cook, a maid or a footman. She was not a housekeeper or game warden like her mother and father. She labored for her gems, she worked with her hands, her body served her masters, but the conditions were different. She was free to come and go. Servants didn't ride down Broadway in ticker tape parades or take rockets to Scotland, and they didn't fuck their Rulers.

It felt like fate. For sex, her choices weren't good. She would have to turn to the village boys, or the old vampires with their wattled necks, pouring champagne and carrying shoes in and out of rooms, their nervous empty eyes red-rimmed like a pigeon's. They would come up behind her on the stairs, in the hall, or a closet, and slide their hand up her skirt. One actually found time to brush the crotch of her underwear with two fingers before she crushed his chest with her elbow, and said, quietly, "Excuse me, sir."

After the debacle with the Young Long, Ruth decided to bide her time. One of the Rulers had to be a variant. It stood to reason. They were careful to hide it, but it happened to everyone. It wasn't rational, it was the body staking its claim. After all, she had girl crushes, but found the Ruler girls, who wanted her openly, to be repulsive. They were odorless, hairless Amazons, but not Beth Baker.

Beth Baker was a natural girl at school who smelled like warm moss and sage. She was awkward and quiet and dressed in dowdy clothes. The other girls ostracized her. She was the subject of nasty rumors. Ruth didn't care for gossip and cruelty, so she let her alone. But she felt the same disgust and disdain for her as the other girls did. There was just something about Beth Baker. She looked at the ground. She was dirty and mean.

One day, they were running five miles and she saw Beth Baker sitting on the side of the track under an old birch tree, smoking a cigarette. Up until then, she wanted to do well in the race. She didn't have to win it, but place well, in the top five. She was four back with enough reserve to make third, she was sure. But Beth Baker filled her eye and she stopped running. The girls behind her didn't break stride; they stared straight ahead. She knew what they were thinking. She was going to fuck Beth Baker.

Beth Baker wasn't looking at the ground, she was looking at the tip of her cigarette, blowing smoke on it and watching it glow. She had a dark unhappy face with round black eyes. Beth became Ruth's hero.

She started to sleep over at Beth Baker's house. They made out in the barn and sucked each others tits. They never did anything else. Beth called it practice and Ruth was fine with that. She wanted to practice as much as possible.

It was strange to see how humans lived. Beth's mother and father worked on riverboats and made tinctures. They cleaned their own house and cooked their own food. They raised too many babies by themselves and yelled a lot. All the kids had to do chores. They raked leaves in the fall, spread manure in the spring, cut grass and wood in the summer. In the evening, after dinner, the Bakers sat on the porch, or in front of the fire, drinking and playing cards or board games, laughing too loud.

Ruth realized she was human of course, but over time she became a Ruler in her mind. She was expected to be haughty and disdainful. Strong mothers were required. The Lady Ruler, who had her own business to attend to, could not be burdened with the task. Surrogates were meant to model the ideal behavior of Rule.

Phaedra was blamed on a Hungarian servant of the Ruler Bánffy's house, who attended a Lord visiting for the summer. Doc Hughes explained that she didn't have to worry about height, hair, or the other obvious mutations, because they were recessive genes. Both parents had to have the same product for it to be heritable. He could turn off most of the other stuff. The proprietary genes wouldn't show up in an instant genetic field test, but once a scan was processed, it would come back saying illegal mutant. All he could do was alter the data before upload, so Phaedra's official record would show a clean natural human genome. Phaedra's passport would be issued based on that record. As long as she evaded scans and had the passport, she would be OK. Only Doc Hughes, Sargon, Renee, and Robin knew. They would protect her.

Ruth was eighteen when she and Sargon started sleeping together. Long before that, throughout her entire childhood, he would visit her. Sometimes daily, sometimes not for months, when the Senate was in session, or he was traveling. They would play four-handed piano. He gave her a Gibson guitar and came to her room after dinner to teach her how to play it. They would play songs and sing. It was said of Rulers that they played perfectly, without feeling. This was not true of the Sargons, who had more than a whiff of Romanticism in their style. When they improvised, she felt like they were reading each other's minds.

Sargon didn't feel like a father to Ruth; he was more like a friend. When they were together he would relax, drop his shoulders, and laugh, telling long stories about the politicians he knew growing up. He told the real stories of Iocle and Sara Istar's wars with Ocba's Martian spaceforce, stories she had known as adventure tales from cartoons and picture books. As she matured, the stories darkened. History was littered with the corpses of interstellar sex slaves and drug-addicted ship captains smuggling illegal genetics to robot labs buried deep in the blue aquifers of Europa and Ganymede. It was more fantastic than any fairy tale.

Then came the day when everything changed. They were in the room with the eyebrow window overlooking Larchmont Harbor in Hommocks Cottage. Balfour was barreling about and Duck was yelling *shuszche*. Sargon was unusually quiet and distant. As they said goodbye, he took her hands and they felt different. They were warm. She could feel his pulse beating and a charge coursed through their fingers. She was aroused. It never occurred to her that she could have any interest in him at all. He was sixty-five years older, her Ruler, and someone she had grown up with, a folksy, grumpy, delightful playmate, not sexy or romantic. But when he left she felt a stab in her heart and a stirring in her groin that made her queasy.

Ruth was to bear his clone soon. When she thought of that, and of their relationship, she realized that since the age of seven they were preparing her to be his bride, not his daughter. She imagined them together as Consorts, descending the grand stair of the Winter Palace in full dress, her hand in his. They would be secret lovers. She would do all of the things she had learned in kitchens and in barns. Deep kisses. The images that staggered through her mind when she masturbated came to the surface all the time and she found herself staring at walls and out windows, distracted by erotic reveries. It consumed her rationality and sense. She realized that she could have him as her lover. Then she would remember the rejection of Long, the cold stream and that awful empty look on his face. Their conversations were awkward. Laughter was replaced with silence. Something had to break.

It was the August Recess but he had not visited in two weeks. She thought then that he would never come, that she would learn he had relocated to Europe and would only return when the clone was implanted, or that he was to be assigned to a Martian mission and would be in space for two years. She lost him each night lying in bed, staring at the moths banging the window, soaking the sheets as she rubbed herself to sleep.

Finally, when the first thunderclouds rolled in,

building up to the fall storms, he came. His hair was lit up and his eyes were pulsing. She met him at the hallway door, put her hands into his and opened her mouth to speak but said nothing. He kissed her gently on the cheek and then the lips. He was trembling. Duck moved into the other room. He was so old and yet he was as timid as a boy. How odd, she thought. She returned the kiss. They furtively groped each other but did nothing else.

Days later, he took her on a long sailing trip aboard the *Rosamund Fair*, a forty-five foot yacht. They anchored for the night off Shelter Island. Chee Min, the chef of Open Dory, a seven-star sushi restaurant in Vancouver, prepared a meal for them in the galley kitchen. They ate fish caught that afternoon and sipped aged sake in their bathing suits, watching the gold and magenta light of the sun, sinking beneath piles of cloud, pour out across the water. The crew vanished and they lay out on the deck talking. Around midnight Ruth got up, stripped, and dove into the black water, phosphorescent plumes streaming through her fingers. Sargon dove in after her and they swam on their backs looking at the stars.

The cabin creaked and smelled of ropes and rime. The bed was long but narrow and low overhead. He was too large for a confined space. They didn't have much room to maneuver. They were clumsy, but they persisted. By the time they returned a week later they knew how to fuck each other. She decided that sex was the best thing ever. Unfortunately, she was also pregnant.

✶

It was now late afternoon. With the longer days, the galleries and halls of the Winter Palace were lit by shafts of saffron sun. Phaedra was hungry, tired, and wound up. She clung to Ruth, whining. On cue the Baby Sargon awoke, looked around, and sneezed twice. Eyes owl-wide, he stretched open his mouth and howled. She went to the Great Hall and searched for a place to sit. The busts were grey in the shadowed niches, their stern profiles stacked in the distance, a whispering chorus of stone. She tried to shush him, rocking back and forth, but he was squirming to be free. Phaedra dragged her forward by the finger. Ruth needed to lie down. She could ignore the howling but not her bursting breasts. "Phaedra," she said.

"Mama."

"Stop pulling Mama." They were at the foot of the grand stair. The chandelier was turned off, and the dull glass threads hung like a rag mop over the atrium. Phaedra pulled her down the Great Hall towards her favorite indoor garden, with the concrete toadstools and a covey of jade quail. "Please Phaedra, stop." She stopped and looked up at her Mama. She puckered her lips and shook her head dramatically. "No Mama can stop me."

Ruth couldn't answer, not over the thrashing of arms and legs in the sling. As she used to do when he was an infant, Ruth put the tip of her pinky in his mouth, but it only infuriated him. The bitter, salty taste, she thought. He screwed about in her arms. She held him to her chest and whispered. She looked up the stairs. Would Phaedra walk? Usually she insisted on it. She couldn't carry her, that was certain. She must get her to walk up three flights of stairs to the nursery. It would be so much simpler to just nurse him down here.

There was nowhere to sit. It was a corridor of stone by day, devoid of faces and candlelight. Gigantic ballrooms, private parlors, a tap room, a banquet hall. Some she knew from official functions, when she appeared with the family, and some through adventure when she was little. She learned to walk a path between what was permitted, what forbidden, and what tolerated. As she grew, that changed from basements, attics, and crawl spaces, to sailboats, roofs, and offices, and finally, beds, couches, and any surface sturdy enough to take their weight thrusting against it.

Ruth felt it was not permitted to go into these rooms. But she had no choice. Baby Sargon cried harder, pushing out his belly as he arched his back in pain. He had knotted his feet up in the carrier and she couldn't lift him out.

The Parlor was near. She opened the doors to the pitch-black room. Blinded, she entered and the lights faded up to a comfortable reading level. She sank into a couch by the cavernous fireplace and disentangled the screaming baby from the sling, her ears ringing and numb, and opened her blouse, waving a nipple in front of his mouth. He reached out with both hands, grabbed hold and sucked. She leaned back. Phaedra climbed up and sat beside her, her face drawn, lips mouthing words. Blue and turquoise flickered in her eyes with streaks of green like April grass, and dots of red. Phaedra rocked gently, leaning into Ruth's body, touching Baby Sargon's head with her pudgy hand, his fine hair pulsing with a contented blue glow.

"You'll have to wait to nurse. He'll drink both sides." Phaedra's expression didn't change. Ruth smiled at her little Stoic and lifted her with her free arm over the baby and down on her other side, so she could lean into her lap and chest. "Our friend's a hungry fellow," Ruth said. As the Baby Sargon nursed she tried to think of what to do. If Mrs. Tucker knows, everyone does, she thought, feeling suddenly tired and thirsty. Sargon would be mad at her for exposing them. She was in danger and had to do something about it. Rulers protect themselves first. She had to get money. She held Phaedra closer, as if shielding her from fire, and said, "When we get upstairs, let's send down for ice cream. Would you like that?" It was all she wanted at that moment. Cold vanilla ice cream melting over her tongue.

★

Renee was waiting for her nine o'clock briefing from the Ruler Euclid. Her office was on the fortieth floor of a utilitarian glass box on Battery Place. It was a building distinguished only by its poor climate control system and unreliable ambient lighting. Flickers were common, blinding flashes and blackouts, less so, but unnerving in lifts and lats. She had a commanding view of the busy New York Harbor and she sometimes felt like a choreographer watching dancers perform her ballet. She could see the ferries cross to the Statue of Liberty, Brooklyn and Hoboken. The ships of her fleet passed by, sailing up the East River to the Brooklyn Navy Yard, or up the Hudson to the West Side Piers. Tugs hauled barges bearing heavy equipment, cement, and goods up and down the rivers. She watched two head up the East River to the Bronx, the Kuiper Belt Corp. flag, of a golden belt encircling eight silver planets on a black background, flying. This was all her Rule, her Command, the Second Fleet in her own safe harbor. When she was with Fleet Command in Norfolk she was exposed, but in her chair in her office she didn't have to think about such things.

Down the hall, also with a view of the harbor, was Captain Euclid's office. He was attached to the Expeditionary Combat Command (ECC), which, among other things, conducted naval intelligence; insurgency, assassination and sabotage campaigns; and logistical support for all naval actions from the North Pole to the 38th parallel north latitude, or somewhere north of the Chesapeake Bay and south of Philadelphia. There were different ways of finding out exactly where the line wavered, but they were to be avoided.

Captain Euclid knocked on the door. She swiveled her back to the window, facing him as he entered the room. She was unnerved by his grass-green eyes, which were very rare, very old, and his lizard-like appearance. He was the quietest man she had ever met. He didn't raise his voice, he didn't pontificate, he didn't hold forth, he didn't rage against fate, or self-dramatize; he betrayed no sense of persecution or slight. He hid behind those eyes. No one could hold them long enough to penetrate the surface and get to his meaning and intent.

"My Lady," Euclid began. "There is a report from the Winter Palace. A cook evidently noticed a strong resemblance between the Ruler Sargon and Phaedra von Doderer. She betrayed you. She was afraid not to." He smiled. "I have attracted a number of flies not worth swatting, but this one is dangerous."

"Which of the cooks was it?"

"Mrs. Tucker."

"*Scheisse*! She's our Chef de Cuisine. Like one of the family." Renee turned and stared out the window. She was expecting something like this, but her hands were tied. If only Sargon were not so enamored of the girl. A mistress was annoying but an acceptable danger for a dalliance. Such things had always happened. She understood the attraction of wild human flesh. His Sire certainly indulged his passion for forbidden women, but the rumors of bastards were untrue, and he never kept one around for more than a few days. There were rules. "Keep an eye on her for now. Did she come to you?"

"Yes. The child is safe in New York, but I wouldn't send her to Texas."

"I wouldn't send the Devil to Texas. Is there anything else?"

"Yes." He paused, choosing his words with care. He looked out the window and pointed to the barges creeping up the East River. "It appears that Senator Maximilian and Senator Imogen have struck a deal to allow Kuiper Belt Space Transport Industries to build a transfer station on his Co-op City holdings in the Bronx."

Renee looked out the window at the barge and felt nauseous. "Like hell they are." The impact of the news scattered her thoughts. Try as she might, she could not school them. She forced herself to think, to push through it. "Don't tell anyone."

She turned in her chair, grasped the sides of her head and stared at the tugs pulling the barge slowly up the churning grey delta. Never, not for one second, did she think Maximilian had the balls to try such a thing. It was Imogen, with Iocle's backing. Iocle was provoking a fight between them. So they had a choice. Take the bait or refuse it. But if they did not fight for their Rule, what was the point? They must strike back.

"Did you want options, My Lady Admiral?"

"No, Captain. That's it for now." Any options would not be worked out with Euclid. He came to her when Aeppar approached him to spy. He did not have to do that. But she had to be careful with a double agent. She only fed him what she wanted them to know. Still, if it should prove to be true, he would earn her confidence.

Admiral Renee called in her adjutant, Lieutenant Naram Sin, an ambitious collector of subordinates, and quite beautiful. She contented herself with imagining her dripping cunt pressed up against her chin. It was not professional; actually, it was wrong to initiate sexual relations with sailors under direct command. But, there were circumstances.

"What does My Lady Admiral desire?" Lieutenant Naram Sin asked, crisply.

"Dispatch a drone to surveil Co-op City and send the report to me, for my eyes only. That is, no one else, do you understand? No one. Get me the Senator, and conference Robin in."

"Yessir."

Sargon crackled irritably into being in the center of the office. Robin projected out of a wobbling plane of static. "We've got a problem," Renee began. "Maximilian gave Imogen Co-op City for his seat on Council. She's got her transport station." She looked carefully at Sargon's oscillating image, unable to discern his reaction, until it violently contracted.

"No bill has come to the floor from Council, much less passed the Senate," Sargon screamed.

"Keep your voice down. It isn't a bill, it's a deal."

Robin said, "Sire, Lady. I shall go to the Senate and see what I can discover and get back to you."

Sargon darkened. He said, in a low, cunning voice, "It's too late for that."

"Maybe," Renee said. "But we don't know."

"Lug is right. I should have killed Max."

"He's kicking you in the balls for centuries of quiet humiliation. You don't have to kick back."

"Sire," Robin said. "It will only make things worse. Darius was right. It will cost you everything."

"This costs me everything."

Renee sought to assuage him. "Think, My Lord," she urged. "Don't overreact. We have options."

"Perhaps a blockade," Robin suggested.

"Yes," Renee agreed. "A blockade is better than an assassination, certainly, but it has its own dangers."

Sargon said, "It's intolerable."

Renee reluctantly nodded her head. Maximilian had the right to that land, and the development rights as well. Moreover, NYC was a free port. Ships and vehicles by law and custom had a right to engage in legal trade. A blockade would be illegal. New York ships would be refused at ports around the country and the world. "I can blockade the supply ships. We control the airspace, the roads and the rails. They would have to go to war to build it against our will. But it would be an illegal blockade, and bad for business. The Longshoremen get restless if they're not working. We would be embargoed. It would be the Northeast and the West against the rest of the country, the world. Can we do it?"

Sargon's image stilled like water. "My instinct tells me to crush him."

Robin said, "Don't do that. Go to Iocle."

"He's right. Go to Iocle first. The President allowed this. He can stop it."

"I don't see how, but if you insist, I will go to DC."

5

The Wilderness

Iocle 5, Ruler of Delaware, Maryland and Virginia, and of the Mid-Atlantic Region, 113th President of the United States of America, sat in his wheelchair, which at the moment faced the Oval Office windows of the White House. He was watching birds fly in and out of the dense wall of foliage that lay across the small lawn, landing and taking off from an array of feeders, gabled wooden houses, platforms, impaled corn cobs, sagging bags of beef fat, and glass tubes spilling seed on the ground.

Remaining in Washington, DC kept him well removed from the irritants of parliamentary process, a charade he did not care to endorse by his participation. He had been President for sixty years, an exceptionally long term for an office that was difficult to attain and hold. Rulers inevitably emerged weakened and humiliated by the experience.

Knowing this history, President Iocle's first maneuver was to leave the UN building and reoccupy the White House, which for centuries had been used as a stage set for state ceremonies and nothing else. For a hundred years it was maintained as a museum, but the museum closed because of safety issues in 2389. The problems ranged from falling ceilings, to black mold, to rabid bats. The nation's Capital had moved in all but name to New York, where the Presidency had been dominated by Bard and Sargon for long enough. Separating them from the office and each other was his passion, but also a key part of his greater strategy to hang on to power long enough to pass it on to his Scion.

Iocle didn't give a damn about the White House's condition. It beat a slow mining ship wending its way from asteroid to asteroid, suspended forever between Mars and Jupiter, Earth not seen for decades, with nothing but time to rehearse grievances. He got a rabies vaccine and moved into the first floor, stationing his army around DC, and the Mid-Atlantic Navy on the Potomac. The entire District was enclosed in a nanodome. That was in 2451.

Next he went about restoring it, starting with the West Wing. But he did nothing to tame the forest of swamp trees that had grown up between it and the old Capitol building. The monuments on the Mall were in ruins. The great lawn was a lethal wood, dense with palm and cypress and a solid understory of thorn bushes, brambles and stinging nettles, laced with poison ivy. A jungle grew down to the Potomac, through a malarial mangrove. He would have built a wall three miles high if it would have helped.

From this fortress, he forged his power, by elevating and purging factions, one by one, until only he remained, his antagonists beneath him in balanced opposition, maintained by small adjustments and compromises, borne of provocation and restraint. It was the Art of Ruling, and he was its master.

Iocle was 141 years old. He had a catheter and a colostomy bag. An oxygen tank fed him sweet air through the nose, over the copious folds of his face. Beneath this blanket of flesh, he could feel the brittleness of his bones. Like burnt calcified metal, they would crumble in the undertaker's hand.

Iocle's back was turned on Utburd, Aeppar, and Utkasting.

"Must I really see him?" Iocle asked through his

voice simulator. He could speak with his vocal cords if he wanted to, but he felt it a strain. Still, he knew the value of spoken communication. He perfected synthetic voices, so that they emanated from him. When he was younger and more mobile he could lip-sync himself with utter ease, and provide an accompanying pantomime of gestures, taking on the gravitas, if he so chose, of a stentorian orator. Unfortunately, as he lost mobility he lost apparent affect, and now glared silently at them as the proxy voice by turns wheedled and pleaded in a fit of self-pity, pitched to elicit guilt.

Utburd, his toffee-colored bullethead reddening, said, "Mr. President, Sire, he is the Ruler of New York."

The President switched off the simulator and croaked, "I know bloody well who he is! I saw him in diapers, playing croquet on the Hudson in that pompous Palace full of old junk and marble. They piled up gems and gold in those goddamn New York vaults of theirs, preening while we battled…" His voice shrank and the folds of his face lost color and became fungal. "Adrift! Forever floating out in space. Sara dead in Ocba's dungeons. That mutant prick Vesuvius sitting in his Martian barrow, brewing up apocalyptic mutations in transgenic clones. We corked the bottle and sucked space for it, while Bard and Sargon sat on horses and attended conferences. And I lost my darling Consort, Sara Istar, watched her drift away." He paused. "What they say is true, her spirit does roam ships." Tears swelled in his eyes. "Then Sargon goes, in the first generation, when we most needed him in the wars, to Hungary or wherever the fuck. This one here, the Third, abandons California to do what? Run a city? Make money? No. To challenge me. But I know what his weakness is. *Pussy.*" He spat out the word.

"Sire, we haven't time for this now."

"Knock it off. I know what I know, I have sources. Sargon's got a little bastard tucked away. Didn't I tell you that? We can rid ourselves of him anytime we want, you're thinking. And Imogen's got her transport station. When he finds out, he won't sit for it. I wouldn't! Would you? Hmm? Was that in the meeting?"

"Mr. President, Sire, he will be here," Utburd pleaded.

Aeppar said, "You are Renee's Commander in Chief, and your Scion is the Supreme Commander of All Naval Forces, she will do as ordered, I will see—"

Iocle interrupted her. "She's a warrior. Sit with your back to the wall when she's around." He jutted his thumb backwards at the wall and inadvertently, at them.

"Mr. President, Sire. Shall we go over the talking points?" asked Aeppar, her yellow crew cut pulsing at the roots.

The President put his long insectile fingers down on the navigation pad and turned the chair around to face them across the *Resolute,* a 600-year-old desk used by JFK and FDR. Now the three bay windows were to his back and he was framed by the black leaves of the jungle. He hoped the desk would humble the three leeches, and that the view would remind them that the jungle was where they came from, and the jungle was where they'd go when he was done with them. At the very least, it might compel them to show some restraint, some respect, if not fear. "The talking points." He chewed, his perfect white teeth flashing between dry, flapping lips. "I don't need any fucking talking points. If Sargon can put his bitch on the Executive Council, so can I. And there goes his seat, and there goes his Presidency."

Utburd said, "There is some apprehension, tension, negative anticipation in the Senate regarding the succession. Bard's return is seen as a direct challenge to your magnificent Rule."

"Where are Bard's Council votes now? Without

them, he'll lose. I'll defeat him when I'm unconscious on a ventilator. With blinks of the eyelid, I'll Rule him. And when I die, Souvanouphong will be President. He has ambitions of his own."

"But we've agreed that Everest should become caretaker before an election. To preserve order. We need a firm hand at the tiller, a Ruler with authority, experience, maturity."

"Who agreed to that? It would be illegal. Souvanouphong is Vice President. I would ask you to define his function if it is not to succeed the President in the case of his death or incapacity?" He leaned forward and wheezed, coughing weakly, exhausted by the sentence he had just uttered.

"We all understand the succession, Mr. President, Sire. It is self-evident that Souvanouphong should appoint Senator Everest Vice President and then resign, allowing Everest to accede to the exalted office of President," Utburd said.

Iocle took a breath of oxygen through his nose, as deep as he could manage. "Souvanouphong may not want to do that. You'll shoot him, no doubt, and dissolve his body in acid. Even so, Everest won't defeat Bard."

"Now that we have Maximilian instead of Sargon, Everest could win a first ballot in the Council."

Isle of Dogs, Part 1

Iocle dissected his face and made him feel the knife. "Everest may come close, they may tie, but you boys don't have the votes yet for what you want to do. And you won't clear the Senate. That's where Sargon is, waiting for you, because we really pissed him off. You idiots don't see that you *need* Rulers with bastards to vote for you. Yet you run around threatening to hurl their little darlings into acid tanks. Maybe you think you can bank on hypocrisy. Let me tell you, they give you just so much of it."

Iocle sucked in air and gurgled, barking from his gullet. He said in a bare whisper, "You people have ignored the Martian Quarantine. You forced Ocktomann, that eruption of stupidity, on me in my sleep, and I awoke to discover that I'd approved it. He is irrational, he is asinine, he is uneducated. He has no common sense! And yet, yet, yet," he huffed, "he is given the Martian Portfolio. Would anyone care to ask why? Why? To feed Imogen's insatiable maw." He gasped and sucked air in through his nose, several deep and unsatisfactory inhalations, his chest tightening as if there were a band of metal around it, constricting with each breath. He put on the machine. His voice came out in a strong harangue. "Bastards Rule, they live among us, always have. Look at Otis. A Lord, and cloning well. Totally legal.

You can't hunt down the Deadbeats without hunting down yourselves. And, while I would never admit it in public, the fact on the ground is, the President cannot Rule without the consent of the Senate. They grant me my power and they can take it away. We don't generally adjudicate elections with civil war in this country, and when we do it goes badly for both sides."

Utkasting stood and paced, rubbing his cheek. Aeppar uncrossed her legs and crossed them again. Utburd said, "I believe that was the bell, Mr. President, Sire."

"What bell?" Iocle looked about suspiciously through the convolvulus of flesh that enclosed his eyes. He shook his head and clutched the red plaid wool blanket covering his legs. Through the voice machine, set to *irate*, he said, "I had perfect pitch and could sing three octaves. I could sing 'The Star-Spangled Banner!' Look at me. I can't even hear the fucking doorbell."

Aeppar, with severe impatience, said, "Mr. President, Sire, this is the White House. There isn't a doorbell. That was the Page ringing Sargon's arrival. It is extraneous to your decibel range."

He could still stare down a face and hold an eye. "Adrift! Forever floating in a vacuum. They sat on horses and attended conferences. I saw him in diapers."

Aeppar, Utburd and Utkasting looked at each other. They didn't dare move or say anything. President Iocle observed them, happy that a slight paralysis meant he could no longer smile, and that his cheeks hung off of his face like curtains. There was also a minor palsy that caused him to twitch periodically and this made the loose flesh quiver. Smiling within, dribbling without.

He allowed the image of time to affect them. Iocle had no choice but to placate Everest, to protect his flank. He needed his vote on Council, but he did not have to kiss his ass or the asses of his sycophants. He didn't need them to manage pricks like Sargon; he could manage that in his sleep, had been doing so his whole life.

Iocle was positioned generationally to observe them grow into their Sires, very unpleasant work. His Sire and Grand Sire had been vigorous in passing down their memories. He stockpiled Sargon stories. His was a hatred nurtured and grown and preserved by five generations, becoming stronger, purer with each distillation. It was the social component of the Ruler system, the honing of the razor, one neglected by the recent generation, who behaved as if all this would be here forever. The dithering blathering alcoholic sex-obsessed Morons couldn't remember their own names. They were an easy herd to manage.

Iocle knew that the old ways were the best ways and added his diary to the memory horde, which he frequently shared and used as a basis for conversation with his Scion, whenever he was home on vacation from school. The Charlottesville St. Anne's was as good a place to get laid and play sports as any other. As far as he could tell, it was also a better place than most to learn how to read, write, calculate, and recite the Ruler glories back at bored humans who were inwardly consumed by fear and anger. But you would not learn how to think.

Sargon was convinced of his insanity. Let him think what he wants! It was another effect of the neural event, lucidity punctuated by bouts of chaotic thoughts and short-term memory loss. It was just by chance that every time they spoke he would have a synaptic meltdown. Maybe they had incompatible quantum states. That happened. He certainly felt that level of agitation when he contemplated sharing the room with the Ruler of New York again, a slow, electrical churning in his gut and a storm in his brain.

"Please tell the Senior Senator from New York that

I'll see him now," Iocle said. "And turn off the air conditioner. It's giving me a headache."

An aide wheeled him out from behind the desk and down to the fireplace on the opposite side of the office. Swedish ivy in pots decorated the mantelpiece, over which was hung a portrait of George Washington. The aide disconnected him and lifted him into one of two facing moss-green armchairs. His Geneticist, Dr. Nerval, a 275-year-old clone beginning to show wear at the edges, was seated off to the side, on a chair with a vermillion silk cushion, examining the readout from his monitor. President Iocle rubbed his fingers together as if to snap them and the logs lit. The door opened and he sat upright, but did not turn to watch Sargon enter the Oval Office. He gazed up instead, at his portrait of Lincoln, and then at a bust of Brutus in the veristic style of the Late Republic, which he had carved out of Marte Vallis columnar basalt, in the gravity room on his first mission to Mars. Again he wanted to smile. *Republican leanings.*

"President Iocle, Sire," Sargon said, reaching down to shake his hand.

They have such big hands, the President thought. How do they ever learn to play the piano so beautifully? "Senator Sargon, my old friend. How are you?" He raised his hand and Aeppar marched over. "Can I offer you a drink?"

"Mr. President, Sire, thank you. Jasmine tea."

Aeppar spoke to a servant dressed in a dark-crimson wrap and a white turban, then turned to Sargon. "What brings you to Washington on such a busy day? Surely you have your hands full in New York?"

The servant returned and poured a little tea out from a rough clay pot with a bamboo handle into a small bowl, which Sargon lifted to his lips with a slight bow of the head. He drank and said, "Thank you. Now, Mr. President, Sire. In March, you fucked me face down in front of everyone. I still don't have an explanation. That seat is mine. Maximilian doesn't run for it unless I tell him to."

The President took the full measure of Sargon and thought he looked more like a puffer fish than a lion. "Drifting," Iocle said. The air in the room was growing warm and humid as the Washington summer seeped in through the ancient building joints. Webs of fog spread out from the corners of the bow window.

Aeppar spoke: "I think the President understands your frustration. But really, the blame lies elsewhere. Within your delegation."

"Senator Everest has had no dealings with the New York delegation that I know of," said Utburd.

Utkasting added, "I would know if he had done so. Many things are attributed to the Ruler Everest. You can't believe everything you hear."

"Excuse me," Sargon snarled. "After forty years in the Senate, I am well aware of the difference."

President Iocle set the voice machine to *sigh* and remonstrated, his eyes glowering, "Civility, my friends. Remember where we are. The Citadel of Democracy."

Sargon said, "With due respect, Mr. President, Sire. That would have been the Capitol Building, whose charred ruins lie just down the road."

There was a silence, broken finally by the President. "Max was elected. That is not the business of this office. Go home. Bring it up with your beloved Senate and leave me out of it."

Sargon said, slowly, "Why did you approve a space transport station in the Bronx without talking to me? A slave ship transit point in New York City, where it is repugnant to all. I'm surprised our wise President would yield so easily to Everest's and Imogen's designs."

"I don't know what you're talking about. What transit station in the Bronx? Have you got pictures?"

"Of course I have. Dated and timestamped." He showed him the pictures.

"That could be anywhere! It's a pile of sand."

"Barges of concrete and steel, turbines, earth-moving equipment, cranes. It's all going up the East River."

"Perhaps they are rebuilding Co-op City? People can wear their hip waders."

"What is it you want? To supplicate these—" he pointed at the three aides.

Iocle's eyes burned through the fallen flesh of his face. "I am not asking for anything! You came to me, asking that I restore a Council seat as if you held it by right, and block some deal I've never heard of."

"Come to New York and discover what I hold by right," Sargon said. He smiled furiously and marched slowly towards the President's Secretary's Office door.

Iocle said, "You should fear the fires of Everest, my friend."

Without turning around Sargon said, "Every decent person does," and left.

★

When he was gone, President Iocle smashed the *indignation* button with his thumb and the voice box thundered, "Can you believe that! Through the President's Secretary's Office door!"

Iocle started to wheeze. The display in Dr. Nerval's hand glowed and be-beeped. Nerval looked up, his glasses fogged. "I'm taking him out of here. He needs to rest. Do you want him to have another bleed?" Sweat that had been beading on Nerval's forehead cascaded down his face.

An aide lifted Iocle and lowered him into his wheelchair, connecting him to wires and tubes, while Dr. Nerval reviewed the data. Nerval had a mane of black hair that pulsed with ultraviolet light and stayed in place no matter how he moved. "This isn't good." Dr. Nerval shook his face back and forth, beneath and between the immobile hair, and pushed the slumped Iocle out the door, sweat running down his chin.

Utkasting, Aeppar, and Utburd went down to their private offices, a suite of renovated rooms in the West Wing, close to the bathroom. Members of Iocle's gold-clad Scythian Guard closed the glass doors behind them and they took seats in black wingback chairs around a low Jovian gas table that didn't exactly glow but seemed to be alive. Aeppar set out a bottle of bourbon and three glasses. They poured shots. "Do you think this is it?" she asked, her hair at full tilt.

Utburd raised his eyebrows and rubbed his chin. "I hope not. Everest isn't ready to make his move. The old man is right. He doesn't have the votes to beat Bard. Imogen voted with us to seat Maximilian because she was after his land in the Bronx. It was not out of loyalty to our cause, or to our Ruler. We all assumed Sargon had her vote. Who would think—"

"—she would cut a deal with Maximilian!" Aeppar burst. "Right?"

Utkasting bent over his thighs and breathed out slowly. Then he sat upright and said, "The President tipped his hand at the end. Do we even know for sure there's a bastard?"

Utburd looked at Aeppar and raised his eyebrows.

Aeppar said, "Euclid assures me there is."

"Upon what evidence?" Utburd asked.

"A cook in the house," she said. "It's a rumor no doubt, but one we can verify with a tissue sample."

Utkasting's face twisted slightly to the left, as if his neck had been overtorqued. "Good luck with that!"

Aeppar, taken aback, winced with anger and said, "All we need is a hair."

Utkasting said, "If you had a hair, you should not trust the result. If you plucked it off of her head yourself, what would you learn, really? And what would you do with it? Arrest him? How? We can't touch him in New York."

Aeppar waited him out and said quietly, "It is a capital crime. Surely it would turn his few allies away, even Bard. Sargon is already isolated. We have to hope he takes the bait and blockades the transport station. That's a crisis that works in our favor."

Utburd, the ambient light gleaming dully off his skull, said, "Everything is in place. Everest will be President and the stage will be set for a great purification of our people. He'll be too weak to stand in the way. We will Rule a nation united by blood and God."

※

On the train back to the city, Sargon, reading a newspaper and drinking a glass of Idaho Zinfandel, asked Robin, who was seated opposite him on a plush, beet-red sofa seat, "Did you hear what he said? That son of a bitch. What do I do now?"

"Sire," he answered carefully, knowing his Sire's vulnerabilities and temper, but also that he expected an honest answer, would in fact be more angry if he flattered him or lied, "the exchange was pointed. Your response was clear. Now you must wait and let things settle." Sargon's anger made way for an abashed smile. He bowed his head to Robin and Robin bowed back, again saying, with a different inflection, and a familiar falling cadence, "Sire."

The two men resumed their mutual silence and Robin continued annotating the current draft of *The History of the Rulers Sargon and Renee*. It was, first and foremost, to be a repository of the line's memories, as recorded in diaries, oral histories and memoirs, handed down from Sire to Scion. But it was also to be a respectable history of the origins of the line, its synchronic and diachronic dynamic contextual relations, and role in the general history of the Rulers up to the present day.

Robin had hoped to correct the final page proofs but the manuscript had come back from readers with many negative comments, all conflicting in vital ways. If it were merely a case of fact correction he could resolve the differences, but some were criticisms of his main thesis, one of continuity beneath a surface of apparent change, that events prior to the creation of the lines and the overthrow of the finance system continued to shape domestic and foreign policy, wars, secessions, assassinations, and the closing and opening of universities, newspapers and theaters for a century, until the settlement of the Mars dispute and creation of the Quarantine. Thus it was impossible to understand the rise of the Sargon-Renee and Bard lines in New York without reference to the Bryson Crisis of 2183. All of this he had reviewed again, in the archives of Georgetown's Lauinger Library, during their short visit. He was anxious to wrap up the work and focus on the oral history.

It was there that he met Tiriel Hargrave, a reporter from the *New York Times*. They were standing together at the information desk, Robin with a leather-bound notebook, and the reporter, a young woman in flamboyant wraps with a flamingo headscarf trailing ribbons down her back, depositing file folders crammed with paper. Robin asked, out of genuine curiosity, salted by the way her black hair lay unbrushed against her neck and the skeptical look of her scholarly eyes, "What's that you're depositing?"

"Who wants to know?" she asked.

"Forgive me for asking. I hardly ever see anyone down here." She said nothing and scanned the exits. "I'm here to check some sources for a book I'm working on."

Tiriel Harvale considered the information and replied, "What kind of a book?"

"History. Not propaganda in family archives. I'm after the dirt."

"These," she patted the box on the counter and kicked the stack of boxes on the floor behind her with her heel, "are boxes of dirt. And this," she waved her hands around, "is full of it."

"It's a world-class library, no doubt about it. Are you a journalist? Or an academic?"

Tiriel Harvale smiled. "What do you think?"

"You act like a reporter. I suppose you have a novel in you."

"Drinker's memoir, actually."

"How's that going?"

"I'm still in the research phase."

Robin laughed, but noted her defensive body language. He was afraid sometimes too, that the wrong eyes would find his manuscript. Sargon didn't know or care about a reporter's research or archives anywhere. But he could be made to know and care about such things; his Ruler was a curious and intelligent man who had genuine feeling, but he also had in his employ people whose job it was to know and care about such things and destroy such people and their files. Like Commander Roosevelt, and now, Captain Euclid. Robin didn't trust Euclid, and didn't like Roosevelt.

"Reporters have many enemies, if they're doing their job," Tiriel Harvale said, smiling more naturally, and relaxing against the counter. "I love Georgetown. It's benighted, wet, dark. I know a good bar nearby, The Chapelizod, if you're as thirsty as I am."

Robin looked at the manuscript boxes. Thousands of pages of research. He began to speculate on what the contents were. "Another time, I'm sorry. I have a train to catch. Are your sources named? For the sake of scholarship?"

"Some are. It depends on the arrangement."

"I'm familiar with the New York press. What is your name?"

She hesitated. "You first."

"Robin Micawber."

"Good God, what an idiot I am."

"No no!" he remonstrated, afraid of losing her. "Please, you aren't in any danger. Our Sire cares nothing for the press."

"Harvale. Tiriel Harvale. *New York Times.*"

They shook hands. "Oh, I am impressed. I've read many of your pieces. You really dig into it, don't you?" He held her eye and his heart beat faster. Then Robin did something impulsive. He slid his card across to her and said, "My private number. Next time you're thirsty call me, we'll go out for a drink. If you would still like to do that." He thought grimly of his wife and a shade was drawn between them briefly. Harvale picked up the card and smiled. The light flooded back and he said, nervously, "I know I would."

Tiriel pocketed the card and said, "Expect a call," and they parted.

★

From the Sky Track north of Baltimore, above the upper Chesapeake, he watched a floating city of junks and prows, of pinnaces and dinghies and dories. Then a varicolored expanse of water opened up beneath them. Blooms of rust-colored goop formed a paisley pattern in the blue, turquoise, and purple water that cut deep into the land, carving small islands out of old peninsulas, stretching open river mouths. The Chesapeake solar arrays flashed in the sun for miles, across the upper bay. In Philadelphia they passed a fish factory, its walls reflected in a slick of oil, ground-up fish remains chugging out of pipes into the Delaware. That was a stench he knew all too well. He had grown up on the Hudson, in an eel and shad town. They smoked fish on planks, hung it up to dry from the rafters, pickled it in barrels, and rotted it down for fertilizer in every shack up and down the river. It got in your clothes and hair. It hung in your nostrils half the year.

Isle of Dogs, Part 1

His father was an eelman and his mother was a musician. She directed the annual school play in town and tuned pianos and gave lessons in a couple of Ruler houses, including Sargon's Winter Palace. As a boy he often went with her, as she didn't want him working on the water.

His father went to the Winter Palace too, and Robin always begged to go along, to deliver eels, frogs, snapping turtles, and shad fat with roe. He tapped sugar maples, kept an apiary, foraged ginseng, sorrel, berries, and beech buds, cut fiddlehead ferns, harvested fennel pollen and saffron, gathered morels and boletus, black trumpets, and hen of the woods. The Rulers paid him in gold.

Robin gazed out the window of the train, which had descended from the Sky Track to the waterway. They rode past methane plants with arrays of pipelines tapping into subterranean fermentation tanks, munitions factories, and lots packed tight with walking battle machines, their ten-foot arms and hammers at ease.

When Robin was ten, his mother died giving birth. His father became catatonic and he took over delivery of whatever he could forage, but it was not enough to support the family. He got a job as a stable boy at the Winter Palace. He had grown up with animals, but the closest thing to a horse was his father's mule Hubert. He had been in horse carriages, of course, and sleighs, but he had never ridden one, never seen one up close without tackle and blinders. Robin hung out with the farriers and tagged along with the vets when they made their rounds. Eventually he could shoe a horse and assist at a birth. He and horses liked each other. Horses were better than people.

He was just starting out in the stable, mucking, haying, and watering, when he met the Old President. He'd come down to the stable to talk about business affairs, which neither of them understood in the slightest. The Old President gave Robin his first books, which, it turned out, he fell for more than horses. When he read those and returned them, begging for more, Sargon 2 arranged for his education with the Winter Palace Librarian and tutors—harassed, defeated people, sad-eyed intellectuals with no military acumen, who depended on the largesse of Rulers and their whimseys.

Robin had the run of the library. The Sargons, Renees, and Bards owned a suite of genes engineered to boost intelligence, though it remained controversial whether the BrainPaks, as they were known, actually worked. They were among their oldest products, with leases dating to the twenty-first century. BrainPaks or not, the families read and collected books, supported large libraries, and endowed colleges, museums, theaters, and orchestras. They employed writers, scientists, and philosophers. Not many other Rulers did.

The Old President was well-read for his generation. He knew the classical authors well, quoted Milton, Shakespeare and Dante. Ptolemy's map of Asia was as real to him as a modern one, grown from a monad. There is a soul in an old map, he used to say, captured there in clean lines and legends. The bend of the mind that drew it. What it saw when it looked at the world, what shape it had taken on the horizon and in the eye of the cartographer. The embodied winds, the sad moue of terra incognita.

But Sargon 2 was hopeless with accounts and with people. By age fifteen, Robin understood that he would not have to live in shit and shoe horses for a Ruler if he could learn accounts and politics. The death of his mother, madness of his father, and dependency of his siblings required him to do so, and because there was nothing else he was good at, he did.

Sargon 2 wanted to send Robin to college in Chicago, a city that frightened him. He was timid of traveling that far west, where his people had never been. There were relatives in Vermont, however, and Maine. The Old President knew a Ruler without portfolio in Burlington who would rent him rooms and give him access to his library. He could attend the local university at no cost. Sargon and Renee would take care of everything.

Around this time the Younger Sargon returned from California. He was nineteen years older than Robin and didn't pay him any mind. One day, the Younger Sargon rode into the ring after a long ride and found Robin there and, out of politeness, asked how he liked studying with the Ruler Serling. Nervous and tongue-tied at first, Robin told him about his studies, and by the end of the conversation the words were flying out of his mouth.

The Winter Palace Library had extensive holdings of published books and a world-class collection of maps, as well as invaluable genealogies, but the Serling Library was a researcher's paradise, an unruly trove of documents, collections of correspondence, diaries, newspapers, broadsheets, guerrilla publications, posters, videos, audio recordings, statistical manuals, and analytical censuses, housed in twelve underground chambers reached by means of transporter tube. It sat beneath a castle modeled on Glamis Castle but fallen into disrepair as all the wealth of the family went into the libraries below. The Serlings had ceded political power generations earlier and had invested poorly, mortgaging their licenses secretly. Their homes were hives of bastards, mutant babies grown to adulthood and left to roam the halls.

The Serlings lived on a small pension and the rent from rooms in their castle. They elected to clone in extreme old age so that the only visual memory would be of a 138-year-old man and woman. They abandoned genetic monitoring, updates, and resets and allowed themselves to attenuate through overbreeding of cloned relatives. They stretched thin through the generations and petered out into intellectual torpor, eyes buglike in the semi-dark of the stacks.

Here he found his true home. Serling taught him the ways of the Ruler world as only a bitter turncoat can. He learned Latin and enough Greek to read Sophokles with a crib and a dictionary. They read *I, Claudius* against the Roman historians. Serling pointed at the page with a stern finger, which normally shook but was holding steady, and said, "Livia. You will find more than one in their ranks. I assure you, even in the house of Sargon there is now a slow poison at work."

✯

As they approached the city, Robin looked at the skyline. The summer sky was a dim violet grey. Jersey stretched out on stilts into the water, and Raritan Bay swarmed with boats, scattering away from the train's wake like roaches in the light, as it cut a path through the water towns, veering between docks and decks and hundreds of small, brightly painted fishing boats at moorings, onto land at Perth Amboy, a collection of bent cranes, storage tanks, and access roads atop water pumps. At Jersey City, the jagged rise and fall of Manhattan towers shimmered in a haze of vapor across the river. Sargon broke their silence and said, "It may be an isle of dogs, but it's beautiful, isn't it? That skyline has stood for 600 years."

Their eyes met. A long habit of communication had formed between them, and it operated at speeds faster than conscious thought. There were indications that Rulers were psychic, particularly adept at hearing minds, and able to communicate wordlessly. It was a trait Rulers never disclosed, even to each other. It was common knowledge (but never taught) that Dr. Vesuvius, as he aged, had come to believe in the occult, crystal balls, ESP, and reincarnation, particularly the transmigration of the Ruler soul from generation to generation. And it was later claimed on his behalf that he had designed an ESP suite owned exclusively by the 400. The last thing he did on Earth was attend a seance.

Sargon broke the silence. "Iocle's got me by the balls." He looked away from Robin, out the window, and said softly, almost to himself, "And I thought he was senile." He faced Robin, agitated, confused, waiting for the trap to close.

"You had every reason to believe he was senile, Sire. He is indeed intermittently so, with periods of lucidity. Certainly he was lying when he denied any knowledge of the transport station."

"That's not all he knows. He knows about Phaedra. It's not like he gives a shit about bastards. It's leverage with him. A way to destroy your enemies, control your minions, buy a vote. Killing him might be as crazy as it sounds, but what choice do I have?"

If he's still asking, Robin thought, there is still a chance he will change his mind. "What about the blockade?"

"Doesn't really get us anything but trouble."

"Then I suggest we find a third way."

Sargon shook his head.

"You can't act alone, Sire. You need backing. You have to go to Bard."

Sargon growled. "He will say no."

At Penn Station, they were met by an escort of the New York Guard. They walked over to Grand Central for the private train to Larchmont. On the way, a family in white, with canary-yellow hats and black ribbons, stopped and put their bags down, to watch.

On the train Robin said, "Sire, it is my judgment, for what it is worth, that your position is still quite good. Suppose the worst, that Everest becomes President. He still has no way of making an arrest or harming you or your family in New York. Who would execute the warrant, the Black Guard? Red Suits? And Maximilian is a distraction. Betrayal is painful. When the mind clings to pain, it clouds judgement."

"The transport station isn't a distraction! You must see this for what it is. The coming together. We are are on our hind legs kicking at their faces. If Iocle won't stop it, I will."

"Precisely, but how? Time is needed to clear the mind, so you will know the way."

"What nonsense are you on about now? It's been three months. Bard's done nothing but make speeches no one listens to. He's frustrated. He thought he could make a difference in the Senate and has discovered it's a pit of quicksand. He's fucked me out of the

Presidency and is no closer to it himself. If he'd only come to me first, we could have avoided this mess."

"Sire, You have shown a strong and proper indifference to the pain *that* loss has caused. Remember we did need California's vote."

"I guess for me there's nothing left but dealmaking. If, as you insist, I have to go to Bard, what am I asking for? How do I convince him?"

"Let's review the promises you made." Robin counted out with his fingers, "You and Bard made a pact to vote together; and for you to support him for President; and that you will bring your people with you, on the Council and in the Senate; and that Renee, in obligation to you, will support Bard's claim to the Presidency if he is elected and prevented from taking office. But now that he's alone on the Council he loses vote after vote. He can't turn those adoring crowds at farmer's markets, fairs, and train stations into Council votes. Because he doesn't know what he's doing, and because he hasn't got the Senior Senator from New York for an ally, which he needs."

"You're damn right he needs New York. He needs *me*." He calmed down and reflected, "Shouldn't Ruler of the City and Senator be enough? When I was young—" Robin hit record— "I was indifferent to power. After a few years in LA, I realized I didn't want to be like my Sire, I wanted to be like the First—bold, a conqueror. It wasn't enough to vanquish Everest, I had to destroy him. Hatred kept me alive."

"Did all the soldiers feel that way?"

"Certainly, grunts and commanders alike. Hatred was the glue that held us together."

"Quite different from your Sire. The Old President was most bitter about the way politics had kept him from his morning and afternoon ride. He was at heart best suited to the stable."

Sargon relaxed and took a breath. "He did well in the Senate. The Senate more resembles a stable than an august body of deliberation, the upper house of the world's oldest democracy. It suited him fine, he was a horse among horses. But you are right as always. The Old President loved nothing better than an actual horse, except maybe a long ceremony. He loved a parade in full dress uniform. That was the part of the Presidency he excelled at. I was just a small boy, about four, when we returned from Hungary and they had the ticker tape parade for him. I remember the gangway and the fishy smell of the Hudson as it flowed against the black hull of the ship. We rode in an open carriage from the Midtown piers to Fifth Avenue, and from 23rd Street down Broadway.

Crowds lined both sides of the street, thickening along the way. At Chambers, the flurry of white began with strips of paper hovering, twirling, and wafting down singly to the street. By Wall, it came down like snow, a rush of white ribbons fluttering in the sky, crowds on either side of Broadway waving New York flags and cheering. Naked men and women charged the carriage, and the Old President stood up against the high plush seats," he laughed and shook his head, "his chest thrust out, avidly waving a handkerchief back, the very one he used to wipe the drool off of his goatee, and beaming at individual faces in the crowd, 'so that they would go home and remember,' he used to say—"

"Oh yes, that!" Robin prompted. "He had a healthy regard for his own importance."

"Indeed. That was the high point. The Old President was mauled by the office. Iocle forced him out with a vote in Council, putting that strunze, Bucephalus, in office until he was ready to take it himself. Watching his demise from West Point was agonizing. I had no ambition then. I was drifting."

Robin wondered if it meant anything to *himself* to be Secretary to the President, his Chief of Staff. He would have far greater power. He would live in the White House, in a cubby of chilled, reconditioned air, miles behind a mass of vegetation, separated by suppurating swamps. And there he would wait for supplicants, listening to the shrieks of peacocks over the croaking bullfrogs. Senators, Generals, Heads of State. And a militia surrounding them. Sensors weaving an impenetrable nanodome overhead, while the evening sky burned as if the air were clear. "Sire, it *isn't* enough, is it?"

Sargon shrugged. "No, not with all that power in reach. And I would know how to use it. You and I'd be in it together, wouldn't we? We could change the world. But that is not to be. My boy. My son." He nodded and became somber. "My son will be a Ruler, and he will know what happened, and he will know what to do, because he will have us, and our book to teach him. Prepare for the trip to Tarrytown. We'll ride in the morning. I don't want to waste any time. Is Ruth meeting us at the station with the babies?"

"Sire, they will be there when we arrive." He knew to look away. All he had ever given his Sire was his discretion.

"You know she asked me for money?" Sargon asked darkly.

"Sire, I did not. Surely she has no reason. There is the money on account for her, once she's fulfilled the terms of the contract."

"Ruth came to me, afraid to speak. I coaxed it out of her. She wants her money in case she has to escape. Once she got talking, her fear dropped away and she became steely. You'd expect that, of course. Her arguments were logical, ethical, and practical, and she appealed to reason and, finally, love." He ground his teeth in agitation.

"Sire, allow me. You are too angry. She is right to worry about self-protection."

"Angry? I'm ashamed! When I tell her that she needn't be afraid or worry, that I will protect her with my life, which I will do, she says to me, 'But you cannot even protect yourself.' Her eyes were cold. The blood drained out of me. I am a failure if I can't protect my city and my family. I'm not a Ruler and I'm not a man. Ruth didn't put herself here, I did. Please, each month on the first of the month, deposit whatever she wants into an account of her choosing. Only advise her if she desires it." The train slowed and approached the station.

"Sire, look, there they are."

Down on the platform, Ruth, Phaedra, and the Baby Sargon were waving. Robin watched Sargon run down the steps of the train.

★

Bard lived in the family castle in Tarrytown, originally built in 1839, and added to by every generation, until an insane twenty-third-century ancestor on the Bryson side expended a fortune on bizarre, hallucinatory projects that ran amok, and soured later generations on any change at all. Instead they had to learn to live within the monstrosity created by their forebears, and it eventually became a family joke.

This fortress above the Hudson served as the first headquarters of the Great Rebellion. It was here a treaty of armistice was signed between DC and the Alliance of Regional Rulers. Here, one of the first legal clones was born and given the name of the family's nineteenth-century primogenitor, Bard. Ten days later, in the Winter Palace, Sargon was born, and a year after that Renee, Slim, and Orchidia.

Sargon and Robin entered the grounds on horseback and rode slowly across a wood and iron drawbridge, over a moat of water so black it didn't reflect the sky. There was a plash. Sargon looked down and saw snapping turtles raise their algae-covered heads, and cottonmouth moccasins ess across the water. They passed through an open gate, squeezed between high stone walls, moss-covered, dripping in shade, with armed turrets. Arrays of sensors embedded in the pink rock transmitted the details of their arrival.

As Herculaya galloped towards the castle, a clutch of onion domes, gothic spires, and blunt Norman towers, Sargon remembered exploring the land and buildings with Bard as a child, riding their ponies over many miles of pasture, through woods and along the river. The memory seemed immensely old, like a space rock from the Oort Cloud, hurled over millennia to the earth. And like such a rock, it burned brightly as it reentered his mind. He had no feeling connected to the image, but saw in its halo the sinister glow of nostalgia.

Every summer in their teens, while on break from Exeter, he and Bard would settle down in one of the many derelict outbuildings, cobwebbed and buried beneath woody vines and saplings, riding out by day to shoot and fish as they pleased, swimming in cold streams, drinking and singing all night with friends, fucking townies in dank stone rooms. They were as entwined as two people could be and he found himself longing for the pastoral anarchy of that love.

The road passed through a lightless cavern of masonry. The air grew cold and clung to his face like a damp sheet. Herculaya's hooves struck the cobblestones, and echoed off tiled walls the yellow of unbrushed teeth. The smell of eternal wet remained in his nostrils as he rode out onto an open lawn of many acres, the river rushing grey, low mountains in the distance. Ahead was the entrance to the original neo-Gothic structure, beside and behind which lay the wrecks of rambling, asymmetrical additions. Flags fluttered against a smouldering purple haze laced with crimson tendrils of sun.

At the door of the castle, grooms took their horses. There was no guard. Bard didn't need one. The nanodome extended for miles in all directions. Sargon lifted the brass wolf's head knocker and his breath caught. He didn't want to be a supplicant. That wasn't who he was: one who knocks on doors. Others came to him. Not anymore. He was living on favors. He would not be able to call them in forever. It was intolerable. He chafed against it. And the more he did so, the more the insult festered. He spent his days dead in the Waldorf, a stranded whale stinking up the beach, ashamed to enter the Senate just to deliver impotent speeches to idiots, rubber-stamping bills while the real legislating went on behind the platinum doors to the Conference Building.

Sargon and Robin stood in the Great Hall waiting for the aged butler, creaking on arthritic stilts, to announce them. Suspended like motes in the immense silence of the high-vaulted ceiling and shafts of late sun, they watched the man retreat slowly beneath the stern, pointed faces carved into the columns, and return some minutes later with orders to escort them to the South Garden.

✷

The South Garden was enclosed by a ruined Roman wall, brought to America in pieces by Augustus Bard in 1899 and reassembled by Italian masons, to put the finishing touches on a Tuscan villa they were recreating for the classically inclined robber baron in his dotage.

Bard, dressed in a black Nehru jacket and white pants, was seated on a wicker chair next to Orchidia and Slim, facing a marble pool with a fountain spraying over tarnished coins. Beyond them was a kitchen garden, with rows of vegetables and herbs glowing against the black soil, in raised stone beds. There was a small orchard, patches of berries, and trellises of beans and pumpkins. In the midst of it all was a scarecrow wearing a rubber Frankenstein mask.

They were seated around a rose-tinted Martian-glass table with bowls of figs, blackberries, and almonds. A servant wrapped in folds of white poured ice water into their glasses.

"Sargon." Bard smiled and stood. The two men embraced. "It's good to see you. Robin, always a pleasure. Please be seated." They sat facing the Bards. "I actually see more of Robin than I do of you," Bard continued. "How did that happen? I thought, coming back to the Senate, we would be in and out of each other's hair, such as it is," he laughed, his thinning hair shining bright blue on patches of bronze skull.

"Rustication. I've always wanted to spend more time with the family." Sargon smiled mirthlessly.

"I understand it's getting quite large these days," Bard observed.

Sargon felt himself flinch and cursed beneath his breath. Did everyone know? "We won't implant Renee until another year has passed."

Bard nodded, his slightly amused, enigmatic expression unchanged. He crinkled his nose and held up a fig. "I just picked these. They're still warm from the sun. When they split, the wasps crawl into the crevice to feed. It makes them delirious. Figs and wasps are like that. Of course, I like figs too, but in moderation." Bard popped the fig in his mouth, held it by the stem and bit down, chewing slowly. He swallowed, leaned over the armrest, and said to the servant, "A pot of white tea, and a bottle of grappa, please."

Sargon sighed. "I've been to see the President. It's time to act."

Bard gave in to a rare show of annoyance. It was different from anger. Sargon was one of the few people who knew how to read his moods. Annoyance was a shift in the chair and a slight raising of both eyebrows. The only outward sign that he was actually angry and not simply inconvenienced was a certain barely perceptible rigidity that expressed itself in a slight dilation of the eyes and a tensing of the muscles on either side of his mouth. And if he became incensed, which was rarer still, he would place his index finger across his lips and lightly cup his chin, as if to hush himself.

"Without you on the Council, I don't have the bloc to go against him. Maximilian votes with Imogen and Everest."

"My point exactly. You don't have me on Council. Imogen's cut a deal with Maximilian and we don't have much time to stop it."

"Deal? I've seen no bill—" Bard yielded to uncertainty. He glared at Slim and Orchidia.

"It's not a bill, it's a *deal*. Kuiper Belt Space Industries is building a transport station in Co-op City."

"Without your consent? They can't do that," he stated. "It's unconstitutional."

Sargon laughed gently. "So is a sixty-year Presidency."

Orchidia said, "Imogen's made no secret of her desire to expand space transport. She told us as much at the Birth Night celebration."

Slim said, "Kuiper has been trying to build in New York for centuries. What's the harm of a transport station? It's a hub, likely. We could earn a lot in fees. In principle—"

Sargon raised his index finger and said, "In principle and in fact, Maximilian owns Co-op City. We won't make a dime. But that's a minor issue. The deal is more dangerous than that, and I'm surprised you don't see it. If Everest gets his census and Kuiper gets the transport station, how long before they start testing and rounding up New Yorkers? Think of the harvest of Deadbeats she'll reap."

Orchidia uttered a slight, contemptuous snort and said, "Neither Iocle will go for that."

Slim said, "It's destabilizing."

Bard nodded and looked to Sargon for a response.

"Iocle could die at any moment. We have two choices. A blockade."

Slim laughed. "You must be joking. That would

start a war." Bard rubbed his chin. The three looked at Sargon.

"Then we have to get rid of Maximilian. That solves all our problems. It puts me back on Council, and it ends the deal for that transport station. Imogen will align with us, and we impeach Iocle."

The servant returned with a tea set and served them. Sargon savored it, as he always did at Bard's table. Another servant put down a clear bottle with a blooming branch suspended in the clear liquor. Bard poured out five small glasses and they touched the rims and drank. It was hot on the tongue, followed by the taste of peach blossom.

"Get rid of Maximilian?" Bard's eye twitched and he looked out at the marble pool. Wind sent indigo ruffles across the pale-blue water. Birds dropped down to drink and bathe. Bard sipped the tea. His face grew darker and his hair raced with black light.

Sargon said, "Without Max, Imogen will fold."

Bard said, "Maybe. Maybe not. Iocle is a corrupt old man, a fool. His stupidity will destroy him, if his senility doesn't. Let them build the station and we'll make sure it never becomes operational."

Sargon said, "Iocle's not stupid or insane. He doesn't care about a census, or transporting convicts to space. If anything, he's on our side when it comes to Mars. He's up to his usual tricks, pitting us against each other, thinking he can put the Younger Iocle in. But Iocle won't last long enough to do that. Aeppar, Utburd, and Utkasting are there to ensure Everest becomes President."

Bard said, "America needs a true Ruler, not a shriveled, cynical, vindictive blowhard. Someone who will inspire the people to do great things again. We've been in a 500-year skid, living off the fumes of former glory. Why do we sit here plotting moves and countermoves like mafia bosses? I will restore honor to the Republic, the honor of Washington and Lincoln, of Cicero and Brutus. I will rebuild this country with the force of our ideals and principles."

Sargon felt his fingernails curl back. "That's a fine stump speech. If you were running for Messiah you'd get all the votes, but you're running for President, and you'll be sludge in a drain if Iocle dies and Everest takes the White House."

"I've promised peace. And I mean to deliver on that. I will not let blood run in the street as President, and I certainly won't assassinate a sitting US Senator, a legitimate Ruler from New York, a man *you* elevated, to achieve the Presidency. I won't be the one."

"This is a dog fight, not a move in a chess game."

"The blame would fall on us," Bard said. "Even if we weren't arrested for treason, our support would vanish with our honor. Civil war would follow. Soon there'd be nothing left. And suppose we succeeded, suppose Maximilian's death won us the Presidency, would we ever be seen as legitimate? It would contradict all that I stand for, and taint our lines forever."

★

There was an animal rustle in the fig trees, and then by the sundial. Twenty feet off, a small child of five rushed out, dressed in a white sarong, with a silver kris sheathed in a gold scabbard hanging from a jeweled girdle. His hair glowed blue and purple in pulses of pleasure. He marched forward, leading a pony a little larger than himself. In his hand was a gold ivy crown.

Bard's face lightened immediately and shined on the boy with immense pleasure. "Little Bard, come, meet my oldest, dearest friend, Sargon."

Little Bard looked at Sargon with cheerful curiosity and sang in a high, confident voice, "You and Papa sailed the length of Lake Champlain in a storm."

Sargon roared out laughter. "Sailed? I *bailed* while

your Papa rowed. We weren't much older than you are."

"That's not true, you were twelve. I'm five. That's seven years difference."

"What a smart fellow you are, you know your figures. Excellent." Sargon smiled and thought how stupid it sounded to children when old men said things like that. But they both knew the roles they had to play, too old and too young to pretend otherwise.

Bard slapped his left biceps, leaving a smear of blood and a squashed mosquito, which the servant plucked off. He stood and said, "I'm getting eaten alive. Let's walk in the garden. I have a new lettuce, a ruby leaf that grows in this heat." They all got up and spread out over the paths of the garden. They reached a short row of dark-crimson Bibb lettuces. Bard squatted down beside the row and pinched off a leaf, handing it to Sargon. "Taste this." He ate it while Bard examined the soil, rubbing it between his fingers. The lettuce was sweet and cool. The stalk had a slightly bitter, juicy crunch.

"This is great," Sargon said. "Mine always bolts."

They walked on and Bard picked off a leaf of this and of that, poking the soil with his finger, pulling out tiny weeds. "They're cutting down a cured venison ham that's been hanging for two years tonight, to go with melon and the estate sheep cheese. I hope you don't mind if we open one of your Sémillons?"

"No, not at all. I can't bring myself to open a bottle. No occasion seems grand enough. But the only grand occasion for a wine is the right meal."

Bard looked at his old friend without emotion and said, "I am startled by your formality." They walked towards the castle, ahead of their silent entourage, and Sargon wondered what Bard meant.

They entered the castle, followed by Little Bard, pony in hand, and walked to the dining hall, a pink marble chamber decorated with country murals, tapestries, and a frescoed ceiling. Sargon, his voice echoing, said, "Please, Bard. No one need know we discussed it, but I can't act alone."

Bard stared at the floor and shook his head. His face was overtaken by some lost memory and his eyes seemed to sink into the shade. "I couldn't live with myself," he said quietly.

6

Windows

As Sargon strode angrily down the stone hall leading from the elevator to his office in the Waldorf, he still had not made up his mind fully. But he was at the breakpoint, he could feel it. Right between his eyes, in the middle of his forehead, was a drilling pain. It was actually a known flaw, the "stress fracture," an unintended consequence of broad melanoma protection, essential for deep tanning.

It was really driving him crazy. The main objection everyone had was that the blame would fall on him. But what if it didn't? What if the blame fell on someone else? He said to Robin, "I think I've got a plan figured out."

"Sire." Robin nodded his head and quickened his

pace to reach the thin, translucent mica door first. He held it open and followed Sargon through a small waiting room, nodding at the receptionist, and into the executive office. They took chairs by the south-facing windows. Set among the glass boxes and spires was the Chrysler Building. The points of the steel crown blazed white as the sun struck, and the gargoyles gleamed like space helmets.

He was avoiding his desk, which had become like an iron lung. It was built of the same stainless steel as the Chrysler crown. The legs were worked with identical detail, seven concentric sunbursts pierced with triangles. The platinum top was covered in documents, which reminded him that he still had a city and a state to run, but didn't mean a thing, because there were no Senate bills, no briefs, no memos from Committee heads, no talking points.

From his desk, he could stare at the view all day. He had in fact done so, paralyzed by hatred. He had waited, he had followed Robin's advice and his own inner counsel, which cautioned him to bide his time and do nothing. He, like Bard, also assumed that Iocle's collapse was imminent and that they would carry the day. History taught him that Everest was an outlier. After all, he did fail in California, and even in his home states purges were not popular. Under

Iocle's Rule, everyone had adjusted to the occasional symbolic arrest of a Deadbeat, but no real bloodletting.

Sargon couldn't bear the thought that he had gone to Iocle to beg for what was rightfully his. The sound of the President's cackling contempt was always in his ears, and his own parting taunt had grown stale. It may be the fate of a defeated Senator to sit in an office staring out the window at beautiful buildings, plotting a return to power that will never happen, but it would not be his fate.

Sargon said, "Have a cigar. I won't join you, but I'll have a drink, if that will help."

Robin bowed his head and said, "Sire, I'll have one of each, thank you." Sargon drew a cigar out from the inner pocket of his uniform and Robin took it in his squat hand. He savored the smell and feel of the leaf and lit it with a spark, puffing the tip orange. Smoke filled the light and spread against the tinted glass. Sargon poured two pale whiskeys into snifters. He held his aloft and they toasted, "*Prost!*"

"I've made a decision. I won't have Iocle's guard roaming the streets anymore. The UN will operate under my protection, not his." Sargon watched a flock of grey-and-pink galahs flutter by. He rifled through the chain of events, collapses, and disasters that enabled an Australian cockatoo to thrive in New York at the expense of pigeons.

Robin replied, "We have no jurisdiction over the Red Suits."

"I don't care. I want them out of here. If MacCallister tries to tell us he hasn't got the troops, tell him to go fuck himself. I'm not kidding, say 'Sargon says to go fuck yourself.'"

"Sire, I'll convey exactly those words to him if it should come to that. But I foresee problems. For what cause? Are they creating a disturbance? It will go to the Supreme Court."

"I'll get to that. You see, I've given it some thought. No doubt you've noticed I have been angry for a long time. Ruth certainly has, and My Lady Renee often takes me to task for my foul mood and obstreperous speechmaking. Now, I'm not angry."

"Sire, I am pleased to hear you have moved on from anger. I believe in the *Meditations* last week—"

"Robin, I must insist that we not discuss Aurelius at this time."

"Forgive me, Sire, I am unworthy," Robin smiled.

"Enough. Bard has refused his support. So I'm alone in this. But others will go along if we succeed, Bard included. And this is how we pull it off. Bear with me. Maximilian thinks he's safe, even if his protector is a half-mad old man in a wheelchair. He'll be looking for a direct attack, they all will. But what if the very guard that protects him were to kill him? What then? One of Iocle's Red Suits loses control, starts shooting and kills a Senator in front of witnesses. The Red Suits are already hated. They've raped our people, extorted businesses in the blocks around the UN. Brawled in downtown bars. Beneath the West Side Levee they have sex in public, and urinate and defecate in the bamboo groves. I read the reports." He watched the flock of galahs swoop between the buildings and said, "With such an attack, I can turn things around. The people will mourn and expect revenge. We would have no choice but to confine the Red Suits to their barracks, while we investigate the murder of our beloved Senator Maximilian at the hands of our craven and insane President's troops. And I will take his seat on the Executive Council."

Robin sat rigidly, his lips parted and neutral. Sargon knew he didn't like it. "Bard is against it," Robin said. "He might not support you on the Council."

"All his talk about honor, that he couldn't live with the *taint*, I mean, really. He came East to be President, not to be famous. He was already a celebrity. He came East for power, and power lies with the Executive."

"There are other ways. Maximilian could be persuaded to retire."

"After what he's done? His Sires pledged to serve my Sires. All they brought with them was Co-op City and a few square miles of Yonkers and Mt. Vernon."

"The Cross Bronx Expressway, the George Washington Bridge."

Sargon scoffed. "Where is his army? The park police? The crooked cops who run his precincts? Only the Rule of Law guarantees his possession, a right he has forfeited." His voice rose. "I approved marriages and offspring between his and my lines and so did Renee. He repays me with betrayal? I will take him down if I please."

"Sire. Of course you will. I only advise that you wait a day before issuing the order, and consult again with Bard. A day will not matter. He is your ally. He may have changed his mind. I will talk to Slim and Orchidia."

"Slim and Orchidia! You heard them. They didn't see a problem. They're the only ones that Bard truly listens to. The rest of us are there to admire and adore him." Sargon tried to feel moderation. He wanted to cultivate indifference. But he did have to live in the world, as did Marcus Aurelius. There was a reason for the *Meditations*. "I should sleep on it, of course. But the more I think about Iocle's parting shot, the more it galls me. It was a warning, a challenge. My gut tells me we're too late. Our moment was in April or even March, but we were not prepared to act.

"I'm going up to Larchmont. I want you to stay away from the Senate. Meet Roosevelt privately. Tell him of our plan and show him my seal. Let him work out the details. Then tell him to come to Hommocks Cottage with an attack helicopter. I want him there by late afternoon to discuss the defense of the city, should it come to that. He'll have to move fast. Tell him that." He stood and Robin stood with him. They looked out at the city one more time and finished their whiskeys.

"Sire, shall I take care of this now? You will not wait a day? These are steps that might prove damaging to your interest later."

He knew that. It was clear. Robin's opposition had thrown the business into high relief. He could examine it slow and fast, near and far. He turned it inside out. It looked about perfect. "Stay in town tonight at 1220 Fifth. Order a detail and a chef. Invite Dana down, if she'll come. Assure her we'll not be there. I'll call you when I get in. I recommend the wood-duck breast, rare, with black currant sauce and wild rice. And the sautéed chanterelles."

They walked to Grand Central, where Sargon boarded his train and Robin rushed downtown. On the way, he placed a call to Tiriel Harvale.

✯

Ruth stood on a stool to look out the half-moon window that faced Long Island Sound. The house had been agitated and on guard ever since her Sire's return from DC. She had heard rumors of a crisis. Then he went north to visit the Ruler Bard and things got worse. Sargon was tense and distant when he came to her rooms. The only time she saw him smile was when the Baby Sargon and Phaedra sat in his lap for a book. Either way, she felt more secure since receiving her money from Robin, but she and Phaedra still had no passport or travel papers should she have to escape, and there was never a good time to bring it up. She could tell it hurt his honor that she would feel the need to ask. She didn't want to fight with Sargon, she wanted to talk to him, argue with him about strategy, politics, what they were saying in town, about this and that, the idiot who parked the car in the sun—as they used to. She wanted a husband, not a ghost. If they fought, she would retreat deeper into her rooms and he would disappear.

In her life of windows, she loved this one particularly. She imagined herself to be the eye of the house, staring out from its pinnacle at the world it Ruled. The window was attached at the upper edge with a chain and hasp. On a cool day, she could open it out and let a breeze in. One fall when she was twelve, she watched a hurricane lash the glass. Below, the Sound broke across the seawall, ocean swells on a tidal surge heaving against the yard as if it were a beach, the air wild, obliterated with rain and wind and flying branches. A roar came in through the small window. Lightning flashed across it. She followed the water beads wriggling between blasts of rain while Duck, brontophobic, shook under the covers, emerging only to sip a glass of slivovitz.

Now, the window was shut and the stagnant air of the third floor was cool. It smelled like the attics of great houses always do, of old carpeting, cheap paint, and hand-me-down furniture. The crawlspaces collected the odor of damp plaster, stone, and mildew and exhaled it through the vents. She could hear squirrels scratching in the ceiling, smell nesting mice.

Hers was a dark room, buried in the canopy formed by three ancient oak trees. She followed the life of those trees through a small lead-paned window with textured glass and a worn casement, watching the black, tangled boughs leaf out and disappear, smothering the sky with green. Below were blue rooftops, lilac, and hydrangea. A little beyond was a glimpse of a shade garden, creeping junipers planted between low eruptions of bedrock, and an ivy-covered concrete bridge beneath a weeping Japanese maple. Tucked behind the gable of the dining hall was the pointed top of an English holly.

Of all her rooms, she loved these the best. They weren't cold and prison-like as the Winter Palace was, or formal like 1220 Fifth, which felt like a museum with its eighteenth-century furniture and hideous black paintings of wigged patriarchs. Her bed was comfortable, and she felt safe, wrapped in quilts that smelled like Balfour, reading in the afternoon or watching TV. It had always been her room; she had not been moved around the house as she aged. The babies slept with her, one on either side. Frau Duck slept in the big room, on a single bed beneath the slanted ceiling.

The big room was painted mustard yellow, with white trim, and a grey rug that smelled like a vacuum cleaner bag. The walls smelled of Frau Duckworth's smoke. In the evening, she filled the bowl of a hookah with strong Bulgarian tobacco and lay in her bed puffing, sipping strong Bulgarian wine and watching murder mysteries, many of which were set on Mars in the colonial days, with lurid plots and loud colors. How Ruth loved being sick as a child, nesting in the bed all day with Duck, puking, or hacking up phlegm, listening to the TV, to her clearing her throat and muttering in German at scenes she disapproved of.

On the opposite wall were two overstuffed chairs, and a dormer window she used to climb out as a teenager, to sit on the roof and smoke at night. It was one of the many secret spots she had. Another was a storage room off of her bedroom, with boxes of Sargon toys and books, and the futon her Mama used the time she came to visit from Transylvania. It wasn't till she was gone that Ruth would allow herself to cry. Then she cried as she did the first year away from Castelul Bánffy, and swore she would either go back, or never see her Mama again. But she had no power to do either.

On quiet afternoons, when the babies were at their violin or German brain-stimulation sessions, Ruth liked to sit in a room at the top of the third-floor landing that faced the Sound. The morning light poured in through two large, lead-paned windows.

Isle of Dogs, Part 1

She could spend a few hours in the rocker with a cup of tea, watching the shadow of the house edge closer to the seawall and the sun shine on the hulls of sailboats, glowing dabs of yellow, red, and blue chopped by the waves, the chameleon scales of the Sound changing keys with the wind and light.

This was where Phaedra, in a haughty mood, conducted tea parties with the Baby Sargon and their stuffed animals, seated on chairs about a low circular table in the corner. Ruth played the guitar and sang nursery songs. Sometimes they danced. Duck insisted on strict order, but in this room the babies could strew their toys and art supplies about as they pleased. Ruth found the clutter comforting. More than anything, she wanted them to be free, the Regents of their small world. She had to give them that.

At eight months, the Baby Sargon spoke his first words. They were all on the floor in the big room, rolling a ball back and forth. The Baby Sargon seized the ball and pulled it towards him. "Daddy ball," he said. Then he pushed the ball to the Ruler Sargon and fell over, righting himself like a wrestler. Sargon, laughing hard and loud, cried, "He can talk! Did you hear that, Phaedra? Ruth? The boy can talk! And so young." He clapped his hands and spun Phaedra around until she shrieked.

Next, the Baby Sargon spent his days determined to walk. He pulled himself up and stood on unsteady feet, swaying back and forth, grinning like a drunk in an alley. He had a beery face, jowly and puckish, dark in concentration. He would stagger forward a bit, fall, get up, and assume the posture of ballplayers in a huddle, until the day he could stand erect and charge about, arms pumping, hands in fists, babbling phrases and making jokes no one quite understood.

When the babies slept she would watch the stars, breathe the salt night air through the screen and listen to the bell buoy and the foghorn, and wait for the beam of the lighthouse on Execution Rocks to pass through the window and light up the walls behind her. Below, visiting young Rulers would splash in the pool and yell. She missed swimming at night with them. They smoked a mixture of hashish, opium, and tobacco. She used to stretch out in the moonlight and pretend to sun herself, like in the movies, dripping onto the hot paving stones, stars wheeling overhead.

Phaedra and the Baby Sargon were downstairs in the kitchen with Duck eating cookie dough and chocolate icing and would be back up soon. There wasn't time to do anything but stare, as light and water shimmered grey-blue against the washed-out afternoon sky. A man wrapped entirely in silver electraweave raced by on water skis.

Then she saw the navy ship cruise into the harbor, under the New York flag. It stopped far out, and a smaller boat approached under sail. Materializing out of the distant haze was the shape of a destroyer, and then another next to that. There was a convoy of destroyers on Long Island Sound. The sailboat approached with an escort of small, fully armed watercraft darting around like pond-skaters. She came about, dropped sails and motored to the dock. The Ruler Renee stepped out of the cockpit in full uniform, peacetime white and gold. She tied off the sailboat herself and walked towards the house, followed by four aides. The escort deployed to their positions around the property. Then an attack helicopter landed on the yard, sighing steam. New York Guards in black armor assembled on the lawn. Ruth stepped down off the chair and heard the babies and Duck on the stairs, thinking, *it will be war*.

7

The Red Suit

Robin took the shuttle to Times Square and changed for the Broadway Amphibatrain. It shot through stale, coffee-colored water, its soft wake hissing along the worn, algaed walls of the canal. He was nervous as he called Harvale's number. He hadn't felt the flutter of erotic excitement in decades, not since the first months with his wife Dana, who, after his Sire, was his only friend. Their relationship was vital in its way, but a friend is not always a confidant and certainly not a lover, in whose arms disclosure came as inevitably as exhalation after orgasm.

They had no children. She came from a large Catholic family from New Jersey, with seven siblings, numerous nieces and nephews, and a posse of grands who ran about on holidays, fulfilling for them any need they might have had to bring humans destined to suffer and die into the world. Robin never imagined he would find romance, much less in his sixties, but there it was.

"Harvale," came the snappy voice, like the punchline to a joke.

"It's your friend," Robin said. Out of prudence they didn't mention his name on the phone but immediately would state a public place to meet. "I'm going to the Met."

"Don Giovanni?"

"Temple of Dendur. The bench." There was a bench by the Ancient Playground, just off Fifth Avenue, between 84th and 85th, with a view of the museum ruins. It always evoked a feeling of existential comfort, knowing that all things crumble and fall, even as plants pushed up through the ramparts of concrete poured by people, roots broke through foundations, cracked walls veined with vines, and branches built canopies above dilapidated roofs.

"Should I pack?"

"Yes."

They spent nights together in small anonymous hotels in the city, places where a few silver coins purchased silence. The rooms left stark impressions on his memory, etchings of dirty windows and iron beds, cellophane flowers collecting dust, rust-stained tubs and toilets with chipped bowls, cells that contained a slow and sinuous ascent to ecstasy. He did not know that his body could respond as it did to hers. And when they were finished and lying in bed, they could quietly dissect the thing they loved, politics.

In Georgetown Robin had promised to feed her news, and he did, using her to leak information. The New York press was ratlike, beyond extermination but always under threat, and its hunger for news, mostly scandal, was insatiable. So far, nothing he gave her was important, but as he came to trust her, came to understand what it was to be an investigative reporter in their time, he knew he would reveal the hidden motives and machinations that reporters guessed at but rarely knew.

Robin would never betray his Sire, but he was more than a little disturbed by his mission. His plan was to point her in the right direction. He knew what she discovered would probably end up in the archives, no editor being foolish enough to actually break such a story. And that whatever made it into the papers would serve their purpose.

Isle of Dogs, Part 1

✯

At Broome Street he got out and walked to the Rooster Room, a chophouse also known as Headquarters, because it was across the street from the New York City Police Headquarters. Commander Roosevelt was Chief of Police, but his portfolio encompassed far more than that. He was Unified Commander of all New York City forces: Security, Intelligence, Military, and Police. His offices were in Police Headquarters and he was a creature of the NYPD.

He began his career as a beat cop. He advanced rapidly after serving on the Ruler Sargon's security detail. Roosevelt could feel and smell minute changes in the city's energy and power. It was a beast to him, one he had to wrestle to the ground even if it might one day kill him. There was nothing in its business he didn't touch.

Every day, for two hours, Commander Roosevelt held court in Booth 12, with a newspaper, a cup of coffee, and a beautiful woman, who appeared to be different from week to week but was in fact the same person, Roosevelt's alter ego, a dominant bastard with a highly unusual set of nanophotonic mutations that created chromataphoric tissue, allowing her not only to change the color of her eyes and hair, but also the color and shape of her skin, like a squid. She was always there, and no one, not even Robin, who knew most things, knew where she came from. She was blatantly illegal. Even so, Roosevelt protected her. Perhaps he was harvesting her, trying to start a line. He was secretive, cold to the outside world. No one knew what he cared about or needed. He kept his family in a forty-five-room stone mansion overlooking the Delaware Water Gap and flew his own hovercraft home every Thursday night at eight, returning Monday morning at six.

The restaurant was located behind a bar where journalists and politicians went to drink with gangsters and cops. It spread out in a warren of dark, wood-paneled rooms with low, oak-beamed ceilings, lit by bear oil lamps and candles.

Roosevelt sat in a booth with cantaloupe banquettes, watching two supplicants talk over one another. He could barely hold himself upright as he attempted to follow the discussion. When he saw Robin he sat straight, smoothed his thick, black mustache with a peacock napkin, and announced, "My friends, this will have to wait. I have state business before me now."

The interlocutors hushed and turned. When they

saw Robin their faces dropped, as if he were not worth their attention. He was an ordinary looking, late middle-aged human being, without a strand of licensed DNA in his genome. They had no way of knowing who he was. Robin was accustomed to this, and used his low genetic status to his own advantage. To be underestimated was a great gift in politics.

It had not always been so. When he was young, he was not prepared for prejudice. Dismissal infuriated him and he had to learn to swallow his bile. The first Rulers he knew not only treated him as an equal, they treated him as an adult. That he was a human boy actually spoke in his favor, for Sargon 2 didn't trust other Rulers as he trusted humans, and of humans, only children didn't lie. They behaved towards each other as grandfather and grandson. It was an intimacy he hadn't known before. His grandfathers were both dead before he was born, one in a boating accident, and the other of rabies, chained to a tree, screaming and alone. Robin loved his father, but even before his mother's death he was a silent man. They could go whole days in the woods without exchanging three words.

★

Robin sat down next to the woman. She had long

black hair and was dressed in a charcoal suit, with a shimmering teal fez. The waiter brought him a menu. "I'll have sparkling water and a green salad, no dressing, just lemon," he said. It had become his standard order. He was getting fat. He could feel his cavities fill up. He could taste fat in his mouth. And he had reason to stay in shape now. He wondered how Tiriel would respond to champagne, caviar, and duck. She was not really a champagne and caviar person, preferring peanuts and whiskey. He doubted she'd mind dining like a Ruler. Roosevelt's companion shook out a cigarette and lit it.

"Robin," the Commander said, tipping his head. He had dark, creased eyes, piercing and inscrutable.

"I come on urgent business. How secure are we?"

Roosevelt gazed around the room and opened his hands. "It gets no more secure than this in the city."

"You see I bear his seal?"

"I see that. That's why I asked them to leave. What is our business, if it's actually urgent?"

Robin got out of the booth and indicated the woman with his hand. "I need to speak to you alone."

Commander Roosevelt sniffed the air and said, "Downtown's with me."

"This is for your ear only."

He said, "But I tell you—" Robin raised the seal and

the light focused on the Commander's eye. He started to blink. "Very well. Go to the bar, my love, and I'll meet you there when we're through."

Downtown slid out and walked away, white pants swishing against her yellow shoes.

When she was gone, Robin sat back down and again surveyed the room. It was comfortable, the mahogany paneling polished by flame, and smelling of cigars, bourbon, and grilled meat, evocative human odors. Maybe later he would wander down to the South Levee to peruse the used bookstalls. Tiriel had mentioned an edition of Blake's collected poems she had seen that was too expensive. *Too expensive.* How long had it been since anything had been too expensive for him? He couldn't really remember. Robin said, "Our Sire, the Ruler Sargon, wishes me to convey that you are ordered to follow my instructions. Understand?"

"Understand." Roosevelt fixed him with one black eye, his lips set beneath the mustache.

"Assemble Group D. You are to eliminate Maximilian. It must be a Red Suit who shoots him in a disturbance, begun by them. Then you are to restore order. The City Guard will replace the Federal troops at the UN and all other Federal properties in the four boroughs of New York. Report to

Hommocks Cottage at 4:00 p.m., in an armed attack helicopter with a combat-ready unit prepared to deploy and set up a defensive perimeter with an enhanced nanoweb and a naval link. Do you have any questions?"

Commander Roosevelt experienced a tightening of his entire alimentary track. "Are we to execute this plan right away?" he asked.

"You have until tomorrow evening."

"Then I had best be going. I'll see you at Hommocks Cottage."

"Call when you have a plan," Robin said.

Commander Roosevelt and Downtown followed Robin out the door into the glare, and crossed Center Street, his blue uniform rippling in the hard hot wind, to Police Headquarters.

"What was that about?" Downtown asked.

"They must be fucking crazy. It makes no sense. We don't do this," he said quickly, face to the street.

In front of Police Headquarters, a few steps up the grand entrance stair, she stopped and demanded, "What? Do what?" She looked up and down the street. They were alone.

"I can't say. It's insane is all. Desperate. Stupid. Reckless."

The skin of her face bubbled up and settled into a

new shape, soft, not angular, and the fez was gone. She had strawberry hair and a rosy complexion, one of happy innocence, of Persephone gathering flowers in a meadow. Her face freckled, and she smiled benignly, like a baby.

"Things have taken a turn for the worse, my love. I'll update you later." He kissed the end of her nose and instantly she reverted to the narrow, black-haired Downtown. "I won't be home tonight."

Downtown said, "We'll talk." He watched her walk away and felt a stitch in his heart as her hair and back formed into a scarlet, blue, and purple fan that pulsed like a betta in a bowl.

✯

In the pink marble lobby, Roosevelt walked by officers he usually stopped to talk to and took the stairs, two at a time, to his office on the fifth floor where his assistant, Julien Gracq, sat back in a black leather and faux-chrome office chair, buffing his nails, listening to a Ramayana broadcast from Kuala Lumpur. A long lock of chestnut hair hung down his forehead and into his placid eye. "Gracq! Get up! Stop buffing your nails. I need Group D. Meet me in my office in one minute." Roosevelt was winding tighter now, honing the edge. Rage helped.

Jobs like this turn out bad if planned too fast, yet he had no time and no budget. He stormed his drawers and read files, looking for the proper numbers and protocol for assembling Group D, through a Group D Directive, and a Finding, and a compile of Group D Directives and Findings, so he would know the proper funding forms to file. These in hand, he began barking at Julien, who was waiting in the other room and now entered fearfully. "Quit cowering, you know I hate that. Stand up straight now. There's work to be done. Get that hair out of your eye. We've discussed this. Tuck it behind your ear. I have to assemble Group D. I need a Finding, and a Directive. Have you done that before or no? Say no, if you *haven't*, not if you *have*."

"A Group D what?"

"Never mind! I need you to gather what we call Group D. Group D is only assembled for emergencies and the group disbands to silence or death, never to meet again."

"Silence or death."

"That's right. And you are part of Group D now. We all are. Get me a cup of coffee, will you? Thanks." Julien's head pivoted on a slight neck. He was slim, tall, and stooped in the shoulders. He shrugged and left, made the necessary calls, and returned with a cup of coffee, which he set slightly to the left of Commander Roosevelt's buttocks, which was planted on the desk, legs thrust forward and crossed at the ankles, one boot tapping against the other. His hands gripped the desk. He took the coffee and drank half of it down in a gulp. His mouth tightened against his teeth and he exhaled loudly through the nose into his mustache. There was a knock at the door. He hopped down off of the desk and sat behind it. "When you open the door, don't offer seats. Let them sort it out. Then stand next to me and a few steps back." Another knock. "Go on, let them in."

Gracq opened the door and Colonel Esther Solomon, Commander of Intelligence Operations; Major Wanda Kew, Commander of Manhattan Guard Special Forces, Counter-Terrorism Unit; and Major Gordon MacCallister (Major Mac to his troops), Commander of the City Guard, entered the office. They stood at attention before Commander Roosevelt and saluted. He rose and said, "At ease. Sit." They sat on the three wooden, straight-backed chairs positioned in front of the desk. "I need your advice. I have assembled Group D. Are we all agreed?"

For a moment they were silent. Their eyes were fixed, like frogs in a pond, until a glaze of surprise washed over them. Group D had not met in decades.

And he suspected the same thought that had run circles through his mind was running around in theirs: *But you can't do that.* Then, simultaneously, without turning their heads they responded, "Aye!" as he had, and as one.

"Then we will go to the Situation Room. Did you get the Aye votes, Gracq?"

"Yes sir, Commander sir. I recorded the votes and the forms are signed."

"Excellent. Wait here for further orders. My friends?" He stood and beckoned with his hand. They followed him to the back of the office, where a carved oak bookcase concealed a private lift to the basement, which they silently rode down a glass tube into the bedrock. In the subterranean spaces of New York lay another world, another city. Bank vaults held chests of jewels, precious metals, and rare genetic material. In subbasement chambers, experiments were conducted that would not stand the light of the street. Conspiracies, battles, and gang wars unfolded in its tunnels, aqueducts, and cisterns.

They passed through security chambers with living, sensate walls made of deep-sea sponges, into a secure tunnel to a blastproof bunker of steel and concrete, white painted arches bolted to the walls and ceilings. Off to the sides were rooms. One of these rooms was 12B, which they entered by turning the knob on the door and pushing. They passed through a small pressurized vestibule and into a red-carpeted room with an oval table, data portal, and holographic TV. The ostia of the spongiform walls pulsed light in and out like seawater. Solomon, Kew and MacCallister sat on one side of the table and Commander Roosevelt sat on the other.

Roosevelt began without ceremony or welcome. "You are to assassinate Senator Maximilian. It must look like the Red Suits did it. We have twenty-four hours. Are there any questions?"

Major Kew raised her eyebrows and asked, "On whose orders?"

"Perhaps you need to brush up on Group D," Roosevelt said, baring his mighty, gripped teeth.

There was silence around the table.

"Good. When you have a plan, notify me by phone." He stood. "My friends, goodbye."

He exited through the door. As it hissed shut, they stared at Roosevelt's empty chair.

★

Colonel Solomon was the first to speak. She and the others were dressed in the black armor of the City Guard. Her long hair, red as a stoplight on wet pavement, was coiled on top of her head. "They must be fucking kidding," she said.

Major Kew agreed. "We don't do that. He's not only a Senator, he's our Senator, and we are the host city, traditionally neutral."

MacCallister said, "But he's not our Ruler, and this is an order."

Major Kew said, "If it's an illegal order—"

Colonel Solomon answered, "It's abrogated."

"Nevertheless, our position," MacCallister said. "Granted it is unprecedented, but given the situation, arguably we are defending ourselves."

Kew said, "Aye."

Solomon said, "Aye."

"Then," MacCallister said, "What are we to do?"

Kew said, "Carry out the order. Where do we hit him?"

MacCallister said, "He leaves home in the morning, takes a limo to the UN, gets out and walks across the Plaza, into the breezeway to the Conference Building. Four hours later, he leaves, goes out to lunch, then home. They joke about it. You can set your watch by his lunch—1:22. As I see it, it has to be public. That's the only way to blame the guards. That means either in front of his building, or the UN."

Solomon said, "He's under Federal Guard wherever

Isle of Dogs, Part 1

he goes. But it's only at the UN that all of the security details are together. It wouldn't take much to get them to shoot at each other."

"They've already shot at each other on the streets," MacCallister said. "Over ice, slag, and poon."

Kew said, "We have to infiltrate the UN detail, get the shooting started as he comes out of the building, and place a sniper who guns him down with a Federal gun. Just to be sure."

Solomon said, "Twenty-four hours is short notice. I'll get the IDs, the armor, and the weapons. My agents can infiltrate the scene and start the crossfire."

"I have the snipers," said Major Kew.

"Do we have armor?" asked MacCallister.

"Not in stock," Solomon said. "We'll have to go out and roll some Red Suits to get what we need."

"What I figured," he said. He fired up the flat screen and called the 69th Regiment Armory. MacCallister asked, "What else?" He tapped and spoke.

Solomon asked, "What are the logistics?"

MacCallister said, "Just a minute. Reserve troops are called to barracks, armed and ready to deploy at my order."

Solomon said, "I'll have the suits, the IDs, and the

guns as soon as possible. We'll operate out of the 69th and coordinate there with you, Major Mac."

Major Kew wearily wiped her brow with her sleeve and her face sagged. She exhaled slowly and said, "I don't like it."

"Neither do I," said Solomon. "No good can come of it. Shall we take him coming or going?"

Kew said, "As he walks out. For lunch."

MacCallister said, "One twenty-two. And the shooters? What do we do with them?"

Colonel Solomon said, "Oh no. If my men go in, they're coming out."

Major Kew said, "It *is* Group D."

"I agree with you, Colonel," MacCallister said. "Just because Group D allows it, doesn't make it a necessity. These are good men?"

"I wouldn't go that far, but they're all I've got. And they won't talk," Solomon said.

"Aye," they said, their voices overlapping and low.

★

Solomon was tall for a human, a little over six feet in a crew cut. Now, she wore her hair in the police fashion, long, and the bright red pile on her head made her even taller, so she had to duck getting into her hovercraft, which was parked in the lot nearby on Broome Street. She took off and flew uptown over the river to the roof of Agency Headquarters, a mouldering, 600-year-old brownstone on 95th between Third and Lex that looked like it had been roach infested for so long, their feces and carcasses glued the structure of the building together. But built within the sagging brick facade was a sound ceramic-and-steel cage webbed with a clean modern interior. Climate and power were diffuse; it had a brainfoam light system, living spongiform walls, stone floors, and elegant baths and toilets. She had nothing to complain about.

The hovercraft sucked into place on the pad and Solomon walked towards the port, not breaking stride. She clomped down metal stairs to the sixth floor and headed to her office. She was entitled to a large corner office, with crown moulding, wainscoting, and bay windows, palms, cats, and small horses browsing on micromeadows. Instead, she took a back room with one window looking out on the benighted airshaft, into which six months out of the year a finger of sun wandered every afternoon. It slipped across the wall and shined on the Plutonian Nickel desk, a gift from her predecessor, a minor Ruler who sat in that chair for twenty-five years doing nothing. Solomon was genetically nobody, but she worked, and the Ruler Sargon liked that. He made her his Commander.

Colonel Solomon put aside her reservations and zeroed in on the orders. She called in her adjutant, Lieutenant Midasinti. Lieutenant Midasinti had a soft face, unshaped by wind or circumstance. It still wore the triumphant happiness of the upper-grade student. He was the most obtuse adjutant she had ever had, and she would get rid of him, but the Ruler Midasinti wanted his Scion to go into Intelligence. As a favor to the Ruler Sargon she took him on, and he was an incompetent prick, armed with the invulnerable certainty of his class.

"Lieutenant," she said. "Call in agents Cowrie, Balustian, and Whitehead." They were her best team of operatives. Where she came from, Alabama, which had a sound, centuries-old martial tradition, these three would be seen as clowns. But they were not clowns, just filthy and cynical. New York was so different from the South and it had taken her a while to understand that everything in New York was about money. Of course, everything was always about money everywhere, ultimately, but as George Wallace used to say, there were only two things in this world: "money and power, and I don't give a damn about money." New Yorkers were there to make money, not waste it on the military. She didn't at first understand the alliances of mobsters and politicians and the police; it had to be explained. And Whitehead had done just that, in the office late one night, when he came in smelling of whiskey, tobacco, and patchouli. He proudly laid it all out for her in about an hour, starting with Tammany Hall and the American Revolution. And it was quite amazing, an unbroken tradition of graft, documented for over 800 years.

Balustian, Cowrie, and Whitehead were not what she was used to, but they were honest, loyal, and brave. She soon learned to trust them. They drank, and whored, and behaved in an unprofessional and slovenly manner. But they had not failed her yet, and the others, the well-dressed spies, did nothing at all but play cards with gangsters and landlords and go out to lunch with bankers. They came home with gossip. These three crawled around on the street and came back with actual intelligence. She gave them the freedom to finance their operation how they pleased, and asked no questions.

The door opened and Balustian, Cowrie, and Whitehead walked meekly in, dressed in grey fatigues and black berets. They saluted and Solomon said, "At ease. Please, be seated." They sat on upright chairs and rested their hands palm down on their thighs. "My friends, you are now part of Group D. Group D operates under the highest authority and I am deputized to execute that authority. Betrayal of Group D is a mandatory death sentence. Are we understood?"

"Aye!" they said as one.

Cowrie was a blond-haired man in his late thirties, with grey eyes in a long face with full lips. To his right and in the middle was Balustian, also fair haired, but with dark eyes and a round face younger looking than the fifty hard years it had lived. On the end was Whitehead, whose hair was more grey than white, with black roots, and whose face was covered in tiny wrinkles, like an old leather glove. Balustian was their nominal leader. "What's the job?" he asked, his partners nodding grimly.

"We have to start a shootout between Red Suits."

"Where?" asked Balustian.

"The UN."

"So," Balustian said, "You need different security details to start shooting at each other. To cover what?"

Chief Solomon said nothing. "How many plants do we need at the UN to get this going?"

Whitehead said, "I think the three of us could manage it."

Cowrie scratched his ear and said, "We'll need to get three red suits. When do they change shifts at the UN?"

Whitehead said, "Don't poach from the UN, they'll tighten security. We gotta take a domestic detail. Maybe the Vice President's. It's big enough, and they're fat and stupid. They don't waste the good ones on the VP."

Everyone chuckled.

Balustian asked, "What do we do with the guards once we have the suits?"

Chief Solomon said, "Whatever you want, so long as it can't be traced to us."

"We'll get started right away."

Solomon said, "You are not to start the crossfire until 1:22 p.m., when Senator Maximilian leaves the Senate and takes his car. He's neurotically punctual. Can you be in position by then?"

Balustian looked at the other three and said, "I don't see why not. But how do we infiltrate three different details?"

Whitehead said, "Easy. They change the guard at noon. Noon is chaos, Red Suits coming and going like rush hour. We just float with the crowd, get where we want, land near a couple of details. The layout's perfect. A four-lane circular drive with a fence, and bushes between it and First Avenue. No one will be able to get anywhere. The problem is, what if we start a fucking riot? All those idiots milling about, armed to the teeth with nothing to do."

Commander Solomon said, "Sounds like Alabama."

Whitehead laughed and said, "You said it, sir, I didn't. At 1:22, the only civilians will be Maximilian and his crew, but at 1:30 the congressional staff leave. If there's shooting on the Plaza, we won't be able to control it. People might get hit. What then?"

They stared at her.

"A riot isn't necessary," she said. "An exchange of fire will do."

"Right," said Cowrie. "It's a clean shot, if that's what you're after."

Solomon folded her hands and leaned forward in her chair, regarding each of them carefully before probing Balustian's brown eyes, which were large for his face and melancholy. Balustian, more than the others, felt the job. Everything he did struck his heart. "Do we understand each other?" she asked.

"Yes sir," they said as one.

★

Out on the street, muffled by the heavy air that settles on the island in August and the morose silence created by the task ahead of them, Balustian said, his eyes watering, "They're fucking crazy. This is stupid. Why do we gotta do this? We're fucked if the guns start going off and ten Senators are dead on the pavement."

"Orders," Cowrie said.

"To get one guy, not carnage."

Whitehead said, "She didn't say that."

"Don't make like you don't know," Cowrie said. "You heard what she said, and then she told us with her eyes. I hate when they fucking do that."

"Me too. That's how I got it," Balustian said.

"However we got it, it's an order. Plus, the Feds aren't on our side. It's our city, and Sargon's our Ruler, not these stinking Red Suits of President Iocle. This I do for fun."

Balustian said, "I can think of things that are a lot more fun."

Cowrie interrupted. "How the fuck do we get three suits? Those things are impervious. Are we going to train a missile on them?"

Balustian said, "We have to get them to take the armor off voluntarily."

They smiled as one. "Let's pay a visit to Margery Milk," Whitehead said.

Margery Milk was a Park Avenue whorehouse, with a 71st Street entrance and private elevator. They knew its proprietress, Margery Malkin, a woman from the Bronx. They picked up a car and drove down, over empty, dirty avenues, crossing the canal bridges. It was a brick building with black iron grillwork on the windows and entrance gate. They climbed the stoop and rang the bell. After a short wait, the black door opened. An old man in a linen suit wrinkled by the heat opened the door, his white hair in a warm yellow halo, and face purple in the shade of the street. "Gentlemen," he said in a patrician accent, "Is there anything I can do for you this evening?"

"We gotta see the boss," Whitehead said.

Balustian and Cowrie crossed their hands behind their backs and nodded their heads, bowing slightly.

"Come in, please." They followed him to a small elevator, which they took to the eleventh floor. The door opened on a black marble foyer decorated with dragon ferns and bird of paradise flowers. Beyond lay a bar and tables for poker, craps, and roulette. The old man escorted them up two flights of stairs to an old office door with a transom. Within was a wooden desk, a cotton mattress on a narrow platform, and two straight chairs. Seated behind the desk was Margery Malkin, a woman in her early forties with a serious face, dressed in a white shirt buttoned to the throat. Her hair was brown, tied back in a ponytail, and she wore no makeup. Appearing bored and distracted, she asked, "Gentlemen, what can I do for you?"

Balustian said, "We have to entertain some Red Suits and it's important that they undress. Can we rent a few of your best flies to bring them in? We'll pay you double and there's a bonus for working fast. We need three."

"Bring 'em back here?" Thinking, she shook her head slowly back and forth a few times and became still. "No arrests then, and no killing. I can't have either in my establishment. And you gotta tip the women, even if they don't work."

Cowrie said, "We don't arrest people and nobody's gonna get killed. All we want is the armor and the weapons. And don't worry, we'll tip the bait."

She nodded, and leaned forward, her eyes inked and intense. "Who's the mark?"

"Souvanouphong's detail. Tonight."

Malkin sat up from the desk and smiled. "He lives at One Sutton Place South, out over the water. We work for him all the time. His guard knows us. I see no problem here. Be back at midnight. They'll be naked by then, I guarantee."

After the agents left, Margery Malkin went to her dressing room. There was a chair, a vanity, racks of clothes, and chests of drawers. On the back of the door was a full-length mirror, with scarves hanging from a hook. She sat in the chair staring at the wallpaper, a pattern of trellises twined with vines and flying insects. She swiveled to the mirror and turned on the lights.

As Margery Malkin put on her eyeliner, mascara, and lipstick, she wondered what she was becoming a part of. She did not trust agents of any kind. These were not exactly police, but they all worked for Roosevelt. Of course, he was the boss and the Red Suits were Iocle's boys. She found herself yanking her lashes and she blinked as if something were in her eye. She selected a black Kashmir-goat-hair wig.

The thing of it was, if the Red Suits came back the next day and wanted to know what happened, what would she say? A Federal investigation could be serious. She didn't like Red Suits. They had no place in New York. But she was in business, not politics. Margery Milk made a lot of money. The tax bill was high and then there were all the payoffs to the cops, the City Council, to everyone with a sticky palm in the city. Her clients demanded mutant whores and banned substances like anyone else. Protection was supposed to mean no Feds up her ass.

Margery Malkin tucked her hair up into the wig and brushed it out so it was like a black Persian cat's, and changed into a black leather jumpsuit with the company logo stitched above the left breast pocket. She checked her schedule and went back to her private office, where she called in her guard, Melissa, Norissa, and Maurice, dressed alike in black leather jumpsuits. "I need some good streetwalkers. Women who could make Gandhi beg for head."

The three pondered this. "Melissa," Norissa asked, "What's the name of that new girl?"

"Norissa," Melissa said, with intended malice, "You don't remember anything. Her name is Greyhound."

Maurice asked, "Because she chases coney?"

"I believe she *catches* coney."

"Enough," Margery Malkin said. "This is no joke. Get me that Greyhound and whoever the best earners are. Wake them up if you have to. Unless they're drunk, I want to see the best six right away." One by one, over the next hour, as Margery Malkin sat at her desk reading *Pride and Prejudice,* the whores assembled in the outer office.

They stood in a row gazing blindly forward like

soldiers, in various states of studied deshabille. Greyhound stood apart. She wore leopard-skin capris and a black halter top. She didn't wear an animal wig; she colored and styled her own hair. Each strand etched the air around her head.

"You must be Greyhound. You earn, looking like that?"

"Enough to stay out on the corner all night. I ain't got no house."

Margery Malkin nodded and looked at the next two, bare beneath matching red micro-mini skirts and white, bone-button bodices with black collars. "And what do I call you?"

The one on the left was tall and hefty with a hard, pitted face and a pouffy yellow angora wig. She said, in a hoarse voice, "I answer to Alpha Lambda Pi, all one word."

"Alpha Land of Pie?" Margery Malkin muttered to herself, trying to figure it out. And when she felt she got it she yelled, "Oh! Alfalandopie."

The other was bony faced, heavily made up with white pancake makeup, though her skin was a shade darker than chestnut. She had white fiberoptic hair implants and could glow like a Ruler. She said, "Esther. It's a book in the Bibble."

"Esther, how's earning?"

"I did ten last night and twenty the night before. I got tired, so I quit early. I could have done more."

"And you," she said, turning to Alfalandopie. "How are you earning?"

"Same as she do. We works together."

"I see. And you two?" She asked the next two. They were street waifs, or playing at it, or both. Their few articles of clothing were filthy and tattered. Margery Malkin sniffed the air. There was no funk of dirty armpits and unwiped butt. They bathed, and their clothes were washed. The one on the left was short, underfed, and young. Her breasts swayed in an oversized oxford shirt, the tail torn to hang a single ribbon of fabric against the crack of her ass, while another veiled her pubic hair in shadow. She said, "Izzy, ma'am."

"Hi, Izzy."

The other was dressed in a gigantic grey tank top that reached just to her knees, a versatile garment she could bunch up to piss or shit, or flash her twat at a potential customer, and drop if there was trouble. She mumbled at the ground, "Utopia."

"Look at me Utopia," Margery Malkin said. "Why not Urania?"

"I didn't want to give them no ideas."

She laughed. "Everything's in a name. I once

named a dog Falstaff. He drank all the booze and never stopped barking. So I named the next one Harpo. He ate all my ties!

"I need you to go down to One Sutton Place and pick up as many of the Red Suits coming off their shift as you can. You gotta bring 'em back here and get 'em to undress in a private room. You tell 'em this one's on the house. And if they want one of the house girls, then pass 'em on to me. You'll get paid and tipped anyway. Tell 'em their boss paid for it. There's a bonus if you bring 'em in quick. By midnight, they have to be naked, and I need those suits. Everyone who brings one in gets a shot at working in the house. A shot. You've got to clean yourselves up and mind your mouth. Now go get me those Red Suits."

★

Greyhound, Alpha Lambda Pi, Esther, Utopia, and Izzy loaded into the whorehouse van and drove down to 56th and First. They fanned out across 56th Street, toward the service entrance of One Sutton Place South, a standing Candela building, one of the most expensive addresses in the world.

"I never worked this block before," Alpha Lambda Pi said.

"It's a good-girl block," Greyhound said, lighting a cigarette.

"You mean old bird. Gimme one a those," Esther said, her hair lit up like a party boat.

Greyhound took one out and gave it to Esther, and said to the others, "That's it. The last one I hand out. So don't ask." They watched the coal burn in the dark. The only other light was cast by the night lamps in the doorways onto the stoops and sidewalks, through thick air. Rain hadn't washed the streets in weeks and the reek of garbage seeped into the pavement. Heat radiated off the concrete long into the night. The whores' sweat glistened and mixed with the scent of hair oil and perfume, and the East River at low tide. "This is a crazy ass job," Greyhound said.

They stopped across the street from the service entrance, a caged black door, unlit, buried in the limestone facade. Behind it rose the levee wall and above the levee cantilevered buildings vanished in the sky.

Greyhound looked up and down the street, at the corners. The city was shuttered and empty. There were no people. No people on First Avenue, no people on York. The whole ride down had been spooky, dark, and empty. Bad shit was going to happen, she sensed. She wasn't a stupid whore. That was why she freelanced. Freelance, she could pick her tricks. At Margery Milk, that only came with seniority. She'd rather cruise for pussy on her own than kick upstairs to the Madame. She could get a Red Suit anytime she wanted. Those babes get off their shift and just want someone to make them scream. She was going to land that Red Suit first.

If it was a setup, there was still time to leave. She'd never work Margery's turf again, but there were other parts of the city, other boroughs. She looked for cars, for dogs, horses, and rats. Checked out doorways and subbasements, the edges of shadows and street-level windows. "I don't fuck Red Suits if I can avoid it," Esther said. "They got nasty habits." Greyhound decided to take the unlit stoop two up from her. It was a longer walk to the door, but it would give her time to make her mark, or bail if it was a setup.

Izzy said, "Red Suits burned me with cigarettes when I was twelve."

"When was that?" Esther asked. "Last week?"

Izzy shook her head and wiggled four fingers at her. "Four years ago."

"Damn girl, you suckin' blood?" Alpha Lambda Pi asked.

"That shit ain't funny," said Utopia. "Drinking blood. Fuck that."

"So like," Greyhound asked, "you swallow paste ten, twenty times a day but you won't drink blood? Ain't that funny?"

Alpha Lambda Pi said, "I don't eat no pig liver but I eat chicken liver. For some reason, chicken liver ain't like liver."

Well, why would you think one would be like the other, Greyhound wondered. She can't be that stupid. "Ain't nothing like nothing else. It's all unique," said Greyhound.

Esther, her face scroonched up, worked out the thought and said, "I don't even think God could do that. There's just too damn much of it. There has to be a pattern and we're all just, you know, output." She paused, smiled, and then became puzzled again. "That's not what the Bibble says. I don't want you to get the wrong idea. It's my own interpretation."

The light came on over the service entrance door and the whores scattered to stoops and corners up and down the block to wait. Greyhound took up her post, at the top of the stoop under the arched entranceway. She was entirely concealed in shadow. The area around the entrance was a large bowl of buttery light. One by one, guards in bright red suits popped out of the doorway like gumballs. Their helmets fogged up.

After a twelve-hour shift all they wanted to do was strip down and breathe, wash off the residue of sweat and dirt, the dirt that sifts in through tiny stress cracks. At first they were like poisoned soldiers staggering randomly forward, but a few steps from the door they stood erect and gazed around at the whores seated on stoops up and down the street. She could tell when each had seen through the fogged glass into the night well enough to discern them. People ready to fuck for money.

One guard veered in her direction as if to avoid the other whores. She was both wearier and warier. She strayed towards the street and headed straight to Greyhound, whom she might have sensed as a heat mass, if the gear was fully engaged. Greyhound stepped out of the shadow and down the stairs into the light. "Hey," she said quietly, shaking loose a cigarette. As she drew it out, she stared into the faceplate. She could barely make out a pair of eyes and a mouth. Blue, green, and red sparks crackled off the visor and floated away in a double-convection plume. "Cigarette?"

"I've got to go," said the aerated voice of the Red Suit.

Isle of Dogs, Part 1

"What's your hurry?"

The Red Suit relaxed, as if the suit itself had let out a breath, and no longer seemed like it was being pulled towards First Avenue by peristalsis. "I need a nice hot bath. Can you give me that?" A mouth smiled behind the glass. "I didn't think so."

"I got what you need. And it's on the house tonight. Your boss prepaid, lover."

"What boss is that?"

"The one that's gonna pay for your night at Margery Milk." She put her hand on the Red Suit's shoulder. "Are you coming?"

The helmet wheezed. The fog was retreating from the center of the faceplate. "Why not." They walked up to First Avenue and got into a waiting taxi. The driver looked into the rearview at the Red Suit and the whore, his face worn out, infected with fear and self-loathing.

Greyhound led her in through the private entrance and took her upstairs to a room with a bath, on the fourteenth floor. In the open door she asked, "Do you want me or someone else? I can get you someone more high class, but nobody eats pussy like I do."

The Red Suit was starting the laborious process of removing her armor. The ankles hissed, and she uncuffed the boot layers. That released the pressure from the lower half, and the odor of a day spent in uniform diffused through the room. She released her helmet next and twisted it off. She had yellow hair and a face like a pineapple, scarred from battle without protective gear of any kind. Her mouth was downturned and her stare one of exhaustion. She got off the rest of the uniform and laid it all out on the floor and then, dressed only in her black underclothes, looked at Greyhound, who had left her to run the bath, and whose rear half was framed by the doorway, kneeling naked to adjust the heat of the water gushing into the tub. The guard peeled off the silk undershirt and stepped out of her boxer shorts and entered the bathroom. She lowered herself into the water and lay back while Greyhound wrung out a giant sponge and Balustian crept into the room to steal her weapons and armor.

∗

Balustian awoke on a hard bed in the dark. He did not know where, or even who he was. He wasn't even certain he was alive, except that his eyes hammered in their sockets and his mouth tasted like dog shit. Lights flashed in fading sheets, in his head, in the air. He coughed up something thick and slippery and swallowed it. The next cough was bone dry, hoarse. He swung his legs off the cot and rested his body on his forearms and knees, face to the floor. His stomach burned. He belched. Bile surged into his throat. In his ears, the groans of Promethean pain. He must be alive. He tried to remember where he was born. All living things are born before they die. But his date and place of birth were a blank. He blinked and teared up as he saw red runner lights, and the outline of bundles in the dark. He smelled the snores and farts of dreaming soldiers and concluded he was in a morgue. Either he was dead or someone had fucked up. Except he wasn't in a shroud, he was free. He searched his mind for a memory but his mind was pitch black and soundless except for the voice, which he assumed was his own but might in fact not be. Out of the dark and beyond, the voice-images stirred. He was crawling on the floor towards a light. His heart started to pound. Margery Milk. The Red Suit! Where was the suit, he wondered. Memories lit up like fireflies and faded in the dark. He started to put it together.

He, Whitehead, and Cowrie had gone out to wait for the whores to come back with the suits. They ate pork steaks and french fries at a dive called Dr. Chang's on Lexington Avenue. Then they moved on to Nelson's Pillar, an Irish toilet around the corner, to get drunk and shoot darts. On the way they smoked a few joints.

After that, the images fell apart and became disjointed in time. He drove. The windows were open and he was hunched over the wheel, stuporous, tunneling into a smear of lights in blind terror. The terror hadn't gone away. It was like part of his brain was still driving.

There was a man in a bow tie, eyes popping out, saying, "Room 1409."

Balustian watched the doors swim around and tried to find the handle to the hallway door he was to take to reach Room 1409. The hall buzzed like a wasp, magenta walls with black stripes and yellow fixtures. The doors were cockeyed. He lurched by, staring with one eye at the numbers, bumping off the walls, until he located 1409. Behind the door lay an inscrutable darkness, woozy with objects resolving slowly into a pile of crimson armor, black satin sheets on the bed. Beyond was light in a doorway and the sound of two women talking. He crept in on his hands and knees. Noisily he gathered the armor and weapons up and left the room as he had come, on his hands and knees, dragging them behind him.

After that, nothing. And now? Not nothing. Not something.

Balustian's eyes adjusted to the dark. He felt he could lift his head without vomiting. His skin was clammy with sweat. He took a grumbling breath and looked up and knew where he was. It was not a morgue and he was not dead, he was in the 69th Regiment Armory on Lexington Avenue in Manhattan. The bundles weren't corpses in body bags, they were sleeping soldiers. He had made it home.

Balustian stood. He was naked below the waist. His pants were on the floor, covered in vomit. He looked around and saw a pair of clean sweat pants, neatly folded by the cot of a soldier. He staggered over, swiped the pants and put them on loudly, the sleeping soldiers rolling over, mumbling *shut up*. He stood at the door, listened, and yanked it open. A throng of soldiers and civilians, Rulers and humans, rushed by. High above, the windows blasted sun.

He oriented himself and headed down to the mess, a tiled windowless expanse of tables and food behind glass. He took his tray and stood in line with soldiers and civilians coming off the night shift. There was laughter. Gossip. He saw the woman engineer from Charlie Company in her short shorts, off duty. He tried to catch her eye and then thought better of it, given what he must look like. He wore no insignia, he had no rank, no known mission. He smelled of vomit and booze. He was disheveled. Cringing, Balustian looked away to hide his face. He couldn't even be sure he was there. Then he reasoned, if I can think that, I must be here. Of course, he had to be here to think that. They weren't necessarily the same thing.

If he did fuck the woman from Charlie Company, what would his wife say? Wife? Oh no! He was married, to Colonel Luanne Schwartz, of the New Jersey State Militia, Troop One, Capital Region. Lulu. They had two children, Barb and Dan. If he fucked the woman from Charlie Company in the short shorts, Lulu would kill him. Or fuck someone else. Maybe even leave him. That's what *he'd* do. And then? He'd lose his children, and she would hate him, and fuck other guys, and he would be hurt and hate her. Maybe get drunk every night and kill himself. *Never fucking mind*, he thought.

It was early, there had to be breakfast. He stared at the trays of food. Yellow mashed potatoes showed through cracks in the heat-lamp crust. Meatloaf and gravy. Pizza. A man in a chef's toque dumped a bucket of black beans and a bucket of yellow rice into trays, shaking the last bits out and scraping the pot with a spoon, the steam rising into his face smelling of dirty hood vents and blocked drain traps. "Where's breakfast?" Balustian asked, his stomach pitching.

"This is breakfast. If you were looking for the pork chops smothered in gravy, we ain't put them out yet."

"Can I get a couple of fried eggs and toast, to go with those black beans and yellow rice?"

The chef's posture stiffened. "Do I look like a cook to you?"

"You'll forgive me for misunderstanding that hat and apron."

"*Toque.* A cook is what I ain't." He scowled indignantly and marched away with a pot in each hand.

There was fried chicken, braised greens, Pock-Marked Grandmother's bean curd, and then, finally, a breakfast station, where he loaded his tray with eggs, bacon, potatoes, beans, tortillas, and seven cups of coffee. Balustian picked the tray up with trembling but capable hands, and transported it with a slight lurch to the register, where an amused young man with long legs and very large teeth was joking with a doctor in a white coat. All he heard was "…gas." Was it grim laughter that followed, at the prospect of a gas attack, or a weak joke about gas? He couldn't be sure. The young man counted the coffees and looked up. "Thirsty?"

"Just ring it up." He scratched his cheek and cleared his throat, sending a squib of mucus onto the tray.

The cashier stared at it as it hung off the edge and stretched. "What's your charge?"

"I'm on my own account. I pay silver."

"I'm not equipped for silver. Just give me a name."

"Commander Solomon." He walked away and took a seat, avoiding the others. There was much to do. He had to cough the food down and take a shit if he was going to do any of it. At first he ate dutiful small bites, but as his strength returned so did his hunger and he wolfed it down, his mind reeling in and out of focus, as disconnected memories were dealt out on a table and returned to the deck to be shuffled. Who was the dealer, Fate, or Chance, or a capricious deity?

As he was sopping up the last of the yolk and refried beans with the last tortilla, Cowrie and Whitehead arrived, looking like boiled owls. They sat down across from him.

"Where'd you get the pants?" asked Whitehead.

"Why'd you make me drive?" Balustian replied. He now felt certain that he had suffered persecution at his partners' hands. The paranoia, tamed by his meal, roared.

"Because," Cowrie said, "you were in the bathroom puking while we did two more rounds of shots."

Whitehead said, "You were the sober one. Remember? We talked about it, I think."

"It's a good thing I don't remember; it was the most terrifying night of my life. I'm still shaking. Look." He held up his hand. It trembled. "Where's your food?"

On Whitehead's tray was a candy bar and two cups of coffee, and on Cowrie's was a glass of orange juice, a glass of water, and a cup of coffee. Cowrie said, defensively, "It's a Continental Breakfast. What they serve in France." Whitehead snickered into his palm and unwrapped the candy bar, with the mesmerizing smile of an imbecile.

"I'm going to shower and dress. I'll see you in the bunker," said Balustian.

After an explosive bowel movement, a hasty and incomplete shave with blood that stranded patches of grizzle, and a shower, he walked the halls in search of a Red Line elevator, the only lift with access to the bunker. He got off on Level B5. The way was dark and smothering, as the perpetual wet of the Manhattan underworld closed in, dense with the odor of puddles and mold collecting in tunnels deep in the bedrock. Something between a possum and a rat, with glowing eyes, lived in the walls and pulled its pink tail into crevices when anyone went by. Insects darted out of the corner of his eye, large winged arthropods with pincers, and masses of larvae contracted as his light passed, bugs brought back from the Martian caves on waterships.

Finally, he came to a grey hallway with a yellow stripe painted down the middle. People pushed carts back and forth, keeping to the right of the line. He crossed into the human traffic and motored forth until he came to the office used for classified meetings, and took his seat at the table. In the corner was a clothes rack with six full sets of red Federal armor. Only Solomon was there, staring at her baton. She was absorbed in thought and seemingly unaware of his presence. He took a seat across from her and she pushed her fingers into her hair and gripped her skull. "Where are the others?"

The Commander sounded severe and unhappy. "They'll be here," he said.

"What I have to say I have to say to all. But between us, that was fine work. I suppose. Of a kind. Ah, good." The door opened. He didn't turn around to look. What was the point? He was to die for his transgression. It was a vague feeling of terminal guilt. It will be now or later. And what is later? What is now? His partners sat down on either side of him. They too had bathed and clothed in simple cotton pants and a tunic.

"You are to deploy immediately. Carry out your mission as planned. As to the uniforms, I commend your results, but criticize your methods, which are shameful. Balustian, you staggered into this base covered in vomit, ranting uncontrollably. You had to be subdued and carried to the barracks. You drove here! What if you had been pulled over with the armor?"

They looked at the table and pouted. Whitehead raised his hand a little and muttered, "Sir."

"Whitehead? Have you something to say?"

"With all due respect, we got loaded. Things got out of hand, I don't know how. I'm sure it will never happen again."

"Commander, I apologize," said Balustian. "I shouldn't have had those last five shots. You know how it is when they're going down?"

"Exactly," said Cowrie. "It went down like water, while we waited for those whores. It was uncanny how it went down without effect."

"I agree," Balustian said, nodding his head and looking up at her with marbled eyes. "It was uncanny."

Her eyes were piercing now, and she directed them at Balustian's soul. "I need you to carry out this mission, and we cannot have a bloodbath. Timing is critical. You do what you have to do to get them shooting and that's it. When your mission is done, your role in this Group D ends. But Group D is never dissolved. Subsequent related findings may reband the group. Under no circumstances do you divulge any knowledge of Group D, its constitution, actions, or the existence of a Group D designation at all. Failure to observe this condition will result in immediate live execution by acid."

"Aye," exclaimed the three.

★

Balustian hated armor. That was why he went into intelligence services. None of that military bullshit, like what he had just endured. Squeezing into another person's suit sucked. It smelled like them. It was shaped to their bodies. Creased where they were creased. And the datafeed was formatted for their eyes, their brains, their ticks. He spent a few minutes teaching it to fit him, and then, once he got the kink out of the breathing hose, adjusted the air to his liking. It actually seemed to help his raging stomach and hammering head. It made him feel less vulnerable, less shaky and terrified. For the first time that day, he felt safe.

8

"I'm Going to the Senate."

Reaching down to scratch Balfour and feed him a biscuit, Sargon announced, "I'm going to the Senate." It was 6:00 a.m. They were seated at a table on the small deck outside of their bedroom, in the shade of two 400-year-old red oak trees. The air was still cool. Dew coated the leaves and iron rail. The sun rose into a smoky grey sky.

"Don't be a fool," Renee said. "You know Robin would say that, if he were here. You haven't been to the Senate in months. It will arouse suspicions if you show up on the day a Senator is killed." She dipped a spoon into a small china bowl with a gold rim, full of raspberries, blueberries, and peaches mixed with sheep yogurt.

"I am capable of making decisions without Robin. I am not feeble-minded!" He sipped a glass of iced espresso and tossed small handfuls of berries into his mouth.

"I said you were a fool, not feeble-minded. So you insist on going through with this?"

"It's the last day of the session. It will arouse more suspicions if I'm not there."

Renee laughed deeply and said, "Killing a Senator is what will arouse suspicion."

"I told you, it won't look like we killed him, it will look like they did. And for all practical purposes they will have."

"No one will believe it." she observed. "Robin is right. There is a third way."

"You didn't tell Euclid, did you?"

"No, of course not. But you have to admit, he proved himself with that business with the chef, and he told us about the transport station."

Sargon contemplated the truth of her statement. Certainly Euclid had warned them of the danger. But so what. That meant nothing. "Like we wouldn't have discovered on our own that they were building a transport station in the Bronx? I trust my people over an ancient, lizard-eyed Ruler any day."

Renee took little exasperated bites of food, chewed

hard and fast and then stated, having mulled it over with her jaws and teeth, "You should have packed that child off to Hungary when I told you to. It complicates everything and clouds your mind with a meaningless passion." Sargon knew she was protecting him, but that did nothing to assuage his anger that she didn't love Phaedra as he did. It was unreasonable, of course. How could he expect her to care at all? But he did. Renee was cold, that was all, devoid of emotion. She erupted, "The way you dote on her!"

Sargon blushed. "She is my child."

"Don't go to the Senate. If things go wrong, you'll be arrested right away and we'll all be killed including that little bastard."

"As the Ruler of this city, I can't have New Yorkers saying I cowered in the Waldorf while the Red Suits shot up our streets and killed our Senator. My mind is settled." He wiped crumbs from his mouth and drained the iced espresso. "This is quite good."

"So you insist?" she asked. Her face was becoming the mask of their Lady, the terrifying official face, behind which the person disintegrated.

"Where's Albion?"

"Sire?" he asked, standing at the French doors leading to their bedroom suite.

"Albion, I'm ready for my shave. I'm taking the launch to town."

"Sire." Albion bowed his head and vanished indoors.

Renee said, "I'll stay in the city to monitor things. The carrier groups are in place outside of Philadelphia. If you change your mind we can cordon off Co-op City in a matter of hours. Iocle will know that, they all will. The deterrent is enough. Good luck."

Renee's morning clothes fell away from her body revealing chalk-white skin, always more vivid in the summer. Sargon admired her and felt a twitch of attraction. She was still strong. Her flesh was in an autumnal state, beautiful in its fading to winter, love's graves written in the margins of her mouth and eyes. He stood, as if to salute her going. She smiled. "My Lord," she said, tipping her head and he replied, "My Lady," and then, "Come, Balfour."

Sargon eased into the barber chair. Albion wrapped his face in hot towels and stropped the razor. He worked up a brush full of lather, removed the towels and covered his cheeks and neck with soft fragrant suds. Sargon sank out of consciousness, feeling only the scrape of the blade against his whiskers. For a moment he stood at bliss's door. Then Albion said, gently, "Sire, it is time to dress."

"Come, Balfour."

In the semi-dark of the dressing room, Albion held up Sargon's grey hemp suit and brushed the shoulders. The shoe kit was still out. A pair of polished black boots stood in the corner. Albion opened a paper package and handed Sargon a titanium electraweave undershirt, effective armor for non-combat settings, and a white button-down shirt. Albion knotted his tie and brushed the lapels again, tugging the jacket and pants into place. As he did so, Sargon felt a prick in his eye.

"I'm going to stop upstairs to say goodbye to my babies."

Albion was motionless beneath his fez. "Sire," he said, nodding.

"Stay, Balfour." Seeing his eyes glisten with worry, Sargon remonstrated, "I know, but you don't want any part of this, believe me."

★

Sargon ducked, going up the stair to the attic, stooping beneath the sloped ceilings. Straight ahead was the room that had been his art studio as a child, where he painted and drew seascapes. It was Ruth's now, scented with her sadness. He pushed open the door and looked at her rocking chair, the mug on the floor with a dried teabag, the guitar, the children's stuffed animals and tea set, crayons, colored pencils, clay and paper, and a calf-bound volume of Dante's *La Divina Commedia*, in Italian, with engravings by Hillerman. He had given it to her for her twentieth birthday.

Sargon shut the door and opened that to the quarters on the left, entering a scene of morning bedlam. All were awake, Frau Duckworth, Ruth, Baby Sargon, and Phaedra, as well as Simon, a large orange cat seated on the bed, and Cawdor, a tiny white Jack Russell mutt he gave them when Doc Hughes finally assented, who raced after a robot mouse they had bought for the cat. He thought, they need a couple of birds and an iguana.

Standing on the stool and gazing out the eyebrow window was Ruth, in loose white shorts and a tank top. He gazed at the back of her thighs, her pale heels and tanned ankles, the muscles of her calves. Frau Duckworth was in a robe and slippers, sipping a bowl of tejeskave and filling in a crossword puzzle. The Baby Sargon was seated on the floor playing with his toes. Phaedra chased Cawdor around the room. All, babies and pets included, paused to look at him, deferential and expectant. Then the dog resumed running around, Phaedra took up the chase, and the Baby Sargon grabbed his feet.

Sargon said, "I am going to the Senate now. I wanted to say goodbye."

Frau Duckworth put down the crossword and said, "Sire. Your permission. This kaffee," and marched off to the bathroom.

He knelt down, feeling stiff in his suit and boots. A rope of drool depended from the Baby Sargon's lower lip. He grinned at his Sire, cried, "Papa!" and stood, staggering towards him, spit swinging from his chin like a pendulum.

"You are quite the walker now. But can you still give kisses?" Sargon asked, holding out his hands to catch him. The toddler, with a puckish smile, stopped and paused as if to think, then reversed his direction and stalked over to Phaedra. He wrapped her in his arms and planted a huge wet kiss on her lips.

A long silence followed until Sargon whooped, "Ha! Ha!" and swept the babies up, perching one on each hip. The Baby Sargon grabbed at his face. Phaedra sat on her mighty throne and took in the world. He searched for himself in her face but saw nothing. He set them down and asked, "How's Mama?" Ruth looked caged. *The gunboat landing, the navy*, he thought. Visible through that window. He hadn't considered that.

There was some part of her that bulged out of her eyes when she wasn't aware of being watched. If he came upon her suddenly in the garden he would catch them shrinking into their sockets. It was so strange! Even as a child they bugged a little when she played with her trains and dolls. After a while, he realized she was merely intent on looking at something. Sometimes, as she argued with herself, he could see the two sides in them, one frowning, the other suspicious. There was a longing in her look, as if she were always measuring the distance between herself and the world. Ruth was a stranger who had never fully accepted her life here. She didn't complain of isolation or loneliness, but even the nursery songs she sang to the children were in a minor key. After all, she lost everything, her mother, her home, her language. Even her accent had vanished long ago. Ruth only had Frau Duckworth, and she had come to her in America. "I've missed you, *Mausi*," he said, touching her tentatively.

"May I?" she reached forward to take his shoulder.

"Please, take me from this," he said. She stood on the stool and kissed him, gripped the back of his head and pulled herself to him. Phaedra stared at them and resumed her march.

"Do you have to go? Can't you stay the morning with us?" Ruth pushed the flat of her hand on his chest and kissed his lips. "We can go to bed while they nap."

Sargon shook his head. "Sorry, *Liebchen*. After this is over, we can cruise down the Donau and spend our days in bed if we like. We'll be free to live with the babies as we please. But not today."

Ruth's eyes bulged and shrank quickly. She smiled but he could see her working it through, the sadness welling up inside her. She turned, petrific, and said, "I can't wait that long. And what is 'this' anyway? You talk about *this* being over."

"Petulant?" He smiled. "You are becoming royalty, my love."

That hit a nerve and she angered. "I would know what '*this*' is if it is ending and affects the babies. I do not even possess legal papers of my own, or for Phaedra, which Doc Hughes promised me she'd have. Foolproof papers, and a legal genome on file. Is that not right?"

"These are matters of state, Ruth. I can't discuss them. As for your papers, you will have them when you need them." Black silence pulsed between them.

"I apologize, Sire." She bowed her head and stepped off the stool.

Sargon touched her hair and placed his hands in hers gently. "Please, don't do that. I apologize. Come. Can we sit on the floor with the babies for a few minutes? Then I must leave. It's going to be a difficult day."

Ruth bowed slightly and sat down by him on the floor. Baby Sargon chased after Phaedra, who chased after Cawdor, who chased the mouse. The cat stayed out of it, content to watch from Duck's bed. "How so?" she asked.

Sargon smiled and shrugged. "We'll find out."

"There didn't used to be secrets between us. You used to tell me what was going on."

"Come here, little Ruler." He reached his long arms toward Baby Sargon. "Help Papa up." The Baby Sargon gripped his index fingers and pulled. Sargon rose to his feet. "What strength! Heroic resolve in the face of battle. That's how it will be written about you one day, and it won't matter what you did. You could wheeze in a corner and take heroin all day and they'd say the same thing." He smiled and squatted down to his Scion. He took him up in his arms and the baby clung to his neck. Then he picked up Phaedra, and she yelled, "Papa!" He walked them back and forth and said to the Baby Sargon, "What I do today, I do for you," and then to Phaedra, "and for you." Reluctantly he relinquished them to the ground and they ran off, oblivious. "My friends," he bowed his head. Frau Duckworth came in from the landing and tensed to find herself standing inches from her Ruler. "Ah, Frau Duckworth. I hope you will join us when we visit Castelul Bánffy."

"If it pleases my Sire," she said, gazing at his feet.

Frau Duckworth maneuvered about him and sat on the edge of her bed, dislodging the cat. She took up a piece of knitting and put on the television. Frau Duckworth liked game shows and didn't let anyone get in the way of her morning round. She was emeritus. If she chose to snore and fart her way through her final years, she had earned it.

"Goodbye," said Ruth.

Phaedra ran and grabbed his leg. "Pay the toll!"

Sargon pried her from him and held her aloft shouting, "Yow!" He swung her around by her hands twice, then hugged her tight and covered her face with kisses. "Goodbye!" He looked at Ruth and said, "Goodbye. And don't worry. I'll be home for dinner." They kissed, her tongue soft and gentle. He squeezed her hand and left.

✶

"Come, Balfour." It was a still day, thick and hot, already ninety-eight degrees and headed for one twenty. He dragged himself slowly across the lush grass, Balfour running ahead and circling back a few times. He fed him a biscuit and said, "Stay," walking down the swaying gangway to the dock, where the navy launch to the city awaited him.

At the East River pier, he was met by a squad of Red Suits who escorted him to the UN. Red Suits were milling about the Plaza. He passed through to the Senate's elevator and made his way to the Chambers.

The summer session was nearly done and Souvanouphong was anxious to vote on the rush of bills that had emerged from the Executive Council and had to clear the Senate before going on to the House for final approval. However, the opposition, led by Bard, had insisted on a Joint Session of Congress to debate the Census Bill before going back to Chambers and voting.

House members and Senators were bustling around schmoozing, hobnobbing in the lobbies. The US Congress had come alive, a corpse reanimated by fear and greed, revived by the imminent death of a President without a clear succession. Rumors had spread that Iocle was dead and being kept on ice by Utburd, Utkasting, and Aeppar. For the first time in sixty years, the field was open. There were 556 contestants, Machiavels, Philosopher Kings, pretenders, beards, figureheads, dark horses, handicappers, side-bet takers, hedgers, back-room dealers, hacks, well-meaning-simple-minded dupes, fellow travelers, undecideds, puppet masters, cynics, pragmatists, ideologues, and assorted others. The whole gang showed up.

There was a commotion. The Senators who served on Council were taking their seats. He caught Bard's eye when he joined the California delegation. Maximilian sat next to Sargon, and they exchanged pleasantries. He took his own pulse again, searching for regret, or a bad feeling. Contempt and revulsion were his friends. He didn't feel sorry for Maximilian. He would kill him himself if he could. And, even if he did have second thoughts, it was too late.

9

UN Plaza

At noon transports and limousines pulled up to the curb, one after the other, and soldiers dressed all alike in red armor poured out like ants, swarming to their positions on the Plaza. Among them were Balustian, Whitehead, and Cowrie. Simultaneously, every guard stationed on the Plaza flowed out to the red transport vehicles that would return them to their base, the 7th Regiment Armory on Park, commandeered by the Federal Guard while Congress was in session. They did not pause to speak to one another, although individuals touched hands or nodded as they passed by.

Red Suits. Red Suits everywhere, in clumps. Some were talking on the phone, some stood at attention guarding nothing, some milled about gossiping and guffawing through the windows of their helmets. Each was weighed down with grenades, batons, a rifle, and two pistols loaded with implosion rounds. Balustian was close to the main doors leading out of the General Assembly Building, the route Senator Maximilian would take.

Balustian gazed up and down the Plaza, scanning his territory in a meditative mood. He breathed slowly and took it all in, waiting. Because all the guards looked alike, he hoped to discern something about their character and likely reaction from their movements and posture. After an hour of watching two teams across the way, he settled on Mark One, a tense, jumpy Red Suit whose finger never left the trigger of his gun. He would take his shot and the other was sure to respond with a full-on salvo. In the confusion he would break left and take a second shot, at the second team. Team Two were slovenly and not ready to return fire, except for one apparently officious ass who lectured the others, making wild gestures with his hands. Periodically he touched the stock of his rifle and felt for the trigger. He would be Mark Two. Shooting would occur in four directions. Plan worked out, he took up his post and stared at his targets and his partners through the datastream.

The armor, which had felt so comforting at first, had become a clammy, ripe-smelling body bag. His head ached with a sharp, radiating pain and his stomach was bloated with the food he had crammed down his gorge. Stomach acid hissed in his throat. He could feel the toxins venting from his lungs and guts, oozing from pores. He began to drift about in his mind. Periodically sleep overtook him, though he remained standing and ostensibly alert. The Plaza swam in his eyes. Every breath was labored and the recycled air was dirty and hot. It stank of his decay and shame. This was not the life his parents had envisioned for him, no. They thought he would go to school, become an engineer, and run a plant in the Midwest, get out of the city. They had worked their whole lives, never took vacations, saved what little silver they could. And that meant he and Luanne didn't have to support them. For the millionth time he wondered why he was so fucked up. If they could smell him now they'd think he was back in diapers. What if his kids, Barb and Dan, disappointed him as much? He lived for them in the end, but they never saw him. He might as well be a Ruler! The thought made him laugh out loud. The laughter stabbed at his gas-filled gut. It felt like it would pop.

The constant throb of lights in his eyes and the

changing focus of the helmet made him dizzy and nauseous. He felt trapped. The armor and weapons were stupidly heavy, the boots seemed to suck him underground. He couldn't run if he had to. All he really needed was a pistol and a good pair of sneakers. And some attacks he'd rather not survive. Many a broken soldier had been extracted from their heavy armor, only to be euthanized.

By 1:00 p.m., he was wheezing and his mind had contracted to the size of a pea. What could a brain that size do? It couldn't even operate his body. He'd be flopping around helplessly on the floor. Birds were smart and they had little brains but not as small as his felt. His was more like a mollusk brain, a nerve ending, or one of those blind Martian bugs in the tunnel.

He made visual contact with Whitehead and Cowrie. The teams had formed up on the Plaza. The sky burned acetylene blue. The state flags hung like dishrags. Nothing stirred. Then there was the flap and flutter of wings as a flock of galahs burst off the levee wall and circled over the Plaza, filling the air with screaming squawks and tatters of pink and white feathers.

Balustian willed himself to focus. A mere seven minutes had passed. Seven minutes! It felt like seven hours. He watched. Mark One swam around in their five member team. They stood in two wobbling lines of attention, facing the doors. Balustian yielded to nature and let out a long, exhausting fart, which relieved the stabbing cramp but further poisoned the air. He was both relieved and hated himself as if he were another person who had let fly in a closet. What was that about anyway, he asked himself. When you watch yourself doing something, who's watching? Who's watching now? The more he thought about it the more annoyed he became. It had to end somewhere, but he never got to it. Spaced out again! Hypoxia. It was a known defect of red suits. Sometimes the filtration unit failed. Methane and carbon dioxide had destroyed the earth and now they were destroying him. He forced himself to look at the world through his eyes and stop thinking, the way he had been trained. Focus. Receive.

Team Two stood in a loose circle. He looked to where he would have to move after the first shot, a position to the left, halfway to Whitehead. The destination was drenched in glare. From there, Mark Two was a straight shot. Balustian gripped the stock and curled his gauntleted finger around the trigger. He waited to hear the doors opening and the footsteps.

Only when he knew it was Maximilian would he fire. He was not going to aim. He was going to raise the barrel of the rifle and point it at the mark. It shouldn't hit him. And the mark will return that fire, blindly. Of that, Balustian was certain. He blinked the time off from the datafeed and then all the other distracting crap. He watched his mark. The doors swung open. He let out a stinking breath and waited for Maximilian to step into sight. The teams on the Plaza seemed even nearer now. It was a small space, intimate, dense with cars, with guns and grenades and soldiers suffocating in their armor. Balustian's eyes bulged at the window between them and the world.

A Senator was approaching. Two aides passed by. It was Maximilian. No doubt about it. He looked grim, scared even. His skin was drained of blood and his eyes darted about nervously. Balustian paused to scan the Plaza and place Cowrie and Whitehead. They made visual contact. He raised the barrel of his gun, pointed it toward Mark One, and fired, as did Cowrie and Whitehead, their shots echoing apart off the buildings. Then several guns went off, as each of the teams they had fired on returned that fire. The other teams attempted to scatter but the drive was narrow and full and they only plowed into each other like football players deprived of sense and purpose in the midst of a play. Some tried to climb the iron fence and got caught up in the bushes.

In the fray, Balustian and his partners took up their new positions and fired again. Now everyone on the Plaza fell under fire from everyone else and the air exploded. It spread across to the Secretariat, where guards stumbled into the fountain to escape the general melee. Balustian started to laugh when he saw what they had done. The Red Suits fired at each other in all directions. The bullets thudded against their red armor, knocking them flat. Injured guards rose on their feet and attempted to stagger to safety, but there was no safety, only chaos.

In the midst of it all was Maximilian. His red hair, receding badly, was glowing and beaded in sweat. His earlier apprehension had turned to panic. His eyes screamed as the crowd carried him off. He seemed to float on the mob around him. And then, as a red arm handed him a helmet and chainmail tunic, a red spot appeared on his forehead. His eyes widened and his head trembled and imploded, ending the life of the Ruler Maximilian 4.

It was time to run. Balustian looked for an out in the opposite direction, the General Assembly Building, and saw instead a crowd emerge from the building and rush out of the doors, oblivious to the riot. The first salvoes brought down slews of aides, whose bodies began to pile up before the shooting slowed, in heaps of headless, limbless corpses dressed in singed, bloodied business clothes, smoking beneath the blazing sun.

When they saw what was happening, Senators and Reps turned back to the entrance, but before they could reverse the tide, many fell and lay critically wounded on the sidewalk and in the drive. Without immediate medical attention they would be beyond regeneration and would have to clone and start all over again. It wasn't like Maximilian could grow a new head.

Gunfire diminished to erratic bursts and single strays. Sanity and silence settled on the stunned guards. Then the air rumbled with subsonic waves and a shiny black NYPD gunship bellied up to the Plaza. The loudspeaker ordered, in a voice that pierced the chug of the rotors, "Lay down your weapons." Instantly muzzles swung skyward as all of the soldiers on the Plaza fired at the gunship. But their charges and bullets bounced off the armor, or were repulsed by sonic shields. Downtown and uptown, more choppers arrived, landing along First Avenue. Two Scythe cannons emerged from the bottom of the fuselage and the gunner cranked out a volley of rounds that penetrated armor as if it were a layer of skin. Torn to pieces, Red Suits went down. They returned fire and sought cover behind parked vehicles and planters. Mostly they hid behind each other.

Balustian saw no way out. Frantically he ripped away at the straps of his armor and deflated it. The bodies of fleeing guards smashed into him. As he made for First Avenue, trying to undo the armor in small pauses, red-sleeved arms, booted legs, and helmets full of goo splatted across his path. He got the helmet off, and then the upper half.

The bushes were within reach. He could dive for it. That would work. Then he could lie there and get the rest off, make for the street a civilian. That was it, the way out. He took a deep fetid breath and thought about his children, saw their sleepy morning faces, so vulnerable and small. How they loved him! It would not end here. He pulled into himself for the leap to safety, the leap to freedom. Coiled tight, he sprang forward. His feet lifted off the ground and he dove for the bushes. Balustian felt a strange elation as he soared through the air, as if he were borne aloft by invisible hands. At the midpoint of his arc, the muzzle of the Scythe poked through the back of the helicopter and loosed a volley. Balustian fell through a rain of bullets, dissolving into mist before he hit the ground.

10

Iocle 5

The President sat in his chair watching bolts of lightning strike up and down the Potomac and eighty-mile-an-hour winds rip through the burning trees, dousing the flames with torrents of rain. He turned back to his monitor and watched the apneatic gasping of the Joint Session of the United States Congress, on full wheeze into its final hours. There they sat, the whole gallery of assassins. Bard, Everest, Sargon, Imogen. And their chattering henchmen: Pike, Maximilian, Micawber (where was Micawber?), and the hundreds of others circling the desks of the chamber, assembling in the lobby, working the cloakrooms and lunches. Blowflies on a corpse.

A numbing incoherence overtook his thoughts for

about an hour. During that time, nurses took his vital signs and tested for mental activity, which they judged to be suborbital. Any conscious function that is suborbital was strictly theoretical, despite claims to the contrary. Spontaneously he awoke and was vibrantly engaged and judgmental, to a degree abnormal even for him. He jammed the sound pad on his chair and intoned, "Bring me my Scion!"

Within seconds he was surrounded. Dr. Nerval was seated at his side checking over the equipment, squeezing the hand pumps and touching his clammy curtains of skin. Two nurses with clipboards wrote down various numbers. Aeppar, Utburd, and Utkasting arrived in an impatient huff and pushed aside the medical team save for Nerval, the venerable genetic designer. Only Vesuvius had exceeded his art. But Iocle knew that the art of Vesuvius was dangerous and wrong. Rulers were monstrous enough as things were. They hadn't created an ideal race. They'd distilled the human idiocy into ever more powerful forms. That was the only insight he had gained in life, and he intended once again to convey it to his Scion. To that end, he crammed the button again, whitening his thumb. "Where is he? I'm ready to talk. Turn the sound up on the monitor, I want to hear the debate."

Souvanouphong recognized the Ruler Valkyrie, House member from Oklahoma, who rose and said, "I don't understand what possible objection the Senator from New York could have to an accurate census. In fact, he cares so little about the issue he hasn't bothered to grace these Chambers with his honorable presence since losing his seat on the Executive Council. Perhaps he should change his name to Achilles?"

Representative Valkyrie yielded the floor and the Senior Senator from New York answered, without bothering to rise, "My friend from Oklahoma asks what objections I could have…"

Iocle said, "Good God, how they drone on. He doesn't want a census because he's got a bastard. His Sire wouldn't stick to men like any sensible Ruler would do, either, but indulged a nasty taste for women. Drift. But surely you already know that, don't you, Utburd?" He exerted effort to force his cheeks to express scorn, but they remained slack and unresponsive.

"I'm pleased you have such excellent recall of our recent rumination on the issue of bastardy and the blot it casts on the escutcheon of the Ruler Sargon."

"Escutcheon! Charming. You've outdone yourself.

Look at those quislings," he pointed at the TV. And then, "Where is he? Quit stalling."

The door opened and a barrel-chested man in a platinum admiral's uniform marched into the Oval Office and stood before the *Resolute*. He wore a large white hat that extended in a point down his back, which he removed and handed to his aide. President Iocle looked away from the TV and stared at his Scion as if through a monocle. "Everyone out, now."

"Sire," Dr. Nerval said.

"You especially included."

Each for their own reason remained until he uttered, without synthesis, a deep growl that sent a ripple through his face. One by one, they left.

"My boy, sit," he said with the little energy he had left. Lately the bursts came more often, but they ended quickly. "You see what they are doing here? My aides, these clowns on the TV. I need to know. Have you decided about the Presidency?"

The Younger Iocle, watching the storm rage through the Oval Office window, slowly gripped his head and said, "Stop asking me that! No, and for the last time, no. I do not want to be President of this country."

"This country? Not *my* country? I have seized it back from Bard and Sargon and held it for sixty years so you could Rule in my place, yet you say no, again? I don't know who I am! We work for this together, century after century. I battled back from space!"

"Oh my god," the Admiral Iocle groaned, sitting down and leaning his head on his hand. "Are you done now?"

President Iocle switched on the voice synthesizer and panted. "I'm, I'm, I'm…"

"You're going to kill yourself with agitation. You could be healthy, even, if you'd just let go of a few things! What good will it do our enterprise if you blow an aneurysm railing at the Senate? Who cares what they do? You run the show."

"And when I'm gone, who will protect us? If you blow it, we end. The only protection you have is the Presidency."

"I have the Navy of the Mid-Atlantic, and the Army of Virginia too. No one can win the Presidency without me. Why would I want the crown on my head and when I have it in my hand?"

"I taught you to think like that, my shame and my sin. I should have instilled the old virtues. Instead I schooled you at home and took you to the Moon and Mars. And they say old men are fools."

"I shall have to support someone."

"I've arranged it perfectly for you. All you have

to do is follow my instructions. Sargon and Imogen will tear each other apart over that stupid transport station in the Bronx. Everest will push his census and start boiling people in acid and lose support even among the so-called fanatics. Bard will stand before his mirror mesmerized by his own beautiful words and dreams, while Ocktomann destroys his beloved California. Without Everest, Pike will just be another rattlesnake from Oklahoma. So you're a hopeless idiot if you don't support Souvanouphong. He'll be the legitimate President. You'll be safe as long as he is—about ten or fifteen seconds, I'm guessing. You at least have guns and money; he's dead in the water, with that artisanal navy of his. It will give you time to see how things break. But what you do now will determine, if you ever change your mind about the Presidency, your chance of ever getting it. No one has such power, no one behind the scenes, despite what they say. Your biggest foe is your own stupidity and vanity. People believe that horseshit about Rulers. They say I'm a great leader because I've held it so long, but I knew when to take it." His breathing slowed. "Now, you go out there and give nothing away to those assholes. They think they can control you. Prove them wrong."

"It is Bard who will be President."

Iocle snorted. "He's all hat. If he's President, make your alliance with Everest. As for Sargon, he has no army. All he has is real estate and a navy to protect that real estate. Drive a wedge between Bard and Sargon. United, they are your biggest threat."

"I must go," the Younger Iocle said. "But I'll be back in time for dinner, and stay the night. Are you up for a game of bridge and a bottle of Armagnac?" When his Sire didn't answer, he left.

The Old President was absorbed again by the TV. He had railed so long, fulminated so completely against the Senate that it was the only comfort he had left. Hate vivified him. He turned the oxygen up and increased the pressure on his ventilator. With nervous agitation he flicked one bony wrinkled finger at the bag of cherry-red biomass dripping into his heart port. He squeezed the clear bag of GenetiBoost going into his arm. The top of the bag bulged in his grip. To the empty room he said, pointing at the TV, "There goes Imogen's punk. Every day he leaves eight minutes before the rest. I could set my watch by it. You see there?"

Iocle became aware that the room was empty and that no one was listening to him. It sharpened his attention. He had not been alone in a century. He continued speaking to the TV. "You miserable prick." The door closed behind Maximilian. He turned the channel to an exterior view of the UN. It was a wide shot of the Plaza. He said, "Follow Maximilian." Maximilian was searching the Plaza for his car. "He cares for one thing, lunch, at a table at The Jacquard on Central Park South. New Yorkers. Money and food. Look!" He leaned forward in his chair and eyeballed the screen, a slow scream assembling in his head. There were three gunshots all at once. What are they doing? he wondered. He tried to figure out if he was dreaming. Many times he had been told that things he saw weren't real. There were the cats that briefly invaded and roamed the residence for several weeks in the summer of, was it last year? '98? They had eyes of fire and slow meows, but they did not exist. Then the static. He saw static at the edge of things. Encroaching death, they said. The periphery goes first, leaving only a core of bodily function. Soon all of the real would be the size of a dot, surrounded by grey hiss. But this was not that.

One by one, more guns went off and he screamed, "No, you idiots! Don't do it!" The cameras followed Maximilian through the rioting crowd, as he was lifted. He saw a hand stretch out with armor and then the shot to the head. It unfolded in an empty zone of perception divorced from distraction. In his single focus, for a few moments, there was only the image, the slow image, and then the rage he always felt but kept at bay engulfed him. He saw all at once what it was, and heard his and Sargon's parting words of a month earlier and realized he had been warned. Gunfire broke out everywhere as chaos set in. He smashed the voice box and bellowed, "Get in here! We're going to warrrrrr...." He coughed, croaked, gargled, took a breath, and his eyes went still as the wind blew out of his body.

★

Sargon sat down and stretched his legs out. He had spoken long enough. He yielded the floor back to the dingbat from Oklahoma and took in the domed hall. Threat was in the air. Every word uttered was done so looking at the clock. Bard was whispering into the ear of a young professor he had taken on for the summer as an advisor. He sought out Everest. Everest, in full beard, with long white hair brushed out on his shoulders, looked alert, his earlier worry ironed off his brow. Sargon laughed to himself and thought, not for long. He could not look at Everest without the stench of acid filling his nostrils, as if he tainted the air around him. Souvanouphong took the podium and cleared his throat. The floor did not settle but became unruly. House members were standing and jabbing the air with their fingers, overrunning each other's sentences, some shouting invective, even as the Vice President banged the gavel.

"Order, order… will the Honorable Ruler from Oklahoma please continue."

"A census conducted every ten years, which is in the US Constitution, and in the New Constitution, would confirm what we already know…"

The hall erupted in noise again. Everest was now on his feet, looking a little perturbed. That's right, thought Sargon. You don't have a friend in the room. That was starting to occur to a lot of them. He checked the time and watched Maximilian rise from his seat and slowly make his way to the door. Souvanouphong banged the gavel, but the joint session would not come to order. From behind the gold megalith that formed the backdrop to the podium marched a squad of Red Suits. Fear rippled through the room. Within minutes, aides packed up papers and headed to the doors. Then some House Members rose and headed out, followed by Senators. For the first time in memory, Sargon was paralyzed. Hundreds of people fled blindly out of the building and into what he imagined was spreading crossfire.

Souvanouphong was crying into his microphone,

"Order! Order!" But the room had emptied and was quiet.

Minutes later the doors burst open. Senators and Representatives who had left in a storm were returning in a paranoid, weeping, screaming mob. They jammed the hall. The Red Suits became confused and didn't know where to point their rifles. Senator Midas of Pennsylvania, barefoot, carrying broken high heels, walked up to the podium. Her hair was wet and limp with blood. Blood was splashed across the front of her dress. A walnut-sized piece of brain clung to the left strap. She looked like prey in the path of a hungry predator, panting with terror, hypervigilant eyes popping out of their sockets, fingers clawing the air as if she were still running. The Red Suits started to rush her. Senator Midas reared back, cried out, and Souvanouphong raised his hand, recognizing her.

Midas gripped the podium and spoke with anger, not fear, her eyes bent on an invisible presence. "Please," she shrieked, trying to speak above the loud voices. "Senator Sargon, are you aware of what is happening on the Plaza, Sire?"

Sargon stood and surveyed the hall. No one was listening. He shouted to Senator Midas, "Senator Midas, My Lady, no. I am afraid I don't know."

"Federal troops are gunning us down, Sire. They've killed Senator Maximilian, I saw him go myself. Hundreds of others lie dead or injured."

Sargon said, "And you come running back here?" He turned to the nearest aide, one of Robin's boys. "Bring me a phone. I need MacCallister and Roosevelt. I'll be on the Plaza," he shouted. The aide handed him a phone, and he said into it, "MacCallister, deploy your troops." He called Roosevelt and said, "We're on, now." Then he left the room, shoving people aside in the aisles. He ran to the stairs and down into the lobby. The walls shook with helicopter blades. Roosevelt's gunship was pounding the Plaza. Civilian bodies lay buried beneath the guard. The air was thick with smoke and smelled of burning flesh. Flames licked the shattered faceplates of red helmets. The heaped corpses stifled the cries and whimpers of the wounded. At the margins, through the blue-grey haze, survivors crawled to escape. As the shooting ebbed, the Plaza pulsed with the funk-funk-funk of chopper blades.

What a fucking disaster, thought Sargon. A squad of guards had followed him out, but he had no idea if they were there to protect or arrest him. He wasn't afraid. It was something else, some inundating emotional state that seemed to predate the world and surpass his limited compass of reality. Before his eyes, the Plaza flickered with images of the dusty white rubble of LA, hot wind blowing the smell of slaughtered bodies. Children screaming their last breaths and grenades detonating adobe domes. The feeling in his heart grew thin and bitter. It slowed to a throb.

Sargon looked up at the gunship and felt his strength return. He gestured with his hand. It lowered slowly to the street, along with four others, and the City Guard, in their shining black armor, emptied out, taking up positions from 42nd to 48th Street. Navy cruisers patrolled the East River. He addressed those who could hear: "Friends, it is time to end this. Put down your weapons. Return to barracks. You will not be harmed." His voice dropped. Behind him had assembled a few dozen Senators, including Bard, who glared at him with undisguised fury, and Everest, whose face was almost comical in its dismay.

"This is my city," Sargon announced, "I will provide security in it." He turned his back on the Red Suits and civilians who had managed to live through both barrages and said to his colleagues, "The Ruler Maximilian 4 is dead. I will take his seat on the Executive Council, pending an election." As they walked in the door, a sob overtook him. He swallowed it whole and headed to the closest private toilet. He shut the door behind him and sat down in total darkness to let it come. Great sobs convulsed his shoulders and he yawned, squeezing tears out of the slits of his eyes. He blew his nose and turned on the light, shocked to see an old man's face in the mirror, sagging and empty, pocked with grief and guilt. He washed up, thinking, *And what of it?*

He dried his hands on the towel roll, fixed his tie, brushed off his suit and walked into the lobby, where he was met by a squad of the City Guard. They escorted him to the Senate Chamber using a secure lateral through the basement. He entered the hall on the level of the Executive Council, behind the President's Chair, and as he did so, all of the assembled members of the US Senate stood and applauded.

★

Utburd, Aeppar, and Utkasting, who had been watching the events unfold from the President's Secretary's Office, and Dr. Nerval and his medical group, who had been watching from the conference room, were rushing into the Oval Office through different doors when they saw the President seize up. Iocle was slumped forward, his face hanging towards the desk in several elongated folds. He was dead before they could reach him. They couldn't see the TV from where they were and didn't realize that what had killed him was transpiring on it still, until the sound of gunfire and screams emerged from the tiny speakers. All eight of them ran as one into the space between the desk and the bow window and stared catatonically at the screen.

Aeppar's flat top flared yellow briefly and then faded to an amber glow with purple roots. The lines in her face deepened into channels and her eyes became glassy and indecipherable. Her defenses went up like sonic shields. She pursed her lips, and raised her left eyebrow slightly. Utburd, taking the measure of the room, noted it. Dr. Nerval said only, "Oh dear." Then he turned to his subordinates and started issuing instructions.

Collecting and preserving tissue was best done when the body was fresh. And no genome map is complete until the final scan is done. So the doctors and nurses tended to Iocle 5 as if nothing were happening on the TV, upon which the attention of the three aides was riveted. Panic reigned as those still fleeing the building ran over those fleeing the Plaza, like a wave breaking on returning water. Then the gunfire slowed and stopped. Utburd took a deep breath. Aeppar exhaled and saw twenty years of service dissolve like the pink smoke drifting above the wounded. In a crisis, Utkasting remained imperturbably optimistic, his steady smile unsettling those about him.

Aeppar had a fleeting hope that this would be it. They would restore order and everything would go back to the way it was. But her hopes were silenced by the chopper blades chugging in the sky. They watched in silence as Roosevelt's assault on the Plaza continued, until Sargon walked out of the building and called a halt, which was the moment she knew they were done, that Sargon had taken everything. But he didn't know that Iocle 5 was dead. Aeppar said, "Doctor, what are you doing? Have you recorded a time of death? I must ask you to stop and answer my question."

Dr. Nerval was old and wizened in spirit, but his face was smooth and tanned, the skin supple and young even as it expressed his great age with deep lines that formed when he smiled or frowned. His fingers had perfect nails above rising lunulae. His two-hundred-year-old teeth, exposed by a horrific smile, flashed. People joked he didn't know how to throw anything away. He said, gazing up at Aeppar with a look of contemptuous denigration, "I am collecting the necessary samples and scans for a proper clone. Time is of the essence. Drift, my friends, Drift." The rueful word hung in the air. For the first time in any of their lives the drama of Drift was present and unfolding.

They were interrupted when Iocle 5's Presidential Guard entered the room, led by its chief, Arthur Safavi. They called them the Scythians, for their uniforms were gold, designed by Iocle and based on ancient Scythian art. They marched into the Oval Office and faced them across Iocle 5's slumped corpse. Chief Safavi said, "What's wrong with him, is he dead?"

Dr. Nerval looked at him and said, "No. He is resting."

Chief Safavi addressed the others. "He looks dead to me. Dr. Nerval is in charge. No one else gets near him." The four guards engaged their helmets and took out their batons. Light flashed off the gold rivets of their gauntlets.

Utburd said, "Of course. Would you station the guard outside of the doors, please? We have state business to discuss."

The helmet was pulled back from Safavi's face, wrapping the back of his head in brilliant folds of gold, framing his long, bent nose and tight mouth. He examined each person in the room, his black, glaring eyes probing layers of fear and deceit. While he did so, he reminded himself that he had taken an oath to obey civilian authority. That was his mandate and purpose. There was nothing about the quality of that leadership. On the other hand, they had taken an oath of allegiance to the President, and their personal honor was pledged to the Ruler Iocle. He said, "Yes, Sire. But we serve the President."

"Serve him outside the doors," Utkasting said.

The guards faced straight ahead, waiting for Safavi to speak. He pulled the helmet down over his face. The cloth hardened into a shining gold shell with a visor. His deep voice, filtered by the speaker, was flattened. "Take up your posts around the Oval Office. No one gets in or out without my direct order." He stood at attention before the aides. Utburd said, "You are dismissed."

"Yes, Sire." He marched back out of the main doors.

They waited a few moments in silence until Aeppar said, "I will send word to Everest, so that he and Pike can escape New York if we should fail."

Utburd's head was crooked. He looked like a man being hanged. "How can we not?"

"Obviously our chances aren't good."

Utkasting said, "We should go back to Texas, now."

Aeppar asked, "Are we not Rulers? This is our time. It will not come again."

The main entrance banged open and the Younger Iocle, trailed by the Scythians, entered the room in a propulsive rage, his hands balled into fists that looked strangely childish emerging from the platinum sleeves of his uniform. His eyes leapt out of his head, a commanding block that sat atop traps and delts so large it looked like a python had wrapped itself around his neck and shoulders. "When did this happen?" he demanded. "Why wasn't I called?"

Aeppar, Utburd, and Utkasting stopped their conversation and regarded the Admiral of the Mid-Atlantic Fleet, now Ruler of Delaware, Maryland, and Virginia. He surveyed them each, weighing in his own mind what he thought. He had imagined this moment many times, but apparently the enormity had eluded him. Brutal fact. What was true, was irreversibly true. He was dead. Pop was dead. An event long anticipated and planned for. None of the plans had included a kick in the stomach.

Iocle would not break down before these people. But he could not make the calculations in his present state. And he had to. His Sire had told him as much.

But the same question lay before him, honor his Sire's last wishes or do what's right?

Iocle viewed the three aides with mounting disgust. He had always regarded Everest with disdain and that disdain was slowly changing to horror. The influence his Sire had allowed Everest to have, to the point of domination in the later years, was criminal. He and Sargon at least could make a deal. And as for Bard's reforms, much remained to be seen. But he would not let Everest unleash his regime of purges and witch hunts and churning acid vats. They might all be dogs, but siccing one upon the other benefited no one.

Aeppar, hair shining to the roots, said, "We are crushed with grief, Sire. We were preoccupied with the medical procedures. How do you wish to proceed?"

"The constitution is process enough for now. I would like you to pack up your things and go wherever it is you go when you're not here."

Utburd trembled and said, "But Sire, surely. Who, who shall run the government?"

Utkasting asked, "The military? The what have you?"

Iocle glared at them and said, "There is a government, and from the moment my Sire died, a new President. I will go to New York and deliver the news myself. I leave in fifteen minutes. And you're leaving with me. The Scythians will escort you each to a rocket that will take you wherever you like. Thank you for your service, my friends. I will be alone with my Sire now. You have ten minutes to pack."

He turned away from the three and focused on the lifeless pile of flesh on the desk, the finger pointed accusatorially at the TV, a familiar gesture. He reflected on his Sire's ill nature. It was not a quality he saw in himself, so he wondered if it was simply a product of old age, or had they developed differently? Their lives were nothing like each other's. He hated space, it felt like he was gasping for air the entire time, and the g-force didn't agree with him. But mostly it was the view. And suspension was creepy. Sleep for months and months, rather than read? And the cocktail parties! The infernal affairs. But his Sire desired it for him, wanted to share the adventure of their avatars. And now this: a poor, rumpled, lifeless sack. All that pissy, angry, brawling, fist-shaking rage was drained from it. And he was about to make a deal with men the old Ruler despised. A deal for the time being anyway. He could always depose them later if it was necessary.

Isle of Dogs, Part 1

★

The ovation died down and all collapsed back into their seats. The Senate Chambers were full and hot, as the building skin was down. Most Senators and staff were lying back in their seats, their blank faces rivered with sweat. A few paced about gesticulating abstractly about revenge, while others of the opposite party swore they would investigate the causes.

Each side invoked President Iocle. One as the agent of, the other as the one betrayed by, the Red Suit Riot, as it was now being referred to on TV and radio. In newsrooms across the country a hysterical effort was underway to procure as many official statements as possible, in the hopes of finding the official line. But all communications were intermittent and by individuals. There was no official line because the White House had issued no statement nor done what the press had hoped and assumed it would do, send President Iocle out by holograph (or at least broadcast) image to reassure the nation that order had been restored on the UN Plaza.

The newscasters wore black armbands in anticipation of the announcement of a day of national mourning for Senator Maximilian and his colleagues. The first on the scene, Tiriel Harvale, scooped them all by arriving before the shooting began. But even she was reduced to muttering shocked clichés. All of which led to a collective terror, a belief that the Red Suits would redeploy and mow them down as they left the building. No one wanted to leave the protection of the City Guard.

Sargon, with a palpable sense of swimming through time, rose to say, "Mr. President, may I address the Senate?"

Souvanouphong said, "The chair recognizes the Senior Senator from New York."

"Esteemed colleagues, friends, why hasn't our revered Ruler, President Iocle, made a statement? Could it be he is too ashamed of what his guard has done to this institution? Not since the downfall of Sejanus has so much blood run on Capitol steps. I yield the floor to my honorable friend, the distinguished gentleman from California, Senator Bard."

Bard sat cupping his chin and tapping his lips with his index finger, a look of volcanic anger in his eyes. Slowly he stood, tall even in that Chamber. With a somber, severe voice, he said, "I move that the Senate consider charges of treason against the President, and that we act immediately to remove him from office. This was an attack on us all."

The Chamber exploded with verbal onslaught. Half a century of pent-up fury blew through the room. Souvanouphong began monotonously to bang the gavel, his hoarse voice tired and weak, imploring quiet. Everest rose. "Mr. President, would it be possible to debate the issue without violence and intimidation, which violate the ancient rules of this august chamber? The honorable Ruler of California, its Junior Senator and a warrior of great renown, upon whom we have often showered our praises, pays back the Senate and the American people with treason. As if we were under no compulsion to first establish what occurred, and why. Certainly our revered Ruler could reap no possible advantage by such a riot. There is only one person who benefits from the death of Senator Maximilian, a dear friend of mine, and our many other esteemed colleagues who lie on the ground, slaughtered like the mighty buffalo. That is the crime that demands our scrutiny and censure. For, does anyone believe his death an accident?"

Mocking jeers and catcalls punctuated his words, but he continued to speak, silver-maned, over the roar of protest.

The doors opened and the Scythians entered, eliciting gasps. Standing a head above them, in full ceremonial dress, was Ascendant Iocle. He said to the security detail, "I'll take two, the rest fan out in the hall." Then, as he walked briskly towards the President of the Senate's desk, he addressed the Chair. "Mr. President," he huffed.

By his look of deference, it was clear to Sargon that Iocle was not addressing the President of the US Senate anymore, but the President of the United States. Sargon felt his pulse quicken. He avoided looking at Everest or Bard now and focused instead on Souvanouphong, who was evidently not prepared for the news. Militarily, Sargon controlled the situation in the city, but if Iocle went with Everest, there'd be a stalemate, followed by war. He would have to release the Red Suits or start that war.

Souvanouphong's face grew quite still and the color faded from it. His eyes searched out the exits, shifting rapidly from door to door, while the rest of him remained motionless. He gulped and blinked, fixed his eyes on the middle distance, engaging no one. So, Sargon thought, there is no deal.

The Ascendent Iocle said, in a calm, ordinary voice, slightly elevated to be audible throughout the hall, "Mr. President, Sire, the great Ruler Iocle 5 is no more. I watched him die myself. I have ordered my troops to secure Washington, DC, and they have already sworn their oath to President Souvanouphong, who is now Ruler of Delaware, as of old. Mr. President, Sire, Chief Justice Lazar will be here shortly to administer the Oath of Office."

The air deadened as all talk ceased. There was not even the squeak of a chair or rustle of paper on the desks. The rotunda felt like a cosmos. Souvanouphong's eyes swelled and reddened. He grasped the podium in either hand and said with a breaking voice, "We have traveled many miles together, friends. I am honored and pray that God will give me the strength to follow my illustrious predecessor. With his guidance and your help, we will overcome these tragic days." *Uh huh*, thought Sargon.

As Souvanouphong spoke, a cloud of static materialized in the air next to the podium. Soon the holographic alias of the Chief Justice appeared, draped in black-and-crimson robes, the heavy hem in a pile on the floor around his feet, and in his hand George Washington's copy of *The Acts of Congress*. The image of Chief Justice Lazar opened the book and began. "Mr. President, Sire, raise your hand and repeat after me: I do solemnly swear,"

"I do solemnly swear," Souvanouphong repeated.

"That I will faithfully execute the Office of President of the United States,"

"That I will faithfully execute the Office of President of the United States,"

"And will to the best of my Ability,"

"And will to the best of my Ability,"

"Preserve, protect and defend,"

"Preserve, protect and defend,"

"The Constitution of the United States."

"The Constitution of the United States."

The Chief Justice smiled, crackling with small lightning bolts before dissolving to static.

Mayhem broke out in parts of the hall, but like distant explosions on a moonless night, it was isolated by silence, as all wondered what to do next. Now it was safe for Sargon to take the measure of the hall. It was as crowded as he had ever seen it. Souvanouphong gaveled the Senate to order and addressed it. "Given the violence and barbarity of recent events, my first act of office is to request formally that you elect a Vice President."

This was it. They were making their move. Souvanouphong wasn't ready for it. He was going to wait to see how it would break. He and Iocle. Now Sargon and Bard had to move. Where did Imogen stand? Sargon caught her eye. He raised an eyebrow very slightly, and burrowed into her eyes. He flexed his nostrils, and shaped his mouth into an *o*. She puffed out her cheeks and squeezed her nose. He had her. Senator Imogen of Illinois rose. "I place in nomination the gentleman from California, my honorable friend, the Ruler Bard. Who among us has fought greater battles or Ruled longer in peace?"

President Souvanouphong said, "All in favor of the nominee say *Aye*." There was a fairly dense cry of *Aye*, some of it passionate, most of it a good bet. "All who say *Nay*?" There was a fairly dense cry of *Nay*. It was too close to call.

Pike stood. Lisping very gently he said, "As long as we're nominating honorable friends to the post, good friends no less, I put forward in nomination the very honorable gentleman from Texas, an old friend of mine, the Ruler Everest."

When Pike nominated Everest, Iocle, surrounded by gleaming Scythians, flinched. It was noted by more than a few undecided Senators.

President Souvanouphong, who looked more like a croupier spinning a roulette wheel than a head of state with near dictatorial powers, called the vote. "All those in favor of Senator Everest for Vice President say *Aye*."

A moderately vociferous cry of *Aye* went up.

"All those in favor of Senator Bard for Vice President say *Aye*."

Again it was too close to call. In the confusion someone called for secret ballots. Senators dropped to their seats and scoured their hearts for the right vote. Aides rapidly whispered in ears. They read lips and signed in cipher. Faces strained with the effort as they exercised parts of their minds that had atrophied. There was no way of knowing what the consequences of their vote would be, even as they knew losing could be a death sentence. Minutes and then a half hour passed. Souvanouphong urged them to vote quickly. When all of the votes were cast and recorded, President Souvanouphong looked about the room and announced, "The vote is tied." Before him stood the Ruler Iocle. Go on, Sargon thought. Do something. Now he caught President Souvanouphong's eye, as he had done Imogen's. Don't be an idiot, he tried to say.

Souvanouphong took a last look at the guards in the hall. Not a Red Suit among them. He said, "The vote is tied. Therefore, since I am still officially President of the Senate, it falls to me to cast the deciding vote. My heart is heavy, I will confess, with the weight of history bearing upon it as perhaps it has borne upon no other President in the history of our great nation." He paused and swallowed. "In the interest of peace and unity, I cast my vote for my honorable friend from the great state of California, the Ruler Bard."

This was met with silence. Senators again became vigilant.

Senator Pike jumped up and yelled, "This will not stand! Usurper!"

"I protest, I protest," intoned Vizier Holland of Georgia.

Everest wouldn't move in his own defense. He was waiting for a speech of passion and eloquence, one such as he would have delivered, but there was none. While this went on, orderlies wheeled in a US Circuit Judge, the Lady Buckley of New Hampshire, in town to tour the UN, from the makeshift field hospital set up in the lobby of the General Assembly. Bandaged and weak, breathing from a tube, she was nevertheless able to administer the Oath of Office to Bard electronically.

What happened next would long be seen by historians as the *cause* of the riot on the Plaza. A true version of events was known to them, because buried in the private archives at Georgetown is Tiriel Harvale's account of the conspiracy and its participants, but they chose to ignore that, for they served other interests. Outside of Group D (which at its largest was no more than nine individuals), all suspected, but few knew exactly, what had happened. Of that handful of conspirators three lay dead on the ground, indistinguishable from the other guards. The other six never spoke of it again.

President Souvanouphong banged the gavel and said, "Vice President Bard is sworn in. And, my friends," he said, his voice beginning to boom and ring, with the genuine gravitas demanded by the situation, "in the interest of the nation, I am resigning as President of the United States. The justice will now administer the Oath of Office to Vice President Bard." Amidst the anguished, furious cries of half the Senate, *no! No!*, the hapless Judge, blood darkening her bandages, administered the oath. When they were done, again Senator Imogen rose to address the Chamber, though few could hear above the din of fury. "I call for nominations for Vice President."

Senator Titania of Connecticut stood and cried out in a resonant voice intended both to calm and silence the hall, "I nominate Senator Sargon for Vice President of the United States."

Senator Katrina Dean of Massachusetts said, "I second that nomination."

Isle of Dogs, Part 1

"All in favor, say *Aye*," called Senator Souvanouphong.

The room again became silent. Nothing moved. The Scythians that ringed Admiral Iocle looked like tubas in a marching band. The New York Guard held their positions at the entrances and exits, visors down, muzzles pointed at the Chamber.

Senators hunched over their desks to muffle tears. Again Souvanouphong said, "All in favor, say *Aye*." A thunderous *Aye* ensued.

"By acclamation of the United States Senate, Sire, you are now Vice President of the United States."

As it had done when he entered the Chamber earlier, the Senate stood and gave the Ruler Sargon 3 a sustained ovation, with only a few Senators sitting out. For most in the end felt safer with Sargon than Everest, who stormed out of the chamber with his allies. And that is how Sargon and Bard seized power in the year 2501.

END OF PART ONE

About the Author

Jon Frankel is a poet and novelist, the author of *Gaha: Babes of the Abyss*, (Whiskey Tit, 2014), and *The Man Who Can't Die* (Whiskey Tit, 2016), and writing as Buzz Callaway, *Specimen Tank* (Manic D. Press, 1993). *Isle of Dogs*, a prequel to *GAHA: Babes of the Abyss*, is presently being published by Whiskey Tit in four parts. Jon's poetry is published exclusively on his website. You'll also find reviews and personal essays about food and culture. Jon Frankel lives in upstate New York with his family and is retired after 27 years of working at Cornell University Library as a book mover and stacks manager.

About the Publisher

Whisk(e)y Tit is committed to restoring degradation and degeneracy to the literary arts. We work with authors who are unwilling to sacrifice intellectual rigor, unrelenting playfulness, and visual beauty in our literary pursuits, often leading to texts that would otherwise be abandoned in today's largely homogenized literary landscape. In a world governed by idiocy, our commitment to these principles is an act of civil service and civil disobedience alike.